KNOWN BY YOU

VETERANS OF SILVER RIDGE

CLAIRE CAIN

Cover design by Jess Mastorakos - Jess@jessmastorakos.com

PRINT ISBN: 978-1-954005-58-7

EBOOK ISBN: 978-1-954005-57-0

For the tender hearts.

CHAPTER ONE

Elizabeth

When someone smiles and suggests everything happens for a reason, I instantly know three things about them.

First, they have a sunny view of the world and life.

Second, they're likely someone for whom most things have worked out in their favor.

And third... they are diametrically different than me.

I would never be confused for an optimist. I've had my fair share of successes, but when factoring in parental divorce, failed personal relationships, a sister who was kidnapped—even if we'd recovered her quickly—and now the mess I found myself in, I didn't think of myself as living a charmed life. Not to say I'd suffered—I had privilege up and down the street. But I didn't feel the need to fit life events into a tidy puzzle where everything fit *for a reason*.

Sometimes, being a few minutes late doesn't save you

from a horrible car wreck. And relationships end because people don't love each other anymore or don't want to work hard enough to fix what broke. Sometimes, people simply don't click long-term. Sometimes, a freaky fan thinks he has the right to kidnap someone.

Sometimes, work blows up in your face despite your best efforts.

These were consequences of choices, actions, and sometimes world events or outside forces. I refuse to believe they were all for a precious *reason*.

That said, as I stood staring at my baby sister, a tear slipping down her cheek, it felt a lot like *she* was the reason I'd come to Silverton. She beamed at me with her innocent smile that held so much love it made me ache as she slipped her bright scarf from around her neck.

"I'm so, *so* glad you're here. Last summer, it was all such a blur, but now? It's an absolute dream come true to have you here for more than a few days!"

She launched out of her seat, making quick work of sliding out of the booth, then yanking on my closest arm and hauling me into her embrace.

"Okay, Jojo. Point taken. You're glad I'm here." I chuckled through it, ignoring the pinch in my chest and shoving the way I'd neglected her for so many years to the back of my mind.

She released me after a few seconds longer than a normal person would, then slid back into her side of the cherry red booth. Catherine, the waitress who was also part of my sister's girl squad here in Silverton, delivered our lunch.

"Here you go, ladies. Anything else I can get you?"

She smiled kindly at us. Her dark hair was pulled back into a ponytail, her stunningly clear, pale skin fresh and without any makeup. She had the mountain girl natural beauty thing going for her in spades.

"This looks amazing, thank you," Jo said with a grin.

"I'll take some more coffee and would you top up the water, too? I'd appreciate it." I held up my half-empty glass. I'd taken to guzzling water since arriving last night. Dehydration never helped jetlag, plus the altitude had me pretty miserable last summer when I came for a quick visit. I wanted the coffee for the caffeine and to warm my fingers, which still felt a bit frozen after my walk from the small apartment I rented.

Granted, I'd hardly been here long enough to adjust when I'd stopped in six-ish months ago. Not even quite a week. Now, though, I planned to be here at least a few months, both to help Saint Security bridge the gap while Jess Korbel-Rawlins dealt with her extreme morning sickness, and to… enjoy my wintry sabbatical from work.

Yeah. It's a voluntary sabbatical and not a voluntold, paid leave of absence while your subordinate is drawn up on ethics charges that implicate you. Way to spin it.

The burn of frustration and betrayal lit in my chest, but I tamped it down and smiled at Catherine.

"Of course. I'll keep both coming."

She scuttled off to get my beverages, and I turned to see Jo eying me with a sly look. I didn't get to spend much time with her, but I still recognized the expression as one to be wary of.

"Yes?"

"I'm just waiting for you to tell me why you're here and how you're taking more than a month off work and how it went when you showed up at Saint Security and, if we're just going to put it all out there, what Kenny did when he saw you because I *know* he had a reaction based on seeing him at the signing."

I huffed, the barrage of questions so like ten and twelve and fourteen-year-old Jo it hurt. We were sisters with a six-year age gap and had often been stuck in different phases of life. We'd stayed in touch fairly well considering I'd lived internationally for the majority of the last decade, but this instance made a wisp of memory blossom and wither at the same time.

Judging by the cant of her head and the way her eyes narrowed and flickered from one part of my face to another, she was trying to suss out the truth. It had been so rare for us to sit across from each other and talk. In truth, it was rare for me to sit and talk to anyone who wasn't part of my working life. So maybe I should take this chance to connect —make an effort while I was here and let her in a little, knowing it would likely make her day. It was a small offering for the kindness and enthusiasm she'd shown me since we'd sat down.

I could give her some of the answers she wanted without creating a situation I had no control over, and so I did.

"I'm on sabbatical for up to three months depending on a few factors and it's standard practice," I said, but left out a few key details about *when* it was standard practice or the fact sabbatical wasn't technically the right word. "And I'm here because I enjoyed this little town and seeing you and Dad. I like the Saint Security team, and when I reached out to Wilder Saint and Bruce Camden, they indicated I could fill a need."

She chewed the giant bite of burger she'd taken while I was speaking, so I did the same. *Glorious.* Europe had a lot of delicious food, but I deeply missed a few American classics, one of which was a greasy diner cheeseburger with American cheese. The other was Mexican food, which tended to be in the "good try" to "truly abysmal" range where I'd been, and I'd already helped myself to takeout from Guac for dinner last night.

"Mmkay, first, awkward to refer to our step-brother by his full name. Second, this begs at least five follow-up questions, not the least of which is 'why would you go to work for Bruce and Wilder when you're supposed to be sabbatical-ing' but most important is—are you going to say anything about Kenny?"

She made a ridiculous face like she was begging me, eyes big—another throwback to when she tried to manipulate me with her cuteness.

There was no escaping this. I might as well execute. "He appeared very surprised to see me. Just like he did last summer. We didn't speak. By the time a few others had finished welcoming me, he'd disappeared."

Her dark brown eyes, the same color as mine, grew large. "Reeeeeeaaalllllllllly?"

I rolled my matching set. "Yeeeeesssss."

The glare I received was nothing short of sisterly, but she spoke even as she rolled hers right back at me. "Okay, Lizzy, and are you ever going to tell me the deal there? I mean like... did you guys..."

She left off as though I'd fill in the blank with something salacious she could write about in her next novel. "What do you expect me to say?"

She chucked a fry at my plate as though it was a punishment. Foolish move— I would devour every fry in front of me and now I had a bonus fry. *Sucker.*

"Maybe that you dated? Hung out? Are secretly lovers and have been all along? That he's pregnant with your baby and you've come back to be his baby mama? *Literally anything* will tell me more than what I know, which is that he whispered your name in a shocked kind of awe that said *things*, but I don't know what, and I'm left chomping at the bit for more."

I coughed, almost spewing my recent bite of burger at her, but saved myself, and her, in a heroic effort before recovering. I guzzled the water Catherine had stealthily refilled, then glared at Jo. "You really shouldn't say stuff like that out loud. If this is like any small town I've read about, the fact that Kenny is somehow pregnant with my baby will be in the paper tomorrow."

She cackled. "Adorable. And this must mean you've been reading from the list I made you."

I scowled. She'd made me a list of romance novels when I had mentioned finishing all of hers in a few weeks, after I found out she was romance author Josie Wade. And yes. I had been. And no, I wasn't proud of it, but then I also wasn't proud of that attitude because I didn't like the idea anyone would feel ashamed to read one of Jojo's books, so why should I feel bad reading anyone else's?

I shouldn't.

Didn't mean I needed to give her the satisfaction, though.

"Maybe. My point is, what happened between me and Kenny was just shy of nothing."

She let out a "ha!" and slapped the table. "That means there was *something*."

I shifted my focus to my now-cold coffee and drank deep. It was coming on eight p.m. in the time zone I came from though just early afternoon here, and though I'd slept decently well last night, even made it all the way to three-thirty this morning before my first waking, I'd need the caffeine.

"We had a joint operation with the EMU a few years ago. Kenny was on the team we worked with. That's all." Mostly all.

And I wasn't going to say anything else, or I knew what she'd say.

She'd bust out her romance writer brain and figure out a way to throw us together.

He didn't want that, I didn't need it... we were fine like this. Let him avoid me and I could give him space and we'd never have to face the awkward reality.

Truth was, it *had* been nothing. He'd been this gorgeous man-boy on a team of grown men and he'd asked me out. He'd been nice about it, not slimy, but I had... well, I'd laughed. Because he'd seemed so *young*. I wasn't certain of the age difference between us, but he'd been this hot, cocky young spec ops soldier and I already felt like a grizzled creature at the ripe age of thirty.

So when hotshot jokester Barbie had approached, I'd laughed, taken the compliment, and that was the story.

Had he been the kind of attractive that felt unrealistic? Yes. Had I thought, "Maybe in my dreams"? Sure. And had I known that under no circumstances would I get involved with someone like him because my job was my first priority?

Yes, I did.

So I'd brushed it off, and I was certain he had, too. The coincidence of us meeting again *ever*, let alone here in this tiny town where my sister and dad had made their lives, only contributed to the surreality of living here.

Stepping on the plane to the US with no return ticket had felt odd enough. Arriving here and moving into an apartment instead of the inn or hotel had been another level of weird. Sitting across from my heart-eyed sister and talking about a man I barely knew who was now my coworker as though it factored into my life in any way? If I found out I was on the set of some alternate-universe reality TV show, I wouldn't have been surprised. It all just felt so completely unreal.

One more facet of this time that made it all seem like I'd stepped between worlds: I no longer lived the life I'd chosen in the job I had. Right now, I couldn't go back to it—wouldn't know when until they told me. I was stuck in this purgatory, though so far, it was largely without punishment *or* anticipation. It was simply... in between.

I had the sense that I'd exit this version of life when I returned to work, but for now, I was wandering around in the dark. And as much as I regretted to admit it, I hated feeling lost.

CHAPTER TWO

Kenny

Good grief, the sky was perfectly blue.

Just gorgeous.

Winter could be a challenge here, but these blue-bird days? Almost made me wish I knew how to ski. The mountains were snow-covered and even down here in town we had a nice white coating covering long-dead grasses and plants.

"Am I about to hear you start whistling?" Cookie asked, one dark thick brow rising in question.

"Maybe. It would fit. Isn't it glorious today?" I swirled around, arms open wide.

"Sometimes, I wonder if you believe you're being filmed. Like in *The Truman Show*. Or maybe you imagine an audience for yourself?"

He had his usual affable yet understated tone. Luc "Cookie" Doux was one of my best friends, and now that

Beast had gotten married and was helping Jess manage her severe morning sickness, it was me and Cookie, and sometimes Stone.

"I do not. I'm just..." I wondered whether it'd make sense but went for it. "I'm relieved."

He raised another brow. "Relieved Jess is being replaced by a woman you struck out with?"

I laughed loudly, then glanced around, praying no one had heard him. He knew my history with Liz, as did a few others, but I didn't exactly love the idea of him shouting it out as we walked into work. "Aren't the French supposed to be understated?"

"I'm only half-French."

I snorted and patted his back. "If you must know, yes. I'm relieved to see Liz again. In retrospect, I might owe her an apology. And after meditating and carefully considering my approach—" Read: after watching my favorite romcom with a giant bowl of popcorn on my couch under every blanket I owned and letting the movie be my excuse to feel my feelings until I could think logically about coexisting in the same space as the only woman who'd snagged my interest in years... "—I'm looking forward to putting that behind me and being friends. I've got a lot to offer her and I'm sure Jo will be busy. I can fold her in, help her with the lay of the land, and just..."

... get over it.

"Just?" Luc asked, never one to let me completely off the hook.

I shrugged a shoulder because I was that easy, breezy, beautiful about it all. "Like I said, just be friends."

Beast came stomping up the stairs behind us and reached forward to grab the door, but instead of storming through like he might've in the past, especially when he was in the darkest places, he held it wide for us. "After you two dummies."

Well, he was still himself.

"Thank you, Sir Beast-A-Lot. Your noble deeds wilt be remembered." I made a fancy, flourishing bow.

"He's on one today," Cookie said, slipping inside in front of me.

"Well, the sky is especially blue, so I'm not surprised," Beast said, his low voice sounding a touch grumpy even when his words were affectionate.

He'd just told us yesterday that he was going to be a dad, so I knew very well his gruff response was all bark. Lucky for him, I'd already attack-hugged him and Jess and told them to notify me of their preferred baby shower date. Just because I'd never thrown one didn't mean it wasn't my new calling.

"Exactly! You know me well." I liked all days, but blue skies in the winter had to be celebrated. We were usually above the worst of the gray inversion that often plagued the valleys further down the canyon and in the Ogden and Salt Lake areas in winter, but it was still worth actively enjoying.

Beast's lips twitched.

"I love you, too," I said, batting my lashes at him as I passed.

He shoved me forward with his giant paw on the back of my head. The gesture made my heart squeeze just a bit. I remembered my actual brother doing that back when we were kids. It was never particularly good-natured, but I liked that it was predictable. It had been part of our dynamic.

We made our way to our individual offices—probably the thing I liked least about being an adult at a company that respected its employees enough to give them individual workspaces. I used to share with Luc, but when they finished the add-on to the building, he got his own office.

I was Rose watching Jack slowly sink into the abyss despite the very clear space directly next to me. *Come baaaaaaaaaaaaack.*

Alas. He did not. As a man who thrived on togetherness and being with my people, sometimes my cushy office felt like a punishment and my penance was being sentenced to the doom of staring out my large window and leaning back in my ergonomic chair and *thinking*.

Listen, cerebral, I was not. Any personality test I'd ever taken showed the opposite, sometimes to my advantage, and sometimes to my detriment. When you join a special operations elite unit like the Exceptional Mission Unit, you're tested for everything from psychosis to IQ to learning style to leadership capability, and that's before you get out of the room with the very kind, super smart, freakishly insightful psych who sees right through you.

I tended to be an open book about most things, so not a problem. Most of their findings weren't news to me, but having someone confirm my lack of chill had been oddly affirming. It wasn't just that I tended toward restlessness— it was that I was an *activator*. I liked doing things first, learning from them as I went. I liked experiences over stuff, people over solitude. The results and psych evals had spelled it all out, and it felt more like a pat on the back for who I already was than the repeated refrains I'd heard as a child begging me to calm down, be quiet, be a little less *me*.

After powering through the few bits of paperwork and email drudgery waiting for me, I rallied in the conference room for another meeting. Two days in a row was unusual, but nothing alarming. Other than a handful of local celebs who needed personal security while in town to ski and what have you, we were pretty slow.

When my heart rate kicked up as Liz walked in, I chalked it up to the novelty factor. I'd already made my decision. I wasn't going to be embarrassed by my past effort to take her out five years ago, even if she did laugh at me when I did so. It hadn't been cruel—it'd almost seemed like she'd been genuinely surprised. And I'd never forget the way her lips curved up as she said, "You're cute. Thanks for asking, but no. I don't date."

And that was that.

She had no idea what the word *cute* did to me at the time, nor could she understand the baggage she'd tapped into with that one little sentence. So. No weirdness. Just friendship.

She wore a suit instead of the "roughs" most of the staff at Saint opted for—plaid flannel button-up shirt and utility pants, with boots in the winter or something lighter in the warmer months. I hadn't seen her in anything but suits when we worked together years ago, so naturally I wondered... did that bun come out when the blazer came off? Was her chestnut hair on the short end? Long? Against her almost olive skin tone, it looked—

I sucked in a breath when her gaze lifted, then turned and met mine.

Caught me.

Oopsie daisy.

I'd been pretty obvious about checking her out, but I hadn't been doing it in a sleazy way. More just... noticing she looked the same.

The dark eyes... they still had the same magnetic power I'd felt years ago. They held this knowing—an incredible intelligence she'd showcased in subtle ways with suggestions to guide the op we'd cooperated on, and intuition about the situation that had seemed like she'd done the job for thirty years, not ten. She'd been this tough, capable, certain person who was not a bit intimidated or impressed by our unit showing up, which had been its own sort of novelty.

And at one point, when she'd been talking to my team leader, she'd smiled. It'd been small, subdued, but it damn near stole my breath. Here was a woman who knew herself and wouldn't let anyone railroad her.

Those eyes of hers still apparently had the power to make my brain white out and my self-control shrivel up. With her attention on me, I just wanted to look and look.

She must not've felt the same because her gaze jumped away from mine and centered on Bruce.

"Let's get going. I think we have everyone who's not assigned right now," he said, checking his notes then looking up as someone entered the room.

Julian Grenier, our local benevolent billionaire, strolled in with an infant car seat hooked over his left suit-covered arm like a purse. On someone else it might seem odd, but on this man it appeared to be the perfect accessory to his bespoke slate suit and hawkish gaze. He extended a hand to Bruce, who shook it, even as he set the infant seat down. Julian then nudged the forward edge with the tip of his fine leather shoe and made it rock.

Dang. If little Josie had been awake, I totally would've gotten some baby snugs.

"You all know Julian. He's here because the assignment I have is a sensitive one," Bruce explained.

"It'll be a personal favor to me and I'm happy to incentivize as needed." His voice was low and calm, but the fact he'd showed up today meant this really mattered to him.

He'd initially invested in Saint Security when Wilder and Bruce were just getting started a few years ago. He's how the fledgling company was able to provide world-class protection from the jump.

"We won't need additional incentive to do our jobs," Adam said, not quite scowling but... perturbed.

As our medical expert and a man who always did the right thing, it didn't surprise me he'd be bothered. Bruce and Wilder likely wouldn't stand for it either as our resident Saint Daddies with unflinching moral compasses.

"I mean, let the man speak." If a billionaire wanted to give me a bonus, who was I to refuse?

Everyone groaned like I'd made a bad joke, and they weren't wrong. I might not be the Captain America of the group, but I probably was at least, like, Spidey? Maybe? And he followed his sweet lil' moral compass pretty well, too.

Maybe. Not everyone laughed, though. Because—I swear I wasn't looking for Liz's reaction—I did notice her expression didn't flicker and her mouth certainly didn't slide up into a begrudging smile like Luc's. Not even an eye roll like Beast.

Tough audience.

Then Bruce laid out the needs of the assignment and it clicked into place—why Julian would want to be here to impress upon us the situation mattered to him, even though he should know we'd take care of it.

Saint Security would handle it, and if I had my way, I'd be on the team.

____

CHAPTER THREE

Elizabeth

Bruce smiled easily, a bright genuine grin, clearly pleased with my offer to help on this mission.

I'd noticed it on my last visit, but the truth struck me yet again—every single person in this building was beautiful. Just, straight up. And not just on the outside, either. Maybe it was because I'd come from a fairly gray existence where baggy pantsuits and stale lighting haunted my station hours, but they were all so... full of life.

"You don't have to do this. You've just gotten into town. But if you're sure you're comfortable diving right in, I'd appreciate it, Elizabeth."

His tone and mien were genuine. So far, he was a *say what you mean and mean what you say* kind of person, though I knew as well as anyone just how lethal he was thanks to his background in the EMU.

I nodded. "Absolutely. Happy to do it. I know Eddie's

getting ready to head out of town with Bri and this strikes me as one that having a woman on board for would be valuable."

Eddie used to be Kappa, like me, though I didn't know her well. We'd been colleagues, crossing paths a couple of times, though not friends by any means thanks to the solitary nature of the job. Still, it didn't take being a spy to know getting away with her famous pop star husband would be highly anticipated. She needed this break, and here I was, fully available.

Bruce knocked on his desk. "Agreed. I'll get the details finalized in the next hour and we'll push it to your cell. Sounds like they want to leave by Sunday morning, but again, I'll get more to you as soon as possible."

"Good plan. Thanks." I stood and rounded the chair toward the open doorway when his voice stopped me.

"I know it's only been a day, but are you settling in okay? Will that apartment work out?" He leaned his forearms on the desk.

"It's great. Comfortable and simple."

He chuckled. "Simple indeed. I'm afraid we haven't given it much style, but feel free to do what you want to make it your own while you're here."

"Thanks." They'd offered me the lodging as a part of my contract, and I'd had no reason to refuse them. It was a small studio right in town not far from All Booked Up the company now owned and used when overseas employees came for trainings or extended trips. Avoiding the hassle of finding a temporary housing situation or footing the bill for a hotel for a week before I found an alternate location had been ideal.

Yes, my father would've loved to put me up. I knew this. So would Jo. But I didn't... I needed space.

"Excellent. And are you coming to our happy hour tonight?"

I nearly tripped over the carpet. "Uh, I hadn't planned on it. Should I?"

"No pressure whatsoever. Very casual, good chance to get to know some of the other crew, and I believe your sister will be there."

I perked up at that. "Oh. Interesting."

Two birds with one socializing stone absolutely spoke to my soul, so the possibility of actually showing up increased tenfold.

"Again, no obligation to be there, but it's a good time. I'd love to see you fold in while you're here. We've got a good team and we're glad you're with us as long as it lasts."

He smiled, and I took the signal as my time to go, sending him a quick chin tip-up. I glanced at my watch and—

"Oh, crap. Sorry."

Kenny Carmichael's hands steadied me at the shoulders.

"My fault completely." I was the dolt not looking where she was going, anyway.

His handsome face—and let me be clear, it was obnoxiously handsome—lit up and he shook his head vehemently. "Nah, no blame game. Just an accident. It happens. Are you okay?"

I nodded, my shoulders burning with warmth from his contact. Was this man running a fever? "Just fine. You?"

"Great. I'm actually really happy to run into you. I haven't had a chance to welcome you to Saint and say how glad I am to see you."

He grinned and stepped back, releasing me and splaying his hands wide in a gesture that I read to mean something like, "Sorry for holding on so long." It also drew my attention to his left hand where he was missing his fourth and fifth fingers.

That's new, too. I couldn't help the thought. Kenny was different in a few ways I'd noticed thus far, but this was the most overt. What happened to him? Was that why he'd gotten out of the Army before retirement?

"Thanks. Likewise. Always happy to see a familiar face in a new setting." *Okay, robot woman.* I forced myself to add something else—anything else that sounded less trite than my first response. "What's new?"

He must've seen my attention snag on his hand seconds ago, because he said, "Well, I lost two of my fingers, got out of the Army about ten years before I ever thought I'd leave, and moved to a State I'd never been to before, sight unseen. How 'bout you?"

His blue eyes sparkled at me, and he said it so good-naturedly, I barked out an odd half-laugh that sounded as rusty as my casual social skills. "Ha! Right. Yeah. Big changes."

His beaming smile widened a touch. "Unexpected course of events, but crap happens. And in some ways it feels like...."

Illogically, my heart sank. I knew what was coming next. "Don't tell me. Everything happens for a reason?"

He quirked a brow. "No. I think in some instances that's resoundingly true. But then there's the darkest, worst moments. Those things that most people hopefully never see, but for those of us who make a point to go into dark places and shine light on things, we can't unsee them. For those things, it's harsh and awful and untrue. What I was going to say is, it feels like being here, for me, was meant to be."

I studied him, his shiny smile gone and replaced with an expression I could only describe as peaceful acceptance.

This was new, too. Still stupidly good-looking and charming and clearly still a bit of a class clown, but also more mature. He had stories to tell—maybe always had, in fairness, since I hadn't actually known him more than an acquaintanceship—and he'd gained some depth. Again, maybe he'd always had it, but now he seemed willing to show it. The version of Kenny I'd met five years ago had been silly and flirty, a little cocky, and just seemed so young.

These five years, however many hardships they'd thrown at him, looked good on him.

"Hmm. Sounds nice." And though possibly construed as a throwaway response, I meant it. After everything that'd brought me here, I felt it down to my soul how enviable it was that he was so at home and right here.

When was the last time I'd felt at peace about anything?

When I'd accepted my job at the agency, I'd felt it then. I'd had this certainty about doing a job that had a purpose and would be impactful for the country and maybe even the world. I'd loved the sense that even as a twenty-two-year-old college grad I might be stepping into something that mattered. After leaving home and feeling like everything there was in chaos, though in retrospect I could admit the drama primarily came from my teenaged perspective and the hurt I didn't know what to do with over my parents' divorce, the path forward with the CIA and Kappa Sector had felt secure. Comforting. Possibly even a version of peaceful.

What I sensed now wasn't peace, though it wasn't exactly tumult. It was that eerie sense I was in-between—places, jobs, lives, realities, all of it.

"I do recommend it. But hey, I need to run in for a chat with Bruce. Can we hang later? Catch up for real?"

He stepped to the side to give me space to pass him, though the hallways weren't all that narrow, and I stumbled over my response. "Oh, um, I'm not sure—"

His eyes shuttered so quickly, I wouldn't have noticed if I hadn't been watching, then returned to their cheery friendliness.

"No worries. I'll be at cocktail hour if you happen to be by tonight and if not, I'll catch you another time. Have a good one."

I nodded, because rather than being a trained agent in the intelligence community and a woman who held a master's degree in international relations and spoke three languages, I was the girl in the hallway simultaneously stunned by this man's golden retriever energy and my own inability to respond to him like a normal human being.

And what was that flicker of something? Disappointment? Annoyance? Maybe he really wanted me to show up tonight. That was a nice enough thought. At one time, he'd been at least a little attracted to me—enough to ask me out. He didn't seem like the kind of guy to hold that against someone, even if he had seemed more than a little shell-shocked when I'd seen him here in the summer.

But that man?

Yeah, he was *not* weeping into his pillow over me, nor had he ever. I couldn't imagine he'd ever had a bed to himself for space to do such a thing.

CHAPTER FOUR

Kenny

Bruce eyed me. "You sure?"

"Yes. I want this. I don't mind working this weekend. I'm bored out of my mind since Luc's always skiing and Dorian's grumpy right now and Beast is hovering over Jess and holding her hair back—"

Bruce's look said enough.

"I know, sorry. He's right where he should be. But I could use a chance to get out. And like I said—" I pressed a palm to my heart "—I will happily accept a bonus from Julian if he feels so inclined."

Apparently, he was not impressed.

"Just kidding. You know I'm joking. I want to go because this is important and straightforward. I want to help these people, and I can do it without it taking me away from my partner or kids or moody teen sister."

Bruce chuckled. His sister, for whom he served as

guardian, had been particularly moody as she entered her junior year of high school. Kiley was a good kid and smarter than most of us ever had a hope to be, so it was handy she had Bruce's beloved Nikki, an actual genius, around to help.

"That's thoughtful of you, Barbie." His gaze softened.

Oh, boy. I didn't want a talk about *that* right now, but I felt it coming and couldn't scramble out of my seat fast enough.

"You going to work on that for yourself?"

It was as gentle a probe as could be, but I still did my best Beast impression and grunted. "Not worrying about it right now."

Did I want a partner of my own? Sure. In theory.

Did I also know the perils of taking a risk on someone? Yep. Been there, done that, have the T-shirt sporting "I fell in love and all I got for it was a broken heart and this T-shirt" to prove it.

So like... yes. I struggled to enjoy my single status as each of my dear friends found not just someone, but *the* one. I loved it for them, truly. I celebrated them and the future dynasty of Saint children who would provide Silverton and the world beyond with a second generation of badass, emotionally intelligent humans.

But I also ached. I had a tender heart and it felt more than a little battered lately, though I hated to admit it. And the thought of someone who knew me in that soul-deep way...

Eh. Whatever. Some people got a soulmate. Some people had someone they thought was a soulmate take a giant crap on their soul. We all had a story.

"Fine. Take the job this weekend and get out of here early. Go for a run or something to burn off the angst, and

I'll see you tonight? I'll gather all the info on the trip and can give it to you then."

I slid out of my chair and gave an obnoxiously doofy salute. "Roger, Jaws."

Having taken Bruce's advice and pushed myself into a punishing workout that started with a five-mile run and ended with a round at Grit with Warrick Saint doing his best impression of an executioner without actually offing me, I half-limped, half-walked into Craic a few minutes after five.

The place bustled with groups already enjoying the weekend, especially since the town was packed with tourists to take advantage of the crazy good snow Utah boasted. I'd heard people talking about how Silverton and the Silver Ridge ski area had grown so much in the last few years, but it was still far less crowded than the more established luxury resorts, so people felt like they'd found a hidden gem even still.

"There he is," Cookie said as I leaned on the table with both elbows. His handsome face flashed with confusion. "Why are you acting like you can barely stand up?"

"Warrick was working out some of his feelings on me at Grit this afternoon." I tilted my head one way, then the other, attempting to stretch my neck. I'd happily roll out a yoga mat and do another full twenty-minute stretch right now if it wouldn't make Kieran and Gemma kick me out.

"Well, you made your choice, didn't you? Don't go to

Grit if you don't want to feel that way." Adam shrugged a shoulder.

"Aren't you supposed to be compassionate? Do no harm?" I whined.

He chuckled. "I'm a medic, not a saint. And I've done workouts with Warrick and I have fond memories of them... lesson learned."

I laughed, but when his eyes flicked to something over my shoulder, I didn't have to follow his line of sight to know he was looking at Jo. They'd gotten engaged, and we'd be lining up for another summer wedding come June.

I probably had steep competition for the role of ring bearer or flower girl because there were some cute kids around, but odds were good I'd get to play groomsman again. I'd stand up next to Doc and watch him covertly wipe the tears away when he saw Jo coming down the aisle any day. I might've longed for my own person while feeling the futility of such a desire, but I would not cease to celebrate when my friends found what they were looking for.

"Elizabeth, so glad you came."

Bruce's words had my gaze snapping up to see Liz walk in—

I could swear "Dream Weaver" was playing as I took her in. She wore jeans and a puffy black jacket she was unzipping, swiping the hat off her head to reveal a shiny curtain of long chestnut hair.

She had long hair.

In my mind, red alerts sounded. Sirens blared.

She has long hair.

It was a stupid thing about me, but I loved long hair. Not that I saw it from afar and got all creepy or anything, but I just... loved it. In another life, I would be Kenneth

Carmichael, long-haired man with a waist-length mane to rival Cher's, just so I could braid my own hair.

Okay, that got weird.

This came from events in my past. It just did. As much as I didn't love thinking about it—about my ex and how much I'd loved her long hair and how she'd cut it while I'd been at basic training and I probably should've seen that as a sign—sometimes who I was because of it made it impossible to ignore. This love of long hair was definitely one of those things I hadn't shaken in terms of what I responded to on a gut level, shallow though it was.

Also... she was wearing jeans. And something casual on top but I tried to bounce my eyes away so I wasn't straight out staring at her.

"Welcome, Elizabeth," Adam said, and he managed to keep the ring of fear out of his voice.

I'd have to tell him what a good job he did. Liz being his fiancée's very protective older sister meant Adam had a complex relationship with our new coworker. All signs pointed to her being happy for them, but Adam wasn't about to miss an opportunity to show her he was a decent guy.

"Thanks for inviting me," she said to Bruce, then nodded at me.

The teenage boy who lived inside my brain shrieked, "She nodded at me!" He was busy running around in circles, not knowing what to do, when she accepted a beer and took a spot between me and Luc, who slid over to talk to Bruce at the last minute.

Torn between loving the man for doing what was right and hating that he'd made it less than covert, I nudged her elbow with mine. "How does the Utah beverage selection compare to wherever you were last? I'm guessing somewhere different from where we first met?"

Our cooperative mission had been based out of Estonia and slipped into... other places near Estonia. State Department and the fancy folk Elizabeth worked for had advised. She'd been nothing short of magnificent in her management of our arrival, the in-country situation brief, and every aspect she touched. I'd been more than a little enamored of her. Mission accomplished, we'd left, but I'd been keenly aware she had an entire life there.

"Yes. I left Tallinn not too long after you guys came through. And I would say thus far, good, though I'm basing that solely on this one beer." She took a sip.

I did not watch her because that would be weird.

"When did you get into town?" I asked, taking an oh-so-nonchalant swig of my own glass someone had shoved in front of me.

"Thursday early evening."

I choked on my beer. "Really? I guess I thought you'd been here a minute. So it's like eleven at night in your brain?"

Her lips, which objectively were extremely well-made based on the curvature of her cupid's bow and the soft reddish-pink color of them—curled into a slight smile.

"Well past my bedtime, yes." She tipped her pint glass to the side and touched the edge of hers to mine. "But here I am. Being social."

This hit me in just the right way, and I burst out laughing.

"So proud of you." I raised my glass, then took a drink. "I take it you're not particularly fond of social outings?"

As a former member of a unit where at least half the

personnel tested as extremely introverted, I was familiar with the desire of some to avoid social events, especially those that might condemn them to small talk.

"Depends, but generally, something like this—" she looked to her right toward a group laughing just a little too loud, then continued, "—wouldn't be my first choice."

"What would be your first choice?"

The question jumped out before I could stop it. The only solace came in the form of her ignorance about just how high my heart had leapt at the chance to ask it.

She sipped her beer and eyed me, not quite squinting but certainly... skewering me with her gaze.

Wait, can she see how my internal organs just reacted?

They shouldn't be reacting at all. They should be going about their regularly scheduled programming. Beating heart. Breathing lungs. Intestines... well, whatever. They should just be doing their thing and not responding to the nearness of a woman who was simply a coworker.

"I love a good run. I'm hoping to ski while I'm here. And I like watching movies." Her head dipped down, and if I wasn't seeing things, her cheeks tinged with a blush.

No. No no no no. I could not be appreciating things like the color on her cheeks or the way she seemed embarrassed at the simple contents of her answer. I couldn't like that she's a little grumpy and a little shy, not unlike two of my three best friends.

"Would you two step outside with me for just a minute?" Bruce asked, then turned toward the exit as though he knew we'd follow without question.

And of course we did.

"Sorry to interrupt, but since you're both here and I'm selfishly hoping not to go in this weekend, I wanted to brief you here. You'll both have the full details in your secure email, but the most important thing is—you're it. You guys are the team."

My mouth dropped open, then snapped shut.

Bruce chuckled. "You're the team that'll be going to California."

CHAPTER FIVE

Elizabeth

Kenny's energy halted in a way that meant he'd stopped breathing.

Maybe I had, too? Despite the cacophony coming from inside the pub, out here in the chill of the Utah winter, the air fell deadly silent—a bit eerie.

And there it came again—more than a little unearthly. Surreal. Soon, everything would shift into a smear of color and light and mouths would stretch into facsimiles of Edvard Munch's The Scream.

Or, you know, it'd just keep feeling a little odd.

"Any questions for now? Kenny can get you two outfitted with whatever you need, plus I believe Cookie was planning to help load you up. Car should be ready to go, and we'll be here on the receiving end Monday." Bruce glanced between us with a pleasant expression.

"Sounds good," I said, hoping I was right.

"Mmhhm. Yep. All good. We're golden, bossman. Just call us the golden egg and the, uh, you know, the other golden thing from the—"

"Goose?" Bruce offered.

"Harp?" I tried.

Kenny's mouth flattened. "Whatever. We're good. Be free and go smolder at your fiancée."

Bruce clapped Kenny on the shoulder, then shuffled back inside.

The bite of wintry air nipped at my bare arms and hands, but it had nothing on the chill of Northern Germany or even DC. The dry Utah climate helped it not feel like a bone-deep cold, and I greatly appreciated that. Wearing a coat was enough of a barrier here, whereas in much of Europe and the Eastern US, winter was brutal and unrelenting in its quest to burrow down to your marrow and chill you.

Silverton's cold felt lighter—more manageable even. So I'd enjoy it while it lasted.

When we'd stood there alone for a few seconds, I turned to him with narrowed eyes. He'd been a bit squirrely in terms of his energy and overall dialogue. Plus, he'd asked me out and I'd said no. Some men couldn't handle closeness with a woman who'd turned them down, though so far that hadn't seemed to bother him, but I'd rather ask now than have it blow up in my face halfway to LA.

"Are you okay partnering with me?"

His big blue eyes blinked in what had to be slow motion. I shouldn't have even been able to tell his eyes were blue, but even out here in the dark, I could see they weren't dark and stormy, but all kinds of clear and light.

He was just so dang handsome. And it was so annoying to be noticing that right after we'd gotten a work briefing. I didn't think about people's physical appearance all that much unless it was to describe them for a report—height, build, guess on weight, skin color, hair color, eye color *maybe*, affect, accent, guess at origins... sometimes these things factored into evaluating a potential asset or tracking someone.

Noticing how a man's blue eyes sparkled was nonsense and not my norm.

"Of course. I'm happy to work with you. It'll be fun." He stood straighter and shifted on his feet. "The real question is whether you're comfortable working with me."

"Why wouldn't I be?"

He huffed, a billow of frozen breath emerging from his lips. "Well, I asked you out a while back, which you maybe don't even remember, but—"

"Of course I remember. But that doesn't make working with you a problem, especially since we never did go out."

I didn't miss the small wince he quickly covered. So he did have a little bruised ego about it. I wasn't convinced he'd noticed at all, let alone cared when I said no, but here he was worried I wouldn't work with him because of it?

Maybe I'd missed something, but from my perspective, it had all been casual and relatively inconsequential.

Hadn't it been?

"Right. Perfect." His eyes met mine and then he glanced toward the pub door. "We should head back in before we both end up with frostbite. I can't exactly afford to lose any more fingers."

My small gasp made him chuckle.

"Sorry. I forget you don't know me well enough to not be offended on my behalf."

I quirked a brow at him.

He shrugged. "I can't change what happened, nor

would I, really. I lost a few fingers, but in the end, it could've been worse." His expression darkened before he clucked. "So! Let's get back inside before your sister comes to hunt me down."

I followed him in, wondering at his ability to make light of something that seemed like it might be heavy. Was he delusional? Or was the wisdom I'd seen a flash of earlier actually what guided him, and he just couldn't suppress his sense of humor for anything? Or *wouldn't* would be more accurate.

Once we'd settled back at the table, Kenny joined the conversation already mid-step about someone I didn't know, and I decided now was as good a time as any to make my way to obligation number two of the night.

Jo saw me coming and hauled me to her with arms wide open before I reached the table where she and her friends had set up. "I'm so, *so* happy you came! I know you came for work, too, but I'm so glad to have you here."

Dove, the petite blond woman with what I thought might be white owls on a cherry red dress, raised her glass. "We all are!"

"Hear, hear!" Elise echoed. She had darker features than Jo or Dove, and her hair had been pulled back away from her face.

Nikki, Winnie, and Catherine all did the same and raised their glasses, so I joined them, clinking in the middle and glad I'd had the foresight to bring my drink along with me.

"Seriously, it's so good to see you again. I just love seeing you two side by side." Dove grinned, eyes ticking back and forth between me and Jo, who still had an arm around my shoulders.

Something had shifted between us this past summer

when I visited. I'd showed up on a whim just in time to assist with her rescue operation and discover that my own sister was a fairly well-known romance author. More significantly, I'd found out she'd kept this truth from me and the rest of our family because she'd worried we thought it wasn't weighty enough—that compared to my work or even my father's in the bookstore or my mother's as a real estate agent, we wouldn't understand.

It had gutted me on one level, and yet I'd understood her impulse to hide. I still did. If Jo's default was to hide, mine was, much to my dismay, to run.

Not that I'd run here. I'd been forced to take a break and of course I'd come back stateside. Why would I have waited it out there when I'd been told to leave?

Entering what felt like a different planet and timeline had me a little shaky and getting that odd sense one might call the "we're not in Kansas anymore" effect, but it wasn't running.

Keep telling yourself that, Malcom.

For Jo, I'd done what I could to make clear how much I esteemed her for doing something she loved that brought joy to others. I'd instantly purchased all her books and blazed through them, then ventured on to other escapes.

Formerly, I'd been primarily a non-fiction reader, with an occasional dip into a thriller on a rare vacation. Now I could easily call myself a romance girly, much to the teenage version of me's dismay.

"I'm glad to see you all again," I said, meaning it. These women took care of Jo—they'd become her extended family.

It was beautiful, and yet it gave me this gnawing sense I was still standing outside in that chilly winter air, watching it all play out.

"Please tell me you're coming to book club next weekend," Jo asked, and Winnie nodded eagerly. Dove clapped and said, "Yessss" while everyone else assented in her own way.

"Oh, no. I don't—I haven't read the book." I stumbled over the words enough that Jo would absolutely notice.

She did instantly, leaning away from me to eye my face.

Nikki leaned in, her red-brown hair looking surprisingly glamorous considering what I knew about her as a math genius and game developer and how Jo had spoken about her. "You don't have to read the book. We'd be glad for you to come."

"Absolutely," Elise confirmed.

"Sometimes, people are too busy even when they have advanced notice, but they still come. You might not even be the only one who hasn't read it," Dove said.

An invisible hand pressed against my sternum, but I exhaled sharply to banish the sensations. "Not sure yet. I'm working on an assignment starting tomorrow, so I'm not sure how the rest of the week will go. I'll keep it in mind, though."

There. That was good enough to avoid refusing outright, but leave me room to not attend if... I needed to.

They seemed accepting of my delay tactic and encouraged me to read the book but to come even if I hadn't. I drank the rest of my beer and set it down on a coaster, an itch to head home begging to be scratched.

"It was great to see you all, but I need to head out and get prepped."

I took a step, but Jo's arm shot out and wrapped around my waist.

"Thanks for coming. I know this wasn't your favorite," she said low enough so only I could hear.

"Love you," I returned before releasing her.

I thanked them all, wished them a good evening, and swung by the Saint table to do the same. No one seemed surprised or upset I was leaving, nor did they make me feel bad I was slipping out less than an hour after arriving.

"See you bright and early," Kenny said, raising the remaining fingers of his left hand, then turning back to the table.

As I hunched against the cold and made my way down the street to the tiny apartment provided by my new, temporary workplace, an ache settled heavy in my chest.

Oddly, it wasn't one of longing to be back at my usual job or even to be walking the familiar streets of Budapest toward my own apartment. And even though the sting of bitterness had crept into the way I'd been thinking about work and even the city, I did love it. I loved how capable I felt doing the job, the difference I made, and the respect I had there—or, used to have, pending the outcome of this investigation.

But tonight, something else entirely had taken up root behind my ribs and I had no explanation for it.

Once I nestled down into the surprisingly cozy reading chair with my computer, a fire in the gas fireplace, sweatpants and fuzzy socks on my legs, and a facemask coating my cheeks, I waited for the relief of solitude to settle in.

Funny enough, I waited all night, and it never did come.

Kenny

After a decent, albeit short, night of sleep, I rolled into the Saint Security parking lot at ten to five. Knowing what I did about Liz, I shouldn't have been surprised to see another car idling in a spot close to the entrance.

Of course, she ran early. It wasn't just the military that appreciated promptness, and Liz had always given me the sense she would work twice as hard and be ten times as successful. That said, she seemed to have enough raw intelligence and drive, so she didn't spend her time trying to prove herself. She was more interested in doing good work because she believed in it and the results—whether in her success with her job or her connections she could exploit or whatever—revealed that.

We got out of our cars at the same time, and I grabbed my bag from the passenger side while she retrieved one from the seat behind hers. We shut our doors as though we'd choreographed it and walked toward the building.

Did I match my stride to hers? Yes, I did.

Did it give me a weird thrill to be walking in sync with her?

Sure enough, it did.

"Get some sleep?" I asked, voice still a bit gruff from disuse.

"It's almost lunchtime in my brain, despite having over forty-eight hours on ground. I'm ready for my body to switch to mountain time."

The door to the building opened and signaled Cookie was already here. He'd likely parked near the back entrance where the fleet cars were located.

"That's rough. I'm sure this road trip will do wonders for your circadian rhythm." We'd be crossing into Pacific time to pick up the package, then rolling right along back here. Likely wouldn't do anything to help her adjust.

"I'm glad for the distraction." Her gaze cut to mine, then away.

"What—"

"Glad you made it. Let's get your weapons signed out and you can get on the road."

Cookie smacked my hand where I held it high for a five. It might've been juvenile, but I got a kick out of the fact that he would literally never leave me hanging. I'd tested it more than once and he always came through, even when the time was far from right.

Call me sentimental, but it reflected who he was pretty accurately. Cookie would be there no matter what. He wasn't the loudest of us, or the pushiest. He wasn't particularly grumpy, nor was he full of optimism like me. The man was solid, steady, and if you believe the ladies, too hand-some to look directly in the eye.

He was a faithful, steadfast friend, and I loved him. And therefore, I forced a high five on him whenever I could.

We checked out minimal weapons for concealed carrying and gear we hoped we wouldn't need. Cookie had already packed the car with an extensive emergency kit, AED machine, and more medical gear than we'd normally take, but for this mission, we wanted all bases covered.

"You've got rooms reserved at this hotel, which is a thirty to forty-five minute drive to the house where you'll pick them up, and they're planning on an oh-eight-hundred pick up tomor-row. You'll stop in Vegas on the way back because the client needs to break up the drive rather than doing the full trip in one go." Cookie tapped away on a laptop while he spoke.

We both nodded, already familiar with these details, but it was standard to give a pre-mission brief to make sure everyone was on the same page.

"Upon arriving in Silverton, you'll take them directly to their chosen location. I'll likely be the one to receive."

We each nodded, the plan unchanged from when Bruce had briefed us.

"Good. Mission complete is at the listed address, ideally no later than three p.m. on Monday." He held out the car keys between us.

I looked to Liz. "How about you drive first, and we'll alternate, but I'll take the last stint just in case jet lag hits?"

The eleven-hour drive would be long, but if we traded off every three-to-four hours, we'd make it quick. With it being winter, the first stretch would be most stressful as we got out of Northern Utah, and after that it was a pretty clear shot through the desert to Cali. I couldn't think of anything

I'd rather be doing, and I'd get a little bonus for the weekend work despite being on salary, so all in all, there was no downside to this situation.

"Sounds good."

She took the keys, thanked Cookie, and marched toward the rear exit, which I hadn't thought she even knew about.

We got our bags settled. I waved obnoxiously to Cookie even though he was nowhere to be seen, and then we were off.

Liz drove carefully but not timidly. I liked it.

Thus far, I liked just about everything she did, so this was no surprise. Still, she had this confident, focused way about her, and it was more than a little attractive.

The temptation to shut my eyes would've dragged at me more, but the awareness that we had eleven hours alone together was as effective as a shot of espresso.

Speaking of, we navigated down Elk Street and passed both Joe and Glazed.

"Have you tried Joe or Glazed?" I asked, longing for a donut and knowing full well I wouldn't ask her to stop. Plus, I'd packed copious road trip snacks, which were their own delicacy.

"Not yet this trip. I had some Joe last time, but otherwise, I got stuffed with bread from Rise and Shine. I'm pretty sure Jane felt it was my duty as Sadie's step-sister-in-law to eat my bodyweight in homemade carbs."

The small smile on her lips made me smile.

"I like Jane." She was just one of those super likeable people, and if you lived in Silverton long enough, you got to know her. The Saints, along with the Morrisons and a few others, were practically founding families of Silver Ridge, so it made sense. "Is it weird that she's your stepmom?"

Jane Saint had married Liz's dad, Darcy Malcom, a few

years back. They'd literally run away to Vegas and got married and they were freaking adorable. They'd found each other after loss and divorce, and the sight of them around town or at a giant table full of Jane's kids and their spouses and grandkids and Jo and Adam... well, it made a man believe in happy endings.

At least for some people.

"I'm not proud to say I thought it would be. I was really skeptical about her. But after about twenty minutes in her presence, I could see why my dad loves her. She's genuine and forthright. That's not how my mom is, and I haven't really talked to them about what went wrong, but it makes sense he likes that."

She exhaled in a way that made me feel like maybe she hadn't anticipated saying so much.

I wondered if she felt guilty for not visiting sooner, but I wasn't about to ask the question. Instead, I said, "And hey, now you have a bunch of big and or little brothers and such."

She chuckled, and I couldn't resist peeking at her to see how the smile looked on her pretty face.

Granted, *pretty* was like calling the Hoover dam a watering hole. She was... beautiful.

"So true. I was never one of those kids who wanted a big family—that was always Jojo. But I'm enjoying getting to know them all."

Jojo. Damn, it was an adorable nickname, and it gave me this tiny glimpse into what she might be like as a sister. Fiercely protective and determinedly supportive, yes. I knew this and had witnessed it firsthand during her last visit.

But *Jojo* gave me a hint of softness. A clue about what might be under some of her serious, focused layers.

Not to be a total romcom-loving cliché, but I loved a tough outer shell with a melty inside. Grumpy with a cinnamon roll center heroines were not really a trend from what Jo and the Romance Reader Club ladies told me, but... sign me up.

"I'm sure they feel the same."

She didn't respond to that, so I let it lie. No sense in pushing this early, and a Golden Retriever I may be, I could also be a dog with a bone about things.

So I reached into my bag and pulled out the first round of road snackies. "May I offer you a Combo?"

A laugh barked out of her, startling in the early morning quiet and the lull of the road. "Um, no, thank you."

"You have a problem with Combos?" I asked, only slightly mocking in my offense.

"I... didn't realize they still exist."

I scoffed. "Then you haven't been living."

I fished one out and held it up for her. The little cylinder filled with pizza sauce flavoring didn't look particularly appetizing, but they were for nostalgia's sake.

Her gaze shot to me and she shook her head. "I appreciate the offer, but I'll stick with my coffee for now."

I shrugged, then popped a Combo in my mouth. They were insanely salty, and the flavor was more than a little artificial. Really, they were pretty bad. But they were also classic road trip food, and therefore, I persisted.

"I think it's your turn now," she said, drawing my attention to her lovely profile.

"My turn for what?"

"Time to tell me about your family."

Ah. Well. There's the downside.

CHAPTER SEVEN

Elizabeth

Kenny twisted in his seat, visibly uncomfortable even in my peripheral vision.

"Saint's my family now," he scraped out, then flipped open the top of his water bottle and took a long drink.

Obviously, he meant the people at Saint Security and not just the Saint family. He clearly knew Wilder's family, but not intimately.

"And before Saint?"

He stared at the road in front of us as I followed the winding canyon down, down, down. We'd emerge soon and eventually jump on the interstate.

Clearing his throat, he wiggled around before slumping back into his chair. He was so physical about everything, it almost made me laugh. I didn't, though, sensing he might take it personally while he was clearly feeling tender.

"Before, I was born to Mandee and Glen Carmichael of

backwoods, Nevada. Grew up in a trailer big enough for three, but there were four of us." He swiped his hands down his quads. "My brother is two years older than me."

I waited for more. One minute, two. Nothing came.

"Guess you're not in touch anymore?"

He laughed, but it sounded all wrong. I hadn't been around him all that much, but it was enough to know he had a big, free laugh and a charming smaller one, and this was neither. It was closed, hollow.

"Not so much."

"Well, I'm glad you've found your place in Silver Ridge. It's kind of dreamy."

His head snapped in my direction. "*Dreamy?*"

"Yeah. Dreamy. It's got the small-town charm without everyone knowing everyone else's business. And it's cozy while still having great restaurants and shops. It's a nice mix and, of course, the mountains are just... soul-expanding."

I'd always felt that way about mountains. Maybe it came from growing up with Mount Rainier in my backyard or escaping to the Alps whenever I could over my years in Europe, but being near them grounded me. I'd not thought of myself as someone who needed grounding, but right now, I clearly did.

Every morning when I exited my building, I'd gaze up at the snow-covered peaks of Silver Ridge and its sisters and I felt... calm. Less frenetic and anxious about what came next.

The grounding helped me feel normal, even though whatever this was still wasn't normal. It didn't make sense, but I understood his point.

"I like that. Soul-expanding is exactly the way I feel about the mountains and the people there."

I must've made a sound of disbelief, though I thought I'd kept it in my head.

"You don't think people can be like that?" he asked, adjusting in his seat so he was almost sitting sideways.

Did I think people could be soul-expanding?

Hard no.

"I've never met someone who makes me feel that way, that's for sure. I mean, I love my parents and Jo... she's probably the closest thing? But we're still feeling our way back to how to interact in person."

"You two have lived apart for so long," he said, almost like he was explaining our challenge to himself.

And for some completely odd reason, I wanted to explain it.

"We have. I left when I was eighteen and she was just twelve. I didn't mean to leave her, but I had to go, you know? I think she understood that. Or, I always hoped she did."

She'd cried when I'd left for college, and the first time I'd called to say I wasn't coming home for Christmas. I didn't miss every year, but I never came home in the summers like she'd asked.

I'd always felt awful about it—the knowledge I needed to be out of the house forging my own path had helped, but the awareness that I'd left her, even for good reason, had stung.

"I doubt she understood then, but I'm sure she does now. She loves you so much and I'm sure she's told you, but she's so happy you're here."

I glanced at him to find his blue eyes looking sleepy but bright and pinned on me. He had a touch of scruff covering his face, like maybe he hadn't bothered to shave this morning. Even a little haggard, he was gorgeous.

Eyes back on the road, I nodded. "I know. I'm glad I'm here, too."

Intuition made me clench my teeth against what I knew would come. Then I thought better of it and jumped to change the subject right as he spoke again.

"Why *are* you here? Did—"

"So, feel free to nap or whatever, and we'll stop in a bit for a stretch."

I didn't look over at him again, didn't want to see if my overt evasion disappointed him or didn't bother him at all. Somehow, either one would be a problem, so best not to take in that data.

Best to keep my eyes ahead, focus on getting through this mission, this stretch of time outside of the familiar, and soon enough, I'd get the go ahead to return to my life.

"Oh, great. Yeah. Maybe I will close my eyes for a bit," he said, shifting so he faced forward and crossing his long arms. He wore his jacket and in seconds, he'd snuggled down and gone to sleep.

Left to my thoughts, I focused on the road and wondered how many more topics we'd each avoid before this trip was over. The minutes plodded along and soon, the coffee I'd been sipping for the last two hours had caught up with me. As if sensing a shift in the air, Kenny moved, stretching his long arms in front of him.

He'd been still and silent since I'd shut him down. I was fairly certain he'd been fully asleep the whole time, but I wasn't sure I'd met anyone who could just veritably roll over and conk out like that.

"Hey, how we coming?" he asked, tilting his neck from one side to the other and squinting out at the bright sunlight. We'd left in darkness and now we were in the full desert morning sun.

"We're almost three hours in, actually. I'm about ready for a pit stop. Thought I'd find a good place sometime soon."

Standing up sounded heavenly. We could absolutely go farther if needed, but we had all day to make this trek and there was no point in torturing our bodies if we could take it easy. Who knew how challenging the clients would make the return trip.

I was used to human variables in my line of work, but not like this. I'd never had a scenario where I'd be spending days with someone I'd never met. Usually, my job entailed a slow build with someone until they were cultivated as an official Kappa sector asset. Even this little road trip jaunt to Hollywood felt like a kind of dream.

"Sounds good. Happy to take a turn driving if you're ready to swap out."

He continued stretching, pulling his knees to his chest and all kinds of things I'd never seen someone do in the small space of a passenger seat. Granted, he and his EMU active-duty counterparts were known for doing whatever it took to get the job done, so I could imagine road tripping without stopping was one of many tasks they mastered. Maybe the key was passenger seat yoga.

"This looks decent," I said, pulling into a station with a large green dinosaur sculpture. Utah really loved leaning into their paleolithic past, I guessed.

"Perfect," he said, then jumped out while I did the same.

I rounded the vehicle and came face to face with—well, with Kenny's butt.

He was bent over, head hanging down and hands braced on his ankles, bobbing slightly, and I was just... staring.

Thankfully, I averted my eyes as though I'd been

checking the place out all along and had not, in fact, been eying the glorious thickness of his thighs or his very muscular glutes. But honestly, the man was all muscle and athleticism in a way I'd never anticipated. Of course he was fit because that seemed to be the first box ticked at Saint. Incredibly fit? Check. Stupidly handsome? Check, check.

More mature and mellow than I'd imagined? Also, problematically, check.

"One requirement before we go in," he said, a little mischief on his face.

"Requirement?" I took orders from my regional chief and there was bureaucracy a mile long at times, but very few people told me what to do anymore. Having him do it, even in this small way, was... new.

He nodded as though what came next was wisdom and not nonsense. "Yes. Road trip requirement. You have to pick a snack you think I'll like, and I'll do the same for you."

He wasn't ordering me in any way that encroached on my autonomy or even on the mission. Instead, he was creating an opportunity, or more simply, a game. With the stakes set at "snack preferences," I could accept, and so I did.

I chuckled, oddly pleased by this. "Ah, okay. Challenge accepted."

He grinned. "Something makes me think you never back down from a challenge."

I didn't have a response to that, so I turned and made for the entrance, a bit breathless from those crystal blue eyes, the same color as the sky, pinned on me and saying things that definitely felt like a challenge in themselves.

And no. Generally speaking, I did not back down.

CHAPTER EIGHT

Kenny

The woman smiled at me, a sultry, coy thing.

She was pretty, for sure. But I was working, and I had no time for flirting, even if it was a favorite pastime. Right now, I had to figure out which of two items to choose for Liz's snack, and failure was not an option.

"Where are you headed?" She took a step closer and flipped her curly blond hair over one shoulder.

"California. You?" Ignoring her would be outright rude and that wasn't me, but I made a point not to look at her or seem engaged in the conversation.

"Fun. We're heading to Vegas, baby!"

Two women by the beverage fridges joined her in a screechy, "Woooo!" and they all threw their hands up.

I chuckled and grabbed the right snack—I felt it in my gut, this one was for Liz.

"Sounds fun. You ladies have a great time and be safe." I

gave them a smile and nodded at the blond one next to me, who was already turning with a "whatever" look on her face.

After paying, I wandered out to the car, surprised to find Liz already settled into the passenger seat. I jogged over and slipped into the driver's side.

"Sorry. Guess I was taking my sweet time."

She shrugged. "Had to let the ladies down easy." She shot me a look.

I rolled my eyes. "Hey, I can't help if I was the only guy under fifty available to flirt with, can I?"

She chuckled and shook her head. "It doesn't hurt that you look like that." Her hand waved up and down.

My mouth dropped open, and I made no attempt to hide the blazing smile on my face. "Why, Elizabeth Malcom, did you just call me hot?"

She sighed. "Goodness. You are a lot."

"Oh, I am. But I'll grow on you, I promise." I tossed out the retort in my usual breezy tone, but something pinched in my chest.

I had always been a lot. I didn't know how not to be.

She laughed, low and a little breathy. A blessed distraction.

"I have no doubt that's true."

I let myself enjoy her response as I navigated back onto the interstate and turned on some music, but set the volume low. "Okay, I'm ready."

She tilted her head to look at me.

"For our game."

"Ah." She rustled in the bag and pulled out two things. "First, I present to you cheddar and sour cream ruffles."

"Excellent choice. The premium chip flavor."

"Completely incorrect, and yet I somehow knew you'd

say that. And second, I have a Kit-Kat." She waggled it between her fingers.

"Ooh, so close, but my favorite candy bar is a Caramelo."

She laughed. "Oh, my sincerest apologies."

I shot her a grin. "I accept and forgive you. After all, we're just starting out here. It would be different if we'd been close friends and you still got that wrong." I raised a brow.

"You're telling me that Beast and Cookie and Doc all know what you like?" She set the snacks back into the bag.

"Actually, yes. But only because we've been deployed and bored and in circumstances like that you talk about all kinds of useless stuff." Those details weren't what defined a friendship, but sometimes, it was the little tidbits that piled up between the bigger moments that made you feel close to a person.

"Yeah, I get that."

She did? I wanted more. Did she have people like that she worked with? Did Kappa Sector types even get to work with others, or were they little life rafts in a bigger sea of the intelligence community? I didn't really know, despite the many interactions I'd had with agency folk.

She was close-lipped about work, obviously. Just like I didn't want to rehash my glamorous upbringing, she didn't seem to want to discuss why she was taking a months-long break from her fancy, secretive career or, evidently, anything about it.

So, Plan B.

"Okay, so now me, and then we play our second game." I grabbed the bag with her snacks inside and plopped it in her lap. "Open 'er up."

She reached in and pulled out a can of Pringles and a

bag of Nerd clusters. She stared at them for a minute, then slowly turned to me. "Okay, how."

I shrugged. "It's a gift."

"No. Really. How did you do that?"

I grinned over at her for a second, noting the disgruntled gaze, then forced my eyes back to the road. "Honestly, it's a gift. I think about what I know about the person and try to find something that matches their personality."

She scoffed, but it sounded a little like a laugh. "So my personality is like Pringles?"

"Well, a bit. You're salty." I glanced over again and she had a brow raised. "But once you try one, you can't stop. And the same with you, once you get a little, uh... well, taste, for lack of a better term, you can't, uh, stop."

A small flush rose to my cheeks because all the salty and tasty insinuations about consuming felt a little sensual in a way I hadn't planned. "My point is, it's not a bad thing."

"And these?" She held up the bright pink bag showing gummies coated in crunchy purple and pink Nerds.

"Well, those are complex—crunchy and a little sour on the outside, but sweet and, uh, a little squishy on the inside."

I narrowed my eyes like it would help me keep a straight face, but miraculously, she burst out laughing before I did.

"Oh, thank goodness, I was about to lose it," I said, laughing along with her. "I'm sorry. It got weird."

She nodded, wiping her eyes at the corners. "It really did."

We both settled down after a few more seconds, and then I could feel her small smile, even though I didn't let myself look.

"I am impressed, though. They're two of my favorites."

"What would you have picked for yourself?" I had to know.

"If I ever have the choice for Mexican food of any kind, that's it. All the more after living in Europe and being absolutely bereft of options."

The genuine distress in her voice as she discussed this had me completely charmed. "Guacamole is hard to come by there."

"You have no idea."

Dang, I liked her. She was just so... so herself. She came off as so closed and controlled, but it wasn't like she didn't laugh or have quirks. It was a silly thought, but I liked seeing this side of her. And I wanted to see how much more I could learn before we landed in LA and the main part of our mission began.

"Now time for our game."

"Another one?"

"Obviously. While I'm the driver, we will play."

She chuckled. "While you're the driver?"

"Yes. Driver makes the rules. Copilot humors him. On a road trip, this is the way."

I wished I could look over and see what her expression said, but the whole me being the driver thing meant I should do my best to keep my eyes on the road.

She hummed. "I accept your terms. How do we play?

Adjusting my grip on the wheel, I did my best impression of a man who was not overly excited to be playing a game with a girl he used to like.

Used to like was the key here. Because now? Now we were friends.

Sure, she was beautiful in a way that stuck to my ribs and smart and capable and covertly funny and she was warming up to me faster than I'd hoped, but friends.

Obviously only friends.

"Nothing fancy. It's twenty questions. Small stuff only."

"I can do that."

And we did. I learned her favorite fast food and that she had a little bear she slept with as a kid. She got me talking about a tree house a neighbor kid down the street had, and how I'd always dreamed of having one, but we didn't have trees anywhere around our trailer. We covered favorite foods and movies and music and books, favorite parts of our job, favorite celebrities.

We stayed away from everything else—all the things that might make one of us shut down. It should've been pleasantly surface level. Should've kept us right in the sweet spot of a superficial get-to-know you that gave us additional comfort working together, but not much more.

Ah, the shoulds. They got me very time.

CHAPTER NINE

Elizabeth

My eyes popped open when I felt someone grabbing my wrist.

"Hey, sorry. We're here."

Kenny's voice situated me to the moment—in the car, on a mission with Saint Security, and with Kenny Carmichael. "Here" had to be LA, which meant I'd slept for a solid hour. I hadn't meant to conk out entirely, but the jet lag was still hammering me.

"Sorry. Didn't mean to sleep on you," I said, unbuckling and gathering my things.

"That was always the plan. No apology needed."

He slipped out of the vehicle, and I followed. In a matter of minutes, we were checked in and riding the elevator up. If we'd been in one of Jojo's books, we'd end up in the same room and the hotel would be sold out. There'd only be one bed.

And I would... not be mad about that.

My eyes widened at the thought, and I dropped my gaze to my feet in hopes he hadn't seen the thought broadcast across my face.

Yes, Kenny was attractive. He was warm and fun and positive, but he'd also given me a hint of something more. A depth to him I wouldn't have guessed at thanks to his Barbie persona and the cheery demeanor.

He was also not someone I was about to get involved with. My life was falling apart rapidly enough as it was—I didn't need this Golden Retriever puppy stumbling around in it and letting me break his heart. Pile on top of that the fact that I didn't actually know how long I'd be here and it simply didn't make sense.

We arrived at doors side by side in a hallway on the eighth floor.

"Night. See you at zero-six?" he asked, his face looking tired and still yet tinged with that baseline kindness and positivity.

It honestly baffled me. His neutral face was basically a smile.

"See you then."

We moved inside each of our rooms as though choreographed to do it in sync, and I made for the bed with a focus I hadn't had for anything in... a long time. Maybe too long, considering I'd always been someone who liked to and could effectively zero my interest and productivity on work and stay there until I was forced to come up for air.

An hour after readying for bed and subsequently staring at the ceiling, I surrendered to my fate. I couldn't sleep, and after sitting all day, despite feeling tired and desperate for the bliss of unconsciousness, I needed to move.

I'd noticed the signs in the elevator for the gym on the top floor of the hotel, so I took the stairs until I couldn't anymore, and after swiping into a calming reception area void of any personnel, I entered the gym itself.

And promptly froze.

There was one other person in there, and I could sense him before I even saw him. He wore bright blue running shorts, bright blue sneakers, and a determined look reflecting in the window the likes of which I'd yet to witness on the man. The white T-shirt clinging to his back disappeared when he reached behind and stripped it off in one swift movement revealing...

Kenny.

But not the one I was familiar with.

Maybe this was why he'd been nicknamed Barbie—his abs looked sculpted by a mold. All of him did, really. He was slick with sweat and running at a clip I doubted I could maintain on my best day, and I was a practiced runner myself.

He was Workout Barbie. Runner Barbie.

Hot as all get out Barbie.

Also... Gorgeous tattoos I did *not* anticipate Barbie. Like... the man had tattoos streaking from his shoulders and down his back. In the reflection showcasing his Lego-brick abs, I also saw hints of a design slipping down over his pecs.

This reality was far more than I could process right now.

I hesitated just inside the door, wondering if maybe I should just go walk the stairs a few times and call it good. There was a raw energy about him that tugged at me while also pushing me away. We'd spent the entire day together and he no doubt wanted space. I *needed* it.

I should've left.

But I stepped farther inside, choosing a treadmill spaced two away from the one he used. Everything about my time since landing at Salt Lake City airport had felt other-worldly, and this gorgeous human being only heightened the sensation.

So me walking in and joining in for a jog? It wasn't something Elizabeth Malcom would typically do, but neither was taking weeks or months off work. Neither was being investigated for potential corruption thanks to my trainee, despite a thorough report accounting for my integrity, and yet...

Pain lashed through me at that one, but I sniffed and started the machine at a walking pace.

Kenny punched a button and began to slow, his pounding footsteps spacing out.

"Liz, hey. I'm sorry I didn't see you," he said, pulling headphones from his ears.

Good grief, he wore a smile so casually. They just jumped right to his handsome face and made him look friendly and deadly at the same time.

I focused on the speed controls in front of me, nudging the incline higher and glueing my eyes there so I wouldn't cave to the temptation of counting his abs or gobbling up the dark lines of his tattoos.

"No worries. You were in the zone." I gave him a thumbs up.

Why? When was the last time I'd given anyone a thumbs up, and yet I'd done it now, with this man, in this state? There were some mysteries that would never be solved and this was one.

He chuckled and wiped the sweat from his brow, face, and neck. I did not watch because that would be weird. I ticked up the pace and began to jog.

"How far will you go?" he asked, taking a big breath right as I looked over at him.

A cough tripped out because *how? Why? Who, even?*

At least I hadn't said something like, *What do you even do with all those abs?*

"Just two or three. Something to wear out my legs a bit, but I want to get to sleep soon. What'd you do?"

He slung the towel over his shoulder and stretched his arms overhead. I begged my eyes to stay glued to the window in front of me and not drift to the right.

No, eyes. Bad eyes! The Barbie man is not for you!

"I just ran for an hour. Couldn't sleep and figured a good run would help, plus it's always nice to run at sea level."

"The altitude is definitely kicking my butt in my workouts. Hoping I get over that soon," I said, sliding up into a faster jog.

"Takes a bit, but you'll get there."

I had to ask, even though it would probably make me feel like crap. "How far do you run in an hour?"

He sprayed the machine and wiped it down as he spoke. "About eight."

"Eight." So he was running a seven-and-a-half-minute mile.

"Yeah. We trained for times and distances in EMU. You know our assessment includes a forty-mile ruck march which isn't running but it's a ways. So anything under ten can be fast for me. Over ten I start to slow down. Some of the guys are just machines but I was never a natural runner."

I laughed, breathless with the reality of what he and his peers could do and yes, a bit with the increasing pace. "Yeah, seems like you really struggle."

He tsked. "I'm not trying to brag. I work hard but it's also literally part of my job to be able to run fast and for long distances. I need to be strong to carry people, I need hand to hand combat skills to fight, I need to shoot well—just like you, mind you—and all the other stuff. If it wasn't my job, I doubt I'd be able to do any of it."

"*Used* to be your job. They don't keep you to that same standard at Saint, do they?" I asked, finally pushing into a full run.

"Nah. But I am a bit of an energizer bunny and do best when I'm physically exhausted."

That fit. It also made me feel some kind of way I couldn't describe and therefore, I kept running. In the reflection of the window, I could see him moving around on a mat behind me—stretching or abs or something. He was probably about to rip out a thousand sit-ups while I plodded along over here, but I wouldn't feel bad.

I also kind of loved that he caveated his fitness level as being part of his job. He was right. And while I preferred to stay physically fit for my own health and, frankly, mental health, it wasn't a job requirement in the same way. That was one of many differences between working for an agency and working special operations in the military. The expectations and missions were different, but they could coalesce and work effectively together using the strengths each entity offered.

Kenny offered brute strength, stamina, and physical capability. And I?

I offered...

Failure to properly oversee a fellow agent. Failure to complete a mission. Loss of a developed asset...

The words from the report I'd filed hammered me, and I increased my speed. I was close to an all-out sprint now, but

I needed the punishing pace—the challenge and the resistance, the burn in my muscles to shred through the self-pity and regret.

I couldn't take all the blame for my subordinate's failures, but I felt them as though they were my own. It had been my job to make sure he was doing what he should, and when he didn't, I'd missed it.

With one final increase, I drove my body into an all-out sprint for the last minute. My lungs ached for more air, and exhaustion waited to pounce. I pulled off all the speed and let the elevation drop, the treadmill's motor running loudly as it lowered. After a moment, I leaned over and rested my head on the backs of my hands where they hung on to the stability bar at the front of the machine.

The ache in my chest persisted, but it wasn't my lungs. It was my bruised heart—the one that'd loved my job for so long but felt scorched by my recent failings, my boss's response, and my inability to summon a desire to change what I'd done even though I knew the results because I'd done what I'd believed was right.

Where did that leave me?

Well, here. It left me on involuntary leave wandering around the western United States like I was on vacation, apparently.

"Okay there?"

Kenny's voice pierced through the fog of grief and frustration I'd let myself drown in for a few seconds. I lifted my head, knowing I had to look as wrecked as I felt.

"Just dandy."

His smile-prone lips did their thing, sliding up while his eyes practically sparkled. "Dandy, huh?"

I nodded, still breathing heavily.

He studied me, eyes only on my face and not falling to

the now sweaty T-shirt or running shorts I wore. After a moment, he dipped his chin.

"Okay then. Let's get to bed."

He held out his hand and gestured for me to lead the way and I went, no argument. Bed was what I needed. A reset with some sleep, and then we'd meet the people for the mission and we'd do what we were here to do. Another few days and I'd feel better—I'd have clarity, and I'd know what I needed to do.

And in a few weeks, I'd be ready to get back to it.

CHAPTER TEN

Kenny

Liz had been quiet this morning. She'd said goodnight once we got to our doors last night, but nothing else. Something was going on in that head, but we hadn't breached any real, personal topics again and I'd sensed last night wasn't the time to push.

I wolfed down breakfast in the small café at the hotel, head on a swivel in case she arrived. Did I want to talk to Liz for more than a few minutes before we picked up the clients?

Sure did.

Did I man up enough to invite her to join me for breakfast?

Sure didn't.

But the thing was, it would've been weird. We'd planned to meet this morning so any additional communication would seem over the top. I didn't want to come across as anything but friendly and professional. Yes, I'd quite enjoyed the pinch of a blush that rose to her cheeks when her gaze tracked down my torso last night, and that she didn't seem to hate the way I looked, but I also didn't want to seem sleazy.

I just... wanted more.

It didn't make much sense considering she was here temporarily and had a shell she had no intention of cracking. But I'd also seen flashes of her that called out to some part of me I wasn't used to, and all I could figure was I should roll with it and not overthink it.

A small group of businessy-looking people shuffled out the doors and my watch buzzed to alert me of the time. I polished off the last bite of my breakfast and piled the utensils onto the plate before hustling out of there. I had ten minutes to clean up, pack, and get back here so I could be a few minutes early to meet Liz.

Ten minutes later, Liz stepped off the elevator looking—

My heart swooped and sputtered in my chest.

"All good?" she asked, tipping her head to one side.

"Great. You?" Thankfully, I recovered from the swooping, and we walked out the sliding glass doors with bags in hand.

She confirmed she was all good as we approached the vehicle. Our legs moved in sync, and being the cheese ball I was, I loved it.

A small smile crept into the corner of my mouth.

"Do I want to know what you're smiling about?" She popped the trunk.

Not about to reveal the depth of my nerdiness or how inordinately pleased I was she'd keyed in on my expression, I gestured dramatically at the sky. "Gorgeous day." *Gorgeous woman.* "Good mission. It's a good day."

Her eyes softened and I could swear her lips curled into a smile even though her face appeared unchanged. She wasn't as broody as Stone or straight up grumpy as Beast, but her natural tendency was not smiling. Any hint of one gave me a hit of victory and only amped up the internal voice that said, *more, more, more.*

We loaded in and she navigated us onto the roadway.

"I admire that about you," she said, her voice so quiet, I thought I'd hallucinated it.

"Admire what?"

"That sunny perspective. You're definitely a glass half-full kind of guy."

She didn't glance over at me, instead keeping her gaze focused ahead. Her driving was technically perfect—she signaled, moved, chose her speed, and functioned with precision. I wondered how she'd do in less-than-ideal circumstances, but from what I'd seen years ago and in every other instance more recently, she handled stress like a walk in the park.

An image flashed into my mind unbidden. Me and Liz, hands joined and fingers linked, arms swinging, wandering through a park.

Sounds nice, my brain traitorously thought, more than a bit wistful.

"Am I wrong?"

Her voice snatched me from the ill-timed reverie. My mind and I needed to have a serious chat because I could not be sitting two feet from her thinking those marshmallow thoughts for the next day.

"No. I am unapologetically an optimist."

She made a sound—not quite a scoff, not quite a grumble.

"That's a bad thing?" I asked, a teeny tiny pinprick of

disappointment worming through me, even though it didn't surprise me.

"Not at all. If you've had a life that has granted you optimism, good for you. It may sound pathetic, but I envy it."

Ah. "I'm not sure if my life *granted* me optimism. There have been plenty of times I haven't felt optimistic. I choose it. And after losing my fingers, and several other times, it was absolutely a choice, not a feeling." It might be overkill, but I added, "I know it's a little much for some people."

She was quiet for a few minutes and before I'd figured out how else to address what she'd said without seeming like I was downright mining for personal information about her, she parked in front of the hotel where we'd pick up our clients.

I was familiar with her line of thought—that only a person who led a charmed life could be positive like I was. But that wasn't true at all. Most of the people I knew were fairly positive, especially once they'd addressed the things in their lives that had harmed them. We all had something. No, not everyone was as overtly optimistic as I was and that was fine—I didn't really want to hang out with a bunch of dudes exactly like me. But many of my closest friends had a frame of reference that pushed them more toward hope than despair.

Luc, Bruce, Adam... they were generally positive people despite hard things in their pasts. Beast had grown in that area significantly in the last few years, even amidst grief. And Stone? He'd battled his way through the mud in order to hold on to a semblance of hope. His was hard won, and I rejoiced over any moment he could see the world through a lens of hope.

Before exiting the vehicle, she turned to me, pressing the seatbelt eject button as she did. "I'm sorry I was a jerk."

I raised a brow. "How were you a jerk?"

Her eyes flickered around, a frown on her pretty mouth. "Just... with the optimist thing. I'm sure I sounded pretty critical of it, but I genuinely admire it. I'm trying to... be more like that."

No details, but enough honesty that it felt like a victory. "No apology needed. It's okay if you're not an optimist. I'll happily rub off on you."

Her eyes widened.

"I mean, uh—" The reality of just how creepy that might've sounded hit me upside the head. "I just mean I get it. Beast is one of my best friends. Stone, too. So I'm not scared of people who aren't all sunshine and roses, even if I happen to be that way myself. It'd be boring if we were all the same."

My cheeks burned, but the way her lips pressed together like they were working to hide a smile eased some of the heat.

Also, I shouldn't have been noticing whether she was smiling or not—I shouldn't have been looking at her face that closely. *Whoopsie daisy.*

"Fair enough. And thanks." And with that, she got out.

In a matter of minutes, we went through the confirmation protocol with hotel and local security, then arrived at the room on a top floor of the swanky place. It was unlikely I'd ever be super wealthy, but I liked stepping into these spaces I never would've imagined being able to afford growing up, and knowing I could get a room here for a night if I so chose and it wouldn't break the bank.

I knocked twice and after a brief shuffle behind the door, it opened.

Jack McKean stood tall and stupidly handsome on the other side. His face appeared more haggard than I'd seen him outside of the dramatic silver screen roles he tended toward, and he still looked straight out of a magazine spread.

"Thanks for coming," he said, stepping back and letting us enter the suite.

"Happy to help," I said, noting thus far, Liz had made no sound.

Would she be wowed by Jack? I couldn't blame her. I was.

But also a vain little part of me thought... *shoot*. I kept in shape but I was no movie star.

Jack shut the door behind us, then extended his hand to me. "Good to see you."

I accepted his hand and he hauled me forward into a half-embrace. One of those *we shake hands but also hug and pat each other's backs* things only men seemed to do.

Um, hello. My mind was screaming, "Are we best friends now!?"

"Likewise." I hoped I didn't sound as excited by his friendliness as I felt. I tended toward recognizing people and putting them at ease, but in the face of a client and A-list celebrity, I never wanted to seem like I was encroaching on his space or trying to get something from him. Everyone knew Jack.

But also, he'd just half-hugged me so I guessed now we were bffs. Wee!

"This is Elizabeth Malcom. She's new to Saint." I didn't need to explain she was fully vetted—Jack would know that. He was close with Julian Grenier, Bruce, and Wilder, and by now, he knew Cookie and Jess very well after they'd both worked with him personally at different times, not to mention most of the other Saint staff.

"Nice to meet you. Thanks for being here," Jack said, taking Liz's proffered hand. They shook once, then released.

I couldn't resist the pull toward her face, though I internally braced against what I'd find there. Peripherally, I saw them both step back and... nothing. She betrayed nothing but an expression of calm and readiness.

Not that I would've expected her to be ruffled by a celebrity as someone who'd likely met all manner of foreign dignitaries and maybe even celebrities, but her seeming to have absolutely no change in demeanor was nothing short of fascinating.

Jack stepped closer and lowered his voice. "She's almost ready. Please just..." he exhaled, his brow furrowed. "Be kind."

"Of course," Liz said, a rote response.

But also, of course we would. Jack had to know that since he knew the quality of people and values at Saint, but he was clearly worried, and his concern for the woman gave me a little tick of awareness.

This feeling, I knew. I'd always had it, but it'd been honed in battle and had developed in new ways as I'd transitioned to Saint and the danger wasn't always as overt. This sensation told me we hadn't gotten the entire story and any minute, we were about to.

"No issues. Can we grab bags?" I asked, every alarm in my head blaring as he didn't say another word. I wasn't about to show him his words concerned me, so we'd focus on baggage, but when a man like Jack looked this worried... there was cause for concern.

And when the petite blond woman walked in, her belly

rounded by what must've been a nearly full-term child, one look at her face told me why.

CHAPTER ELEVEN

Elizabeth

Kenny stiffened next to me, and I instantly moved.

"I'm Elizabeth. Can I take your bag?" I asked the woman, looking her squarely in the eyes and not letting my gaze wander to the bruising under her left one and across her cheek.

"I'm Evie. And um, no. It's okay. I've got it." Her eyes dropped.

"Evie, let them help. They're carrying my bag, too," Jack said, catching my attention with his serious expression.

I nodded, understanding at least part of what he wanted. Evie needed help, and she wasn't likely to take it unless she wasn't getting special treatment.

Evie swallowed and released the handle to her roller bag without looking up.

Interesting. What was the dynamic here?

"If you'll give us just a minute, we'll meet you by the elevators," Jack said, his voice soft.

"That okay with you, Evie?" Kenny asked.

She startled. "Yes."

Kenny studied her a moment, then took Jack's bag and waved me forward. I exited first, and he let the door close softly behind us.

I had hardly turned back toward him before he spoke.

"You need to talk to her. We need to make sure she feels safe with Jack."

I blinked, not entirely shocked by his vehemence, but a little surprised he'd suspect Jack. I'd gotten the impression everyone at Saint knew and loved the man. They'd even hugged when Jack greeted him. Still, Kenny didn't assume it meant everything was okay.

This raised him several degrees in my esteem, and it'd been rising consistently since the first time I'd seen him again. He wouldn't trust that Jack wasn't the one who'd hurt Evie, even if he was a wealthy, powerful celebrity millions of people adored.

"Of course. As soon as I can." Not that she'd feel safe being honest with me after knowing me for approximately thirty seconds, but I had to ask.

Jack exited then, Evie following behind.

"Elizabeth will take you down first, Evie, and then I'll follow behind with Jack."

Kenny met my gaze, and I nodded.

Normally, we would've all gone together, but this would give me a chance to check in.

"That okay with you?" Jack asked Evie, his voice softened.

She nodded. I moved, wheeling her bag and holding the duffle I'd seen by the door into the elevator, then watching as she stepped in. She nestled into the farthest corner, shifting on her feet and hands pressed to her belly.

"Evie, I need to ask you something." Maybe not the smoothest entrance to this conversation, but there was no time for easing in.

"Okay." She looked over at me, head still ducked slightly.

I hesitated for a second, wondering how best to put it. Ultimately, because we had seconds before someone joined us or we reached the bottom of the elevator's route to the lobby, I went for point blank. "Did Jack hurt you?"

Her mouth dropped open. "No. Oh, gosh, no. He's done nothing but help me."

I waited, knowing that denying someone was being abusive unfortunately often came with the territory. If it was Jack, someone with his status wielded incredible power and resources. She might feel trapped or—

"Really. It was my fiancé or, uh, my ex-fiancé. I work for Jack, and he's been trying to help and when he saw me two days ago..." She exhaled, her lips trembling before she spoke again. "Well, I know it's hard to believe, but it actually looks a little better today."

She tucked her hair behind her ear and met my eyes.

"I'm so sorry that happened to you. You can tell me if anyone at any point makes you feel unsafe while we're traveling, okay? We're here to get you to Silverton, but we're also here for you. *I'm* here for you. And not even Sexiest Man Alive out there is going to stop me from doing whatever I can to help you."

Her lips pressed together before an amused smile hit. "I'm okay with Jack. And the guy seems nice but I don't feel super comfortable with men I don't know..."

"No problem. If we need to divide and conquer, we'll

do it like this, as long as you feel okay with me." It wasn't a given despite my being a woman, though she'd opened up enough to make me hope she felt okay.

"I'm okay. And... thank you. For asking." She swallowed hard and blinked rapidly before continuing. "I know it's awful to ask but honestly, it's so much worse when I think about how many times someone didn't."

I nodded, heart twisting for her and a strange satisfaction flashing through me. "You're safe now, Evie, and soon enough, we'll get you home."

While Jack and Evie got settled in the car, I had a moment to reassure Kenny Jack wasn't the one who'd hurt her. I couldn't imagine how tense their elevator ride was, but the way Kenny's shoulders sagged told a story.

Also, why did this whole interaction make me like him a little more than I already had? Maybe it was his willingness to ascertain a woman he didn't even know was safe, even in the shadow of a man he already knew and who had so much fame? I'd navigated many ethically murky situations in my years in the agency and maybe I'd grown cynical—maybe part of the drag I felt when thinking about returning to work was exactly the absence of this.

Kenny was a good man. It appeared most of the Saint Security staff were upstanding, but I wasn't someone who could just take that as a given. It was why Adam was still working on gaining my approval, even though I'd mentally given it to him the minute I saw how he threw himself in front of Jo when her stalker had her at gunpoint. A man who would sacrifice his body for someone else, what could've been his life... that was someone I'd consider being good enough for my little Jojo.

Kenny would be like that. He was ready to deck Jack and swaddle Evie in a warm embrace if he'd sensed it was welcome. He might've played up the sweet, optimistic guy angle, but he was incredibly observant and cautious.

He had a clear sense of justice in there, too, I suspected.

And I liked that so much, it scared me.

Not really, of course. Not much could get a rise of actual fear out of me anymore, but if I were the kind of woman to get scared by things, then this might've done it. Attraction plus this... affinity?

But it wasn't a real danger because the clock was ticking. In a matter of time, I'd be back to the world I knew where my feet felt fully planted on the ground instead of like I was hovering just above it.

We'd made it a few hours down the road, stopped once for a bathroom break and to stretch, and we'd be arriving in Vegas to spend the night. Looking at Evie as she arched her back and searched for some relief from the roundness of her belly... it must've felt so unearthly and strange to carry a human inside you. I couldn't imagine it, and in so many ways, it seemed like her experience of life was like we lived on different planets.

I abruptly turned to my coffee, and a few minutes later, we were back on the road. We didn't talk, and less than an hour into the next leg, Jack had headphones in, and Evie appeared to be sleeping.

Kenny made a call to the hotel where we'd be staying, letting them know we were less than thirty minutes out. We'd enter through a less conspicuous door than the front grand entrance of the resort, which should save us from anyone recognizing Jack. I wasn't sure whether Evie was avoiding people seeing the bruises or her face altogether, but she'd definitely kept her head ducked, a hat pulled low, and her hair practically in her eyes whenever we weren't in the car with its dark tinted windows.

"All set," Kenny confirmed as he set his phone down.

"Good work."

His low chuckle had me glancing at him. The flash of straight white teeth and those charming creases in his cheeks were lethal.

"I appreciate the positive reinforcement, thank you."

The way he said it almost sounded flirtatious. But he'd stayed away from anything like that, so I wouldn't interpret it as such.

"Happy to provide it."

"I'll be sure to return the sentiments whenever possible, which based on what I've seen thus far will be often."

I did not look at him again. His voice had taken on a silken tone that an innate warning system in me recognized as something dangerous. Not to anyone but me, of course, but still, the way his sentence felt like a caress was just...

Evidence I needed to get out of this car. Simple as that.

I never responded, which didn't seem to bother him, and a few minutes later, we were pulling up to the curb. Jack gently roused Evie in a way that was both tender and brotherly, and Kenny grabbed the bags while I stood guard. My work in the agency wasn't typically focused on personal security, but I had acted in that capacity more than once and wasn't about to shirk my duties now.

We moved as a group led by hotel staff to the VIP elevator, then far above the lobby level, shuffled out and I waited with Jack and Evie while Kenny checked the rooms. He held the door for us as the hotel representative literally bowed to Jack and reiterated for the fifteenth time to let her know if he needed anything, and finally, we closed the door behind us and that leg, at the very least, was done.

The presidential suite was lavish as all get-out. A ten-person dining table, an opulent living room with a gigantic television, a full bar and kitchen, and what I imagined were the bedrooms. This had to be the doing of Mr. Grenier.

Jack walked Evie to a room, then excused himself to another.

That left one.

"We'll take turns on watch tonight," Kenny said, each of us delivering our own small bags to the third room where two queen beds waited.

It didn't matter that we would be sleeping at different times and in different beds. I still couldn't ignore the way my stomach flipped and dropped entering a hotel bedroom with Kenny Carmichael.

It wasn't even a thing. Nothing to worry about or feel this stupid dip like I was staring down a loop the loop.

Semi-sharing a room with this sweet, sunny, and lethally hot man was absolutely not a problem.

CHAPTER TWELVE

Kenny

I nstead of dining at the gigantic glass dining table that looked about as comfortable as sitting on a, well, a chair made of glass, we opted to sprawl out in the *is this really a hotel room?* living area.

"This is delicious," I said, diving into my chicken sandwich with enthusiasm. I'd eaten minimal road snacks and something about a trip like this made me hungry.

"Mine, too," Liz said, tucking an errant piece of lettuce back into her sandwich—also a spicy chicken—before taking another bite.

Evie's head nodded up and down. She had a truly gigantic order of shoestring fries and a Caesar salad with blackened salmon. Her eyes had been wide, taking in every detail of the space when she emerged from her room a while ago.

"This place always has decent food. I like to dine out but figured that's not a great idea this time."

Jack gave us all a look I thought might be... guilty?

Huh.

I hadn't worked with him directly like others had, but every interaction I'd had with him had made me like him more. Now, being reassured he wasn't the source of Evie's injuries, I was finding myself compelled to like him even more.

They didn't seem to be related, or he likely would've said as much. They were also sleeping in different rooms, which could mean they were together romantically and taking things slow, but their interaction didn't feel romantic in any way. There was no tension between them when they got close, no heated glances... nothing. As a lover of love and observer of my fellow man, I dared say I'd notice.

"Please don't."

Evie's words were so quiet I hardly heard them. When I looked up to see her eyes imploring Jack and Jack almost scowling at her before he nodded, my instincts kicked in.

"Did you guys know I grew up not far from here?"

I said it like it was the most interesting fact in the world. It was not. But I needed something to change the subject because the heaviness between Evie and Jack had felt like a black hole and I didn't want them to retreat to their rooms just yet.

"In Vegas?" Jack asked.

"No, a town a few hours from here. I'm a desert child." I dramatically tucked a non-existent lock of hair behind my ear.

Evie chuckled, Jack cracked a smile, and Liz coughed into a napkin as though she'd choked.

"Interesting. I'm from New Hampshire, but I've lived in

LA for the last twenty years." His vision seemed to tunnel as he stared down at his food. "I think I'm finally ready for a change."

"Really? Going to take your place in The Ridge?" The ritzy neighborhood in Silverton was home—or second home —to the likes of billionaire Julian Grenier, famous rock star Jamie Morris, renowned former tech CEO Madeline Reynolds, multiple other A-list celebrities and musicians, and more.

Jack wiped his fingers on a napkin. "I've done some longer visits for the film fests, but much to Julian's dismay, I hadn't bought a place until recently."

My brows perked up. "You've been visiting a lot, so I hadn't realized you didn't own a place there yet."

He shrugged. "It was time."

Though he appeared to be low key, I'd never gotten the sense Jack was quite that laid back. He seemed strategic with which movies he did and which events he attended. Maybe I had him all wrong, but something told me he had a reason for moving to Silverton *now* and it wasn't simply because the time had come.

"I'm from California. I can't imagine living anywhere else..." Evie's words had started out plucky, almost, but faded a bit as though she'd just realized she'd be moving.

My heart sank for her. I didn't know how long she planned to be gone from her home state, but I wondered if maybe the idea was for this move to be permanent. The need to reassure her—to do anything that might make her burden lighter—surged up in me.

"I've lived a few places, but I can easily say Silverton is my favorite. It's given me a sense of home and community I honestly never dreamed I'd love so much. I don't know if that's how it'll feel for you—probably not at first—but I can tell you there are good people in that town, and I know you'll be welcomed with open arms."

Her eyes shot to me, and she blinked away a few tears. "Thanks," she said, voice watery. "What about you, Elizabeth? Where are you from?"

Liz had been quiet, but she spoke up immediately. "Born and raised in the Seattle area, then moved away for college and have only been back to visit once or twice."

She didn't mention how she'd lived in Europe for the last decade, maybe more, or that she was only with Saint temporarily. No need to tell people she didn't know all those details, but it seemed significant now that I thought about it.

Did she miss Europe? Or had she missed the US while living there? She'd missed guacamole, she'd said so. Was she so far down the expatriate trail she'd never want to live in the States permanently again? Could she even choose that, or did the agency dictate such things? Why this made my chest pinch, I couldn't have said.

"Do you like Silverton?" Evie asked.

There was a pause before Liz said, "I do. It's a unique place and..."

Her pause made me look at her just in time to see her say, "It feels more like home after just a few days than any place I've ever been."

The small victory those words brought perplexed me because why did I care how she felt about Silverton?

Oh, fine. Of course I cared. I liked her. I was struggling to keep that *like* under wraps. *Of course* I liked that this incredibly talented, extremely intelligent, ridiculously beautiful woman liked the little town I'd chosen as my home. The fact that she was saying she liked Silverton was, I hoped, true, but she'd been so gentle and thoughtful with

Evie, maybe it was for the woman's sake. It was just one more thing in the *pro Elizabeth* column in my head—she was tough and self-directed and a bit intimidating, but she was a helper. In her gut, at her heart, she was, and I... man, I liked that.

Evie excused herself so she could get ready for bed and Jack followed suit, thanking us both before he shut his door.

"You sure you want to take first shift?" I'd suggested I take the first shift since she was still adjusting to the time change, but she'd assured me she'd had too much caffeine late in the day to sleep.

"All good. Enjoy your rest."

Her smile was all muscle, no feeling, and I kind of wanted to poke at her and see if I could coax something real out of her. Probably not the best idea if I didn't want to confuse myself.

"Thanks. See you in a few hours."

I wanted to go to the gym and burn off my energy, but decided to crank through some bodyweight work like pushups, squats, sit-ups, dips, and so on. Twenty minutes later, I felt a little better and showered.

I should've gone straight to bed, but I couldn't. My mind had been circling Liz's words from earlier and I didn't have the self-control to keep from opening my door and padding into the living room.

She was seated in a chair facing the entryway to the room, a book in hand and only a few low lights remaining on. Outside the floor to ceiling windows, Vegas lights from neighboring hotels shimmered, mesmerizing if I weren't sharing space with her.

"Did you need—"

Her words cut off when I slipped into the chair next to her and grabbed her free hand with mine.

"This may be a bit much but that's me, so I'm going to say it anyway."

Her dark eyes watched, a stern curiosity lighting them as she took in my face.

"I'm glad you see that Silverton is special. I don't think you would've chosen to take your break there or work with Saint if you didn't."

"True."

I squeezed her hand gently once more, letting my thumb glide over the olive skin at her wrist, then released it. "Good."

I rose, the last few words hovering on the tip of my tongue. Before I reached my door, I let them go.

"However misplaced this may be, I just want to say that you deserve to feel at home somewhere. You deserve that feeling of belonging. Maybe you have it in Europe, but..." I shook my head, not certain how to make sure I was making my point. "I guess I just wanted to say that out loud—if you want it, you should have it."

She swallowed hard, her expression inscrutable. "Good night."

Fair enough. Maybe she didn't know what to say in response. Maybe I'd ticked her off and she'd sit there stewing at my over-stepping ass.

Or maybe there was something in her that felt it—the desire for what I'd described having, that I thanked God for every day. I wished it for her, for Evie, and for Jack.

"Night, Liz."

If I could help any of them find it, I would.

Maybe it didn't make a lick of sense, but the thought bounced around in my head as I shut the door... *Especially her.*

CHAPTER THIRTEEN

Elizabeth

I stared at Kenny's closed door for a solid hour. The glossy white surface became a canvas for my imagination in ways I hadn't experienced since I was a girl.

Did I want to feel the way Kenny claimed he did? Like he belonged in Silverton and like he'd found his home?

It wasn't as simple as listening to the distant voice declaring *yesssss* from the rooftops of my mind. I had a career I couldn't give up on, and an entire life I'd established. I'd worked hard to rise in the ranks and get to where I was—to have the relative autonomy and reputation I did. Or the one I thought I'd had.

That was part of all of this mess—I'd felt so secure in my job, so certain my superiors saw what value I brought. Secure in what I offered, too. I was someone who got the job done in creative, efficient ways. I completed the mission, cultivated the asset, got the intel we needed in record time. I was part of the giant wheel ensuring the good guys took out the bad guys.

But the longer I was away from it all, the more doubt niggled. If I was so valuable, would they have put me on leave for this investigation? Part of me said yes, this was the process. Part of me said no, they must not trust me like I thought. And if that were true, what else about my life had fooled me into thinking it was more than reality proved it to be?

Granted, that life felt thinner than ever these days. It was watered down milk in a glass left out overnight. It was pale, sallow, and even in winter, the colors of Silverton beckoned me.

I hadn't told Kenny, or anyone, why I'd come to Silverton for the break. I wasn't sure I wanted to, since admitting it to them would mean admitting I'd messed up. But worse, there was a decent chance cracking open the seal on the issue would let loose a deluge of other feelings I wasn't sure I was ready to handle.

I imagined myself pouring all of the emotional mess this subject dug up for me into a neat little jar. I screwed the lid on, tucked it in a box, tied a lovely little bow around said box, and shoved it in the back of my mental storage space.

There. Spick and span.

And the swirling sensation left on my skin where Kenny's warm, rough fingers had gripped my wrist? Also tucked away. Somewhere, probably not as neatly. Basically just shoved in between other stuff right along with the way my heartbeat quickened and my throat went dry at the sight of his wet hair curling at his neck and ears.

He was so boyish in one second and so... not in the next. Honestly, he was unlike anyone I'd ever met.

My book recaptured my attention by which I meant I

forced myself to read the same paragraph six times until it finally latched into my flittery little brain and the hours ticked by. I stretched, walked the room, and checked the door every half hour. It was likely overkill, but it helped me stay awake.

At three, Kenny emerged. He scrubbed at his eyes and stretched, his undershirt rising to reveal a few inches of that firm abdomen I'd glimpsed at the gym last night. I did not appreciate the stunning architecture of even this part of him and instead turned to pour him a cup of coffee.

"That for me?" he said, crowding into the kitchen and making the fairly spacious area feel, well, crowded. He didn't seem like a large man, but that might've been because he was so often standing next to actual giants like Beast. Even Jack McKean had an inch on him, but Jack was known for being one of those people who was actually as tall as they said and not secretly five-foot-seven masquerading as a six-foot-three god.

I extended my hand to him, and he reached for it, taking it with the three fingers of his left.

"How did it happen?" I asked, instantly hoping it wasn't the wrong thing.

His brow furrowed, and my stomach dropped. *Crap.* He hadn't seemed all that sensitive about it, but his face...

"It was a gorgeous day. I didn't see it coming. The deer took them right off."

I jolted, rearing back to examine his face.

A hint of something... challenge? Mischief? glimmered in his eyes.

"A deer?"

He nodded, cupping the mug of steaming coffee with both hands, then shuddering dramatically. "I don't like to think about it, but yes. Mistook my pinky and fourth finger for early spring rose buds and chomped them right off." He fluttered his lashes.

I... snapped my mouth shut and shook my head. "You are odd."

He shrugged. "Fact."

I laughed at that, the long day pulling at my shoulders and lower back. "Okay, then. I'll see you at seven."

"Sweet dreams."

After a few hours of sleep, I readied myself and packed, eager to get on the road and make it to Silverton. Weather reports showed the snow should hold off until this evening, so we should be able to get Evie and Jack settled before it hit, barring any major issues.

Jack exited his room looking every inch the movie star he was with his dark hair swooping elegantly and yet somehow haphazardly and his clothes casual but overtly more expensive than anything I'd ever owned. Curiously, his wardrobe reminded me of Cookie's, which was odd. Saint Security paid well, but surely not A-lister movie star well.

Evie was already sitting at the bar in the kitchen chatting with Kenny. She laughed in an open, broad way I never would've imagined coming from her when we met yesterday, and especially not with Kenny, whom she'd innately distrusted by virtue of his male status. She'd eased in last night, but now she seemed genuinely comfortable.

He really was a remarkable person.

"I told him he's never going to get her attention that

way," Kenny said, beaming at Evie with an expression that held so much amusement and joy it was blinding.

"But... can't he just talk to her?" Evie asked, clasping her hands like she was fully invested.

Kenny shook his head. "Right? Can't he? But apparently no. For all his experience and advantages, he is an absolute chicken."

Evie giggled. "Sounds like he just needs to take up eating donuts for a living."

Kenny laughed. "I mean, he basically has. I'll get you some tomorrow morning and then you'll understand that part is not a hardship."

Evie leaned back in her chair. "I will accept that offer."

"Yeah? Does this mean we're friends?"

Kenny's voice was so full of hope, I could taste it.

She giggled again. "I'm not sure I can resist. You have that best friend energy coming out your pores."

He gasped. "Are you saying I have big pores? Not all of us can have flawless skin like Jack."

Jack's low chuckle would make a lesser woman tremble. Not me, because I was currently and inexplicably jealous of an eight-months-pregnant woman.

"They literally call you Barbie because you're so pretty. I don't think there's any comparison."

Kenny tsked. "They call me Barbie because my name is Kenny and they decided Ken would be too on-the-nose."

Jack was already shaking his head slowly. "Your very own Jess Korbel-Rawlins told me it was at least in part because you're so cheery, and I quote, 'perfect-looking like a Ken doll.'"

Kenny's lips twitched and Evie hid a laugh behind her hand.

"Fine." His gaze snagged on me as I approached them,

and his eyes held mine as he said, "But I would like to add the caveat that I am very much *unlike* a Ken doll in certain places that shall not be named."

Evie burst out laughing, and even Jack sounded truly amused. Kenny just winked at me like a little creep.

"This is the most fascinating conversation to come upon, I have to say." I meant it. I wanted to know everything about Kenny and these little tidbits were absolute catnip to me.

"Too bad the mold was broken on the left hand." He held up his hand complete with three fingers.

Evie's mouth dropped open. "Oh, gosh. I'm sorry. Can I —is it okay to ask what happened?"

Kenny leaned his hands down on the counter. "Of course. It was a fireworks accident when I was a teenager showing off. So stupid." He rolled his eyes and shrugged, then tossed back his coffee like a shot, and turned to me. "We ready to roll?"

Evie and Jack moved instantly, doubtless unsure what to say about the supposed firework incident and ready to get on the road. I'd have to ask Kenny about that story since it was markedly different from the one he'd told me about the deer last night. But for now, we moved toward the exit.

"Back exit is closed after an incident there with a K-pop group, so we're stuck going out the front. How about you go get the car and bring it around and I'll escort?" Kenny said.

Not ideal to use the front, but Jack had a hat pulled low on his head and Kenny now donned one, too, so they looked like college bros ready to bet on a horse race or something as long as you didn't notice they were both extremely good-looking and well-dressed.

Well, at least Jack looked particularly stylish, but it was

subtle enough hopefully people wouldn't notice in the low lights of the casino floor.

I moved quickly downstairs, using the main elevators, and retrieved the car. In another few minutes, I was parking and exiting the vehicle, a bellman waiting to help with luggage despite my statements that I didn't need any.

As I waited for the group to come into view, I realized they were already standing just inside the pneumatic doors. When the panels pulled wide again, I saw Kenny hugging a kid. *What?*

When he pulled back, his face was blank.

My entire existence went on alert. That was not Kenny.

The man standing in front of a small group of people with Jack and Evie to the side was a ghost of himself. I hadn't known him long, but I knew enough to see something was very wrong, so I moved. Jogging inside, I joined the group.

"Everything okay?" I asked them quietly.

Both gave me concerned looks.

"Kenny, are you—"

"This someone you work with? Introduce us!"

A petite blond woman with a weathered, tanned face extended a hand. "I'm Mandee Carmichael and this is my husband, Glen. This is my oldest son, Glen Junior, and his son, also Glen." She beamed at me.

Kenny stood stock-still.

I extended my hand. "Elizabeth." I couldn't say it was nice to meet them because I had no idea what was going on.

"Can you stay and have breakfast with us, Uncle Kenny? This buffet is the best one and my mom knows the chef so we get—"

"I'm sorry, G. I can't."

Kenny's voice was ragged. His eyes were downcast, and he was an alternate universe version of himself.

"I'm sorry, honeybun. Kenny's always been very focused on his work."

"Yeah, Uncle Ken is working hard to compensate for all the failings in his personal life. It's a him-problem, not a you-problem." The tallest man, Glen Senior, patted his son's shoulder.

"But who are you traveling with, Kenny? Is this an old friend?"

Mandee's voice had a false ring to it as though we wouldn't recognize she wanted to be introduced to Jack, whom her eyes had latched onto and she couldn't look away from.

The muscles at Kenny's jaw flexed and I'd had about enough of this. People had started milling around sizing up the group, likely because they were noticing that the tall baseball cap-wearing man who looked like a movie star was one, much like Kenny's lovely family here.

"Sure you want to have this guy on your team? Pretty sure he's the weakest link..." Glen Jr. said with a chuckle, all while Glen Sr. watched and never spoke a word.

"Sorry, folks. We're on a tight timeline. Hope you have a nice day." I set a hand on Kenny's arm. "Ready?"

He nodded and I moved, ushering Evie and Jack out to the car. I'd left it unattended far longer than I would normally, but since there was no imminent threat and because I'd sensed something way off about the interaction, I'd abandoned it.

Right move, I couldn't help think, as Evie and Jack's doors shut and Kenny visibly exhaled and shook out his hands as he walked away from the group and toward the door. He entered the car and it snicked shut. I checked the rearview and found Evie and Jack looking at Kenny, concern etched into their faces.

"Just go."

All he said, but all he needed to say.

I'd guessed that despite his optimism, there were things he couldn't put a positive spin on. I hadn't wanted that to be true so much as... needed it. I needed to know that someone with hardships could be like him.

But now, driving Eastbound out of Vegas, I'd never wished I was wrong about anything more.

CHAPTER FOURTEEN

Kenny

My eyelids were heavy when I forced them open and checked the dashboard clock to find I'd conked out for a solid two hours.

"You sleep like the dead," Liz said, her voice low enough I figured only I had heard her.

With a groggy grumble, I ran a hand through my hair and rubbed my eyes.

"Sorry." What else could I say?

Sorry I saw my family for the first time in years and it was low-key traumatic!

"You want to talk about it?"

Her question lingered in the air between us and my gut impulse to say no was nowhere to be found. Maybe because I was still tired from my unplanned nap, or maybe because I wanted to talk about this with someone and for the first time in a long time, I felt compelled to, I said, "Actually, if you're up for it, yes?"

She straightened in the driver's seat, hands adjusting on the wheel. "Oh. Good. Okay... so. That was your family."

"Yes." I wasn't sure how to get into the backstory, how to explain everything rolling around in my head.

"I gather you haven't seen them in a while?"

"Six years, and even then, it was very brief."

"That's a long time."

Her voice softened and something about it made my insides twist, whether from the question she hadn't asked, but lingered in the air, or from the frustration that this had come up at all.

My temporary hibernation from reality had been irresponsible at best, and I owed her an explanation.

"Yeah, so, Cliff's Notes version? My nephew? For a while, I thought he was my son." I exhaled a pent-up breath, eying Liz's profile as she drove.

She blinked, focus on the road, but after a second asked, "How?"

She said it so softly, so *gently*, she clearly already knew something bad was coming. Like she was stepping onto an iced-over lake, trying to distribute her weight but knowing any second now, her foot would break through.

Just do it. Get it out there quick and then it's over.

"So I was with his mom in high school. When I graduated, I proposed before I went to basic. We'd waited for years, but we were together before I left. About six weeks in, I got a letter telling me she was pregnant."

I huffed out a breath, my lungs not sure whether they wanted deep breaths or to stop breathing altogether as I remembered the moment I'd received the letter—how my world tilted on its axis and everything in my life changed.

Liz stayed quiet, not interrupting or pushing for more. Just... here with me.

"I was shocked at first, but completely thrilled. She seemed happy, too, and even though we were eighteen and I was at the very beginning of a huge career choice, I felt like it was meant to be. We'd get married when I got home on leave and then she'd go with me to my first duty station. We'd have health care and a housing allowance, and she could work a bit before the baby came if she felt like it... it just seemed like things were lining up for everything I'd always wanted."

"But." Liz's sentence was short, sweet, and the hinge on which it all turned.

"Yeah, major but. I got home and she seemed a little distant, but we'd literally never been away from each other for more than a few days, let alone weeks, so I wasn't too worried. Chalked it up to the time apart and everything changing. We'd planned for a small wedding ceremony—I'd put a lot of it on my brand-new credit card because her parents had said they wouldn't help and mine couldn't."

We didn't need to get into those dynamics right now.

"When did you find out?" she asked, eyes still blessedly forward.

I didn't want to see the pity in her gaze with this next part, so I kept my eyes on the desert landscape as we passed signs for Cedar City. The feeling in my chest now was faint, though. It was the memory of the way I'd felt shredded that lingered, a ghost lurking in between my ribs.

"I'd been home for three days. Went to her house to talk because she'd been distant and found her and Glen making out in his car."

I didn't feel the old twinge of pain anymore. My heart had been thoroughly shattered in that moment, and the ones that followed, but it'd knit back together with time and attention. The distance of years had been a salve, and so had maturing and growing in ways that helped me learn what love did look like. It hadn't been that, despite what my young heart had believed.

"Damn."

I chuckled. "Yeah. It was messy. And the thing that has stuck between me and the family is how everyone defended Glen. I called off the wedding, which everyone was weirdly upset about, and then it was like all the negative feelings funneled toward me. It was my fault I'd left her and she'd needed Glen. It was my fault I'd been too trusting. It was my fault I was now facing down the bills from deposits we wouldn't be using. It was my fault she was pregnant, even though she and I had only been together exactly once and by the time I got home she was having her twenty-week ultrasound."

This was the part I couldn't quite put to bed. I may have realized that my version of young love with Shay had been naïve and foolish, but the way my family had kicked me when I was down, had criticized me for trying to make something of myself in the military... it still stung. And having seen them, confirming their attitudes hadn't changed, scraped me raw.

"I'm guessing it hadn't been twenty weeks." Liz's words were low and dark.

The brutality of that realization had been devastating. So deeply cruel to a kid who'd dreamed of making a life both for himself and the girl he thought he'd always love. Sometimes, just thinking of how innocent and ignorant I'd been made me cringe and even cry, but I was also oddly grateful I'd had a naïve love like that at least once.

I wouldn't ever have it again. Over the years, I'd recognized how flimsy our feelings really were, especially in light of what happened, but as much as it'd hurt, I got it. It was better.

Honestly, it'd freed me to pursue special operations and find my real family, and I never would've taken that route if Shay and I had stayed together.

It was the family element, the way they'd all rushed to Glen's defense and refused to even attempt to see I might be hurting, that still pricked me with a thousand pins.

"Correct. And then it was my fault for joining the military and not sticking around to support my family. It was my fault I'd ever planned on leaving and if I hadn't, Shay and Glen wouldn't have gotten together. Everything was on me, and I'd never been so relieved to have a reason to go and not come back."

The cab was quiet for another minute before she mumbled, "We're stopping for a bathroom break." She pulled the car into a gas station and parked.

Jack and Evie were out of the car before I ever even looked back, which made me wonder if they'd heard everything. Thus far, they'd used headphones, but their quick exit with zero chatting made me guess they might've been listening.

I wanted to stay here and... I didn't know. See what else Liz might say? She couldn't fix it or make it better. I was years beyond that. But I couldn't deny the drop of disappointment in my chest when she slipped out and hustled after Evie.

It made sense. We were here to protect her and Jack. And speaking of, I hurried to find him, waiting just outside the men's room. When he came out, his troubled expression told me he'd probably heard my tale of woe.

He patted my shoulder. "You're a good man."

A knot formed in my throat. "Thanks. You, too."

His bright blue eyes held mine and then he nodded, moving to the aisles of the store. I followed him, noting the two women in the corner whose gazes had already caught onto Jack's identity based on the way they were whispering with flushed cheeks.

A few minutes later, Jack had purchased a candy bar like a regular mortal, and Liz had escorted Evie back to the car. We each took turns in the restroom for ourselves, Liz first, then me. When I got back to the car, Liz was leaning against the passenger side, her black slacks, blazer, and white button-down completely out of place at this worn-down gas station.

"Hey," I said, a flip of nerves twisting in my belly after laying myself bare. I wasn't all that scared of certain kinds of vulnerability, but that story—that she'd seen my family in the flesh, even—left me feeling truly naked.

She just stared, then slid her sunglasses up to reveal her dark, mesmerizing eyes.

"I need to say something."

I halted a foot from her, completely at her mercy, heart rate climbing the longer she held my gaze. "Please do."

She took a beat, her eyes almost steely as she practically glared at me. Her jaw flexed and I was shocked to register she was angry. Then she stepped forward and wrapped her arms around me, squeezing with a mounting pressure that made moisture spring to my eyes.

This show of tenderness made my eyes mist, and I cleared my throat in an attempt to stave off full-on tears as she abruptly released me and stepped back.

"Sorry, I needed that first. Forgive me." She shifted on her feet, probably the first time I'd ever seen her less than a thousand percent sure and steady.

My heart clutched at the gesture—at the idea she'd needed to hug me, for me *and* for her. *There it is again—she's a helper.*

"I need you to know even though I don't know you all that well, I know you're better than most people. You're a good friend, a good employee, and a good human being. If your ex and your brother and—" she scoffed "—your whole family don't see that, it's their failing. Not yours."

The swirling mess of feelings dug up by seeing them, by their words, and how they still wanted me to own up to something I couldn't figure out, stilled. Liz's chest rose and fell under her blazer and button-down, her expression so intense that if I hadn't heard the words she'd just said, I would've thought she was angry with me.

But no. She was angry *for* me.

It felt wonderful to have her want to defend me—to need to comfort me and reassure me. In most senses, I didn't need that anymore. I'd done therapy, I had friends who offered me the stalwart faithfulness and love I'd always longed for from my family, but Liz...

Maybe it made me a fool yet again, but Liz's anger *for* me made me fall just a little bit in love with her right then.

CHAPTER FIFTEEN

Elizabeth

We pulled into Silverton a little past five and arrived at Jack's gorgeous home in the swankiest Silver Ridge neighborhood ten minutes later. Each house we'd passed once we'd entered the gated community, complete with guard station security seemed larger than the next. Surprisingly, Jack's wasn't the biggest, though it had a down-to-earth quality, likely more aesthetic than it was actually homey.

I focused on these details and not on the still-simmering rage I felt in the wake of Kenny's story.

This sweet man had been so mistreated, and it made me want to—

Honestly, it made me want to burn something down. Or get violent. And I didn't tend to be a physically reactive person.

On the whole, I was even-keeled. I handled stress well

and compartmentalized like a pro, because I was one. I'd been doing it since I was a teen, and I'd perfected it once I joined the agency after graduating from Georgetown.

But something about Kenny Carmichael being so completely betrayed by everyone in his family, save his little nephew, incensed me. I hadn't felt so viscerally angry in a long, long time.

I'd hugged him because I'd been compelled to. And I wasn't a hugger. I just... I'd needed to press him close and reassure myself he was all in one piece, even though he'd said as much. When he'd talked about what happened, he hadn't seemed destroyed. It was that hollow expression, the way his energy and light seemed to dry up in the minute and a half we stood near his family. It gutted me.

I pushed away the memory of his empty eyes in that moment and focused on unloading the bags.

"This house is smaller than the one in LA," Evie said conversationally to Jack.

"Right? It's so modest."

The humor in Jack's voice was evident even though I couldn't see his face. Evie's response came fast.

"I'm just glad I'm not on staff here."

Ah. We hadn't pried into their relationship, but I'd gathered there was a working relationship and also a disparity between lifestyles. Evie didn't seem destitute, but it was clear Jack was heading up this move, and she was at least a little uncomfortable with his funding the trip, but anxious enough about getting away from her abuser that she'd acquiesced.

Jack didn't speak, but as I rounded the corner with Evie's bag, I saw him holding her hand with both of his.

"You're going to be okay. We're going to get you settled, find you work, set up a life you can live to the fullest. You're a wonderful person, Evie, and you're going to have a wonderful life."

She sniffed, nodded, and swiped at the tears gathering in her eyes.

"Ready to head inside? Kenny said it's all clear."

He'd texted to say as much after checking in. We'd actually beaten his household staff here, so Kenny had met Cookie at the door and they'd done a sweep before we brought Jack and Evie in.

In minutes, Jack's entourage arrived, a much less flashy crew than I'd expected—one woman who looked to be in her early sixties, another somewhere in her forties, and someone who Kenny and Cookie seemed to recognize as a local doctor. Cookie would hang back and provide on-site security since part of this curious expedition had been leaving Jack's California crew in LA.

"Let's get gone," Kenny said, shooting a finger gun at me.

"Okay, cool guy," I said, a silent laugh following it. For a man who'd been mired in heavy emotion hours ago, he was practically skipping down Jack's front walk.

When we both clicked our seatbelts at the same time, he grinned over at me.

"Have you ever noticed we do a lot of things exactly in sync?"

I searched my mind. "Never prior to this moment."

He started up the car and reversed out of the drive, then navigated to the front of the neighborhood, giving a chin nod or finger lift or full out wave to every car and person checking their mailbox we passed.

"Do you know all those people, or are you that friend-ly?" I wondered aloud.

"Most I know personally to some degree. One or two

are just familiar, and this is a small enough town that you sort of acknowledge the regulars. This isn't a tourist zone, so it's fair to say if someone's through the gates, they're home."

They're home. Why did it always come back to home with him? I wondered if he even noticed how often he said the word, let alone conveyed that Silverton had some kind of magical quality that made it special for home-making.

"Sounds nice." The words came under my breath but he heard them.

"It is nice. Better than, actually. Probably because I grew up in a trailer park with a family that, in the end, doesn't like me very much, I value the feeling of belonging in a place more than the average bear."

A quick glance showed me his sunny expression—eyes taking in the streets ahead and naturally smiling lips curved up a touch as usual.

"I'm not sure it's more than others, but I can see why you like it. Saint's a little family, Silverton's this place you love... I'm happy for you."

His smile broadened. "Thanks. And what do we do about you, Lizzy?"

"No. Only people blood-related to me call me that." Though I didn't completely mind it. And I wasn't about to interrogate that thought right now.

He held up his hands, a gesture of innocence. "Fair enough. Can I call you Liz?"

Something in his expression shifted, an almost shy bent to his gaze. It wasn't the hurt from earlier or the brash smile or the flirty guy... this one made me feel a tenderness I didn't expect. "Uh, yeah, sure."

He'd called me Liz on the mission years back. He'd asked me—*Liz*—out. I didn't have anyone else in my life who called me Liz—family called me Lizzy and work colleagues called me Elizabeth.

What did it say that those were the two main groups in my life? I didn't have that third category—friends.

"Most people call you Elizabeth, right?" he asked, perceptive as usual.

"People from work. It's how I introduce myself." Why did saying this make me feel so squirmy? Why did my skin flash hot, like someone had shifted a spotlight onto me?

"And friends?"

I coughed, a fake grab for time he'd no doubt recognize as a delaying tactic, but it happened nonetheless. "I guess they call me Liz."

His smile started small, a drop in a lake, then expanded and grew, rippling out until it felt like his entire being was beaming over at me.

"That's what I like to hear."

It should've concerned me how much his approval and joy made me happy, too.

"Good," I said, shifting awkwardly and keeping my eyes away from his sunshiny face.

"And so, as your friend, I need to show you around. Give you the best chance at getting to know Silverton."

I scowled even as my heart slipped. "Jo can show me. Or my dad."

He shrugged a shoulder. "Eh. They could. But we both have tomorrow off, and I bet you neither of them does. Let me show you around tomorrow, at least. Give you something to do on a day off." He glanced over at me, but his attention slid back to the road.

He couldn't know I was dreading the day without anything to do. I could go see Jane, whom I liked, but she had a way of seeing right through me and I didn't feel like dealing with that right now.

"That could work..." I said, perpetually cagey with making plans.

Part of me wanted to curl up with a book and some coffee and not move. But lately, doing this pressed down on me and caused a weighty, oppressive sensation. It was old school body armor with the high neck collar and it had the potential to suffocate.

"Oh, it'll work. Perfect. And since I know you heard me raving about the donuts, we're starting at Glazed."

I hadn't had a good donut in a while. Europeans just didn't do donuts the same way the US did, and I couldn't deny the draw of having this deeply enthusiastic person show me the ropes of what must be one of his favorite places based on the way he seemed to buzz with energy now that we'd made the plans.

"Alright, then. You can show me the world of Glazed."

"Great. Then it's a—" he cleared his throat. "Plan."

Right.

A friendly plan.

CHAPTER SIXTEEN

Kenny

It's not a date. Not a date. Not a daaaaate.

I'd been chanting this to myself as I woke, ran on the treadmill, lifted, showered, dressed, and parked at the Saint building. No sense in taking up street parking during tourist season, especially on a snowy day when they'd need to plow regularly.

Liz exited the building where she was staying right as I crossed the street to her block. My stomach clutched as I took in her boots, jeans, and a puffy coat. She tugged a hat over her head and shivered when a gust of wind blew past. She looked so comfortable and normal... and cold.

"Let's get moving and get you inside," I said by way of greeting.

She tucked her arms around her waist and dipped her chin into her jacket. "Works for me. I didn't realize it was this cold today."

The sky was gray and the light on the flat side. Often, the bluebird days could be colder, but this one felt almost like an Eastern cold despite not having any humidity to drill down to your bones. "We'll let Elise's dough babies warm us from the inside out."

We shuffled along the sidewalk past storefronts, past the lure of espresso in Joe—*I'll be back for you, my love!*—and into the bright pink door of Glazed.

A bell jingled overhead, and we heard a cheery, "Welcome in," from somewhere up front, though I could barely see the counter because there was a line six people deep.

"This place is... wow."

Liz's gaze traveled over the bright pink walls, the white tables and chairs, and the neon sign that said *Get Glazed*. The menu ahead was an old-fashioned letter board with donut flavors and pricing per single, half dozen, or dozen. It had an effortless feel to it despite how trendy and bright it was. Somehow, Elise had managed to create a store that said, "Welcome to this cool place you want to hang out, but literally all we sell is donuts." No coffee at all. They did have water and milk for sale, but otherwise, she happily directed patrons next door to Joe.

"It is. Just wait 'til you get your mouth on one of those babies." I nodded toward the display case, then froze.

Slowly, I turned to her.

Her eyes were wide.

I cracked up. "Yeah, I hear it now. Sorry."

A smile broke free on her face and she laughed. "Thank God you heard it, too, and better yet, you didn't mean to sound like a creep."

I held up my hands, pure innocence. "I didn't. I swear. I just mean, when you taste the donuts, you'll be even more impressed."

"Fair enough."

We settled into a comfortable silence between us, but the buzz of the place brought plenty to observe. Quite a few of the people seated at tables were tourists or people I didn't know, but Jamie Morris strode in to grab a box and shook my hand as he exited, and then two others said hello before Aidan Wallace requested I tell Wilder hello.

"First, was that Jamie Morris? And second, do you know literally everyone in this town?" She watched Aidan exit the store.

I grinned. "It was indeed. He's a good dude. And no, I don't. But I do know a lot of people." I shrugged. "I'm a friendly guy."

"You are that."

"Hey, guys, glad to see you! Kenny, thanks for bringing Elizabeth in for her first visit!"

Elise stood behind the register, a bright pink apron on and her hair pulled back into a high ponytail. She looked fresh-faced and happy, and I wanted to give her a high five for finding her passion. Glazed hadn't been open all that long and she'd been killing it. There was nothing better than seeing someone do what they loved.

"My deepest honor," I said, pressing a hand over my heart. "Dailies?"

She pointed to the smaller board behind her, the letters bright pink over the white background in contrast with the black and white of the main menu.

"Maple bacon. Not my favorite, but it seems to be a crowd fave." She smiled. "If you're not into toppings, I suggest a classic glazed or one with vanilla or strawberry frosting. The classics."

"I'll take a glazed, a maple bacon, and a Mexican chocolate." I would likely have a sugar crash, but later Kenny could deal with that.

"And you?" Elise asked while another employee slotted my donuts into a wax-coated bag.

"I'd love a glazed and a strawberry frosted," Liz said, eyes still roving over the case full of delectable offerings.

"Perfect. Anything else for you guys?" She rang us up when I said no, and then we stepped aside. Once we had our donuts in hand, Elise waved.

"Hope to see you again, and Liz, let's get lunch sometime or something!"

The crowd had only grown while we ordered, so after Liz acknowledged Elise's suggestion, we slipped out.

But not before Cookie snuck in. I instantly turned to see if Elise had noticed. Little spots of color burned her cheeks, and she had her head ducked, but I'd bet a hundred bucks she'd seen him slipping in.

"Hey, this is practically my home away from home since it's basically Barbie Land in there. What's your excuse?" I asked Cookie.

He just narrowed his gaze and said, "Hungry."

I raised a brow. *Mmhmm. I just bet you are.*

We walked the few steps between Glazed and Joe. "On to get coffee, and then we head to our breakfast spot."

"We're not eating here?" she asked as we slipped into Joe.

"Nah. I feel weird eating donuts here since they have their own delicious breakfast offerings, plus, my goal is to help you fall in love with Silverton and I don't know how long you're going to give me, so I've got to make a good showing."

"Very strategic of you," she said with a soft smile.

Ethan Carter was ringing up at the register settled on

the dark wood counter in Joe and he sent a wide grin to Liz. "Well, hello, Elizabeth. Kenny."

The guy was charming and handsome and had one of the best brothers on the planet. I considered him to be a friend. He was also looking a little too happy to see Liz and I didn't like the way his eyes were lit with interest.

"Hey, Ethan. Good to see you again."

I almost made the idiot mistake of asking how they knew each other, but she must've met him on her last visit. Plus, her sister was marrying his brother.

They were basically family so them dating was essentially incest, right? Like, *hello, taboo.*

"Likewise. I hear you're in town for an extended stay this time," he said, still hitting her with his perfect smile.

Ugh. Why did the Carter men have to be so handsome and nice?

Actually, no. I didn't like that thought. My dudes were handsome and smart and awesome, and if Liz was interested in Ethan then...

Well, she could go right ahead. Because this wasn't a date, and I wasn't looking for anything from her, and I knew darn well she wasn't looking for anything from me. She had, what? Maybe two months here anyway? What kind of future with someone was that?

So I needed to stop getting all bent out of shape about this and be a real friend to both of these human beings.

"Yep. A month or two at least, probably a while longer."

So maybe a little more than two months? My heart leaped before I crushed the thought.

She glanced at me and I ignored the swoopy feeling in my chest. "Should we order?"

Ethan took our orders and we paid. A few minutes later, we retrieved our drinks and got out of there with another wave to Ethan, and not without him giving me a meaningful look.

Once outside, we moved quickly down the street to the Saint lot and slipped into my car. The wind had stopped, but after being inside surrounded by the coziness of the coffee shop and its warm lighting and espresso scent, exiting into the bitter day was brutal.

Fortunately, the drive didn't take long, and soon, we were parking. I grabbed a pack and strapped it on, then took our donuts and my coffee.

"I promise you this is worth going back out into the cold." Maybe I shouldn't have planned something so outdoorsy on such a chilly day, but if you waited for warmth in Utah winter, you weren't likely to come by it.

She didn't speak but followed me and didn't seem too inclined to revolt. I was getting used to her tendency toward quiet. Two of my best friends tended toward *not* talking, and really, even Cookie's default was not talking, whereas mine was the opposite, to say the least.

The bench I had in mind came into view around a corner and Liz's slightly louder exhale behind me sounded like confirmation this hadn't been a fool's errand.

"This is stunning," she said, her frozen breath rolling off her lips like fog on a lake.

A wanting hit me low in the chest. Good grief, I wanted to steal this very breath from her lips, to touch my chilled ones to hers and warm them up.

Not helpful. Not happening.

"It's nothing compared to longer hikes but those aren't great options this time of year. I wanted to get you outside and give you a scenic view, at least."

In front of us was Silver Ridge Resort and the small town. We weren't high up enough to make the people turn into ants or anything so grand, but we were at a different perspective. Most importantly, we were nestled next to a frozen river and to the right rose the mountains. We were just above the town, and sitting at the feet of the peaks.

"Thank you." Her voice was nearly all breath.

We sat quietly, each sipping our coffees and savoring the view.

I wished I could reach out and hold her hand or do something to connect us. I needed that closeness sometimes and I'd been missing it. But more than a base need, it was the desire to connect with *her*. Right here, right now.

"Thank you," she said again, a little bolder now, and I swore I saw her swipe at her cheek from the corner of my eye.

There it was. A glimpse at something soft inside her— the part of her that called to me in a way I couldn't explain. It was dangerous and all kinds of stupid, but I wanted to dig and pry her open until I learned about that part of her, and every other aspect of the woman who was Elizabeth Malcom.

CHAPTER SEVENTEEN

Elizabeth

I*'m not crying, you're crying.*

Fine. I cried.

I sat next to a nice boy who bought me donuts I hadn't even tasted yet with the perfect view of the mountains, and I cried.

The sun had started peeking out of the clouds, rays of light fanning out across us and beyond, all the way to the horizon. My heart filled with a mixture of heartbreak and hope so potent, I simply couldn't stop it, nor did I try.

These last few days had felt like someone else's life I'd stepped into. I'd been going through the motions, disconnected from myself, until I'd seen Evie. Something about the bruising on her face and the pain in her gaze had yanked me down to Earth. I was in it now. I still felt like a stranger to myself, but the last twenty-four hours had throttled all sense of normalcy from me, and I'd briefly released the countdown to the return to my regular life because...

Because the glimpses of life here were grabbing at me in a way I couldn't escape.

This gorgeous view and the kindness of Elise and Ethan and the bustling energy of the mountain town on a busy morning and this man...

I'd needed this quiet moment, and he'd given it to me.

"You okay?"

His low voice startled me, and I swiped at my tears again. A watery laugh escaped, and I blew out all the rest of the pent-up emotion before daring to look at him. His piercing blue eyes were riveted on me, waiting patiently.

Any plan to keep everything locked away crumbled in the face of his kindness and yet readiness to listen. "I know it'll shock you to learn this, but I'm not really here by choice."

His brows rose. "No?"

I shook my head. "I mean, I'm *here*, but not on sabbatical. And the way that happened was—" I sighed, completely uninterested in delving into those details right now because they weren't the point. "Well, it was bad. I feel small and unsure right now, and I can say with certainty I haven't felt that very often in my adult life."

I'd made a point to avoid anything that shook my foundations. I hated instability. That was part of what drove me so far from home to college—I'd hated the way my parents' marriage was so clearly on shaky ground, and they'd refused to acknowledge it.

I'd fled that uncertainty and run full-tilt toward an institution and a career track that had felt clear and possible. Not that moving up in the ranks of an organization like the

CIA or Kappa Sector was easy or even guaranteed, but it all felt manageable, attainable, and organized.

Plus, turned out I was good at being a spy. Really damn good at it, and the years of feeling like an absent daughter and a mediocre sister had been smoothed, at least a little, by the success and security at work. My job brought results, even if I didn't tangibly feel them myself. But I saw it happen, saw the bad guys being taken down, evil networks collapsed, innocents kept safe, clueless they'd escaped from a terrible fate but that was the point, because it meant we'd done our job and they were none the wiser. People like me worked in the shadows, and I'd been okay with it.

But when I'd booked a flight here, I'd thought it might feel like a quick vacation. I'd assumed I could keep Silverton and visiting Jo and seeing this town and even working for Saint Security firmly on the temporary detour on the route back to my regular life. And somehow, though time was passing and I should be getting an update on the status of my return in the near future, it didn't seem so simple anymore.

"I think—" He stopped, lips pressing together in a thin line.

"Don't start being shy on me now, Barbie."

He sent me a squinty-eyed glare, maybe for my use of his nickname. But I wanted his words—wanted to know what he thought about my confession.

"I don't want to sound like I'm trying to fix anything. I've learned that's not helpful. But I want to say I think it's normal to have times when we feel just that—adrift. We don't know which way to go or what's ahead. We thought we had this plan of how life would look and something changes, usually something unexpected, and we reroute. But it's not automatic, and if you're someone who plans ahead, it can be painful." His Adam's apple bobbed as he swallowed, his eyes back on the mountains in front of us.

"Sounds like you've been there," I said, wondering how recently he'd experienced this feeling, and maybe, how long it took him to figure out what came next.

He nodded. "I have." He held up his left hand and gave me the most pitiable look. "Ever since that witch cut off my fingers for her potion."

I chuckled, grinning despite the eye roll I was giving him. "That would be a sudden change."

"Indeed. Changed the trajectory of my life." He held up the bags of donuts. "We've waited long enough. It's time."

Though I would've liked more from him—more of his insight and more about what he'd gone through—I could see his need for the subject change. He'd been involuntarily dragged into his past once already in the last few days after seeing his family, so it didn't seem fair to push.

I slipped my hand into the sack he handed me, going for the glazed first. It was pillowy but had a good amount of give when I picked it up. The glaze made it shiny, and I could smell the sweetness from here.

Like a woman starved, I took a huge bite into the mouth-watering delight and instantly groaned with pleasure. It was the perfect, toothsome texture, the glaze sweet without being overpowering. It was so. Good.

Kenny, whose attention had been on me as I took that first bite, coughed and pounded on his chest like maybe he'd choked. I watched as his eyes fluttered, then shifted to me, his brow pinched as though in pain.

"Gonna make it?" I asked, curious how he'd choked on air considering he held a fully intact donut in his hand.

He scrubbed his free hand over his face. "Yeah. Yep. I sure will." Then he shoved his glazed donut into his mouth, taking a bite that was easily three quarters of the rather large donut.

"Wow. That was... wow."

He chewed, jaw working in a way I found oddly attractive, which was just dumb. Sure, the man was attractive and not a thing about him wasn't, but since when did I get internally fluttery over the way someone chewed a too-large piece of donut?

Maybe this was my own personal version of altitude sickness.

"So, what's next in your plans to show me Silverton?" I asked, ready for distraction from the inane sensations running rampant.

"We eat our donuts and then flee for warmth. I wanted to just drive you around a few places if that's okay and wanted to hear what you enjoy so I can tailor my plans. How long do I have you?"

Once again, my body responded in ways it shouldn't have.

How long do I have you?

Um, forever?

My eyes widened at the wild thought and his brow furrowed so I rushed to say, "I just remembered I promised my dad I'd stop by today. I haven't seen him yet. I should probably do that around lunchtime."

Especially since Kenny seemed to have some kind of inhibition-lowering libido pull on me I wasn't fully prepared to combat. Spending hours and hours together today wouldn't be wise.

Certainly wouldn't be safe.

"Cool. I should go check in with Stone. I'll take him lunch." He nodded like it was now officially his plan.

"I don't think I've met him, have I? He wasn't there last

week, right?" I searched my memory for someone named Stone and couldn't recall anyone.

Kenny's lips tugged into a fond smile. "He wasn't. He's only part-time with Saint. He's been through a lot and doesn't do well with crowds or even groups all the time. Varies a bit, but overall he's good, just... needs his space."

"So he's your opposite?" I joked.

He chuckled. "Basically. He owns a tree farm and lives a little farther out of town than most of us. He's got his own thing going, but still does some work with Saint, I think mainly to stay connected to the people. He can get too solitary pretty quick." Kenny frowned, inspecting his next donut—the maple bacon one from the looks of it.

"You worry about him." It was written all over his face.

He shrugged. "Nah. I mean, not much anymore. He's doing well these days. But I don't like the idea of waiting until he's not doing well again to check in or pester him, so I make it my mission to be up in his face at least once a week when he's in an off-cycle with Saint work. Especially in the winter months when he's not doing much for the tree farm, he needs someone there to get under his skin."

I snickered, admiring the way he described his checking in and knowing all that supposed pestering and getting under someone's skin came from a place of love for him.

Despite knowing him only a few days, there was no question he had such a deep well of love for those around him, and he gave it out freely. It wasn't something I'd noticed years ago when we'd met, but the circumstances of the mission hadn't lent themselves to a lot of down time where I could observe him. These last few days, I'd easily gathered the truth.

Kenny Carmichael loved with his whole heart, and it was right there on his sleeve. He wasn't scared to say I love you to his friends, he wasn't afraid to be affectionate, and he wasn't ashamed of caring for people.

It was beautiful. Enviable.

Desirable.

And, based on the tug in my gut urging me toward him, incredibly dangerous to me.

CHAPTER EIGHTEEN

Kenny

S tone's property was ridiculously pretty all snow-covered and silent, but it was this quiet that sent a slight chill through me.

He's fine. He's fine. He's fine.

I rang the doorbell again. It was normal for him to take a minute to answer. Totally normal.

He's fine.

Right as I held up my fist to knock, he pulled the door wide.

His hazel eyes squinted out at me, the brightness of the snow no doubt nearly blinding him. He'd pulled his longish hair back so it looked neat rather than like a clue to a puzzle, so this and the clarity in his gaze eased the frantic gallop of my heart.

"Hi, friend."

He stood there for another second before stepping back and making space for me to enter.

"Thank you so much. And yes, I'm doing well, thank you so much for asking!"

My fake enthusiasm for his nonexistent question had him shaking his head.

He led the way into the kitchen and his Alaskan Malamute, Bear, raised his head, then slumped back down on his bed.

"I come visit you and I get no love from you or your dog. *Noted*," I said, but approached Stone's beast of a dog anyway. I took a knee and held out my hand. He nuzzled it instantly and gave it a soft lick, blue eyes looking at me with such feeling, it always made me a little sad.

Not because Bear was sad. Bear had a dog dad who'd be more than willing to *die* for him, he'd *lived* for him. In their story, that was the most loving thing possible, and it was beautiful.

Bear's comfortable energy and those blue eyes drilled me right in my chest, though. More and more lately, I'd felt a longing for my own pet. I could've gotten one by now, and probably should've, but I'd always felt like I'd know the right one at the right time. Like love stories—I'd just know.

This might have also extended to the way I thought about not just a pet, but a person, too. I wanted a person. As more of my closest friends paired off with loving, wonderful partners, happiness and hope filled me up, up, up. But there was the small voice I couldn't avoid hearing that asked when it would be my turn, and the harsher answer insisting it never would be.

"I don't need checking on anymore."

Stone stood watching me pet Bear's soft head, his arms crossed and feet spread wide.

"I'm not *checking* on you. I'm just…"

"Checking on me."

I huffed. "Well, yeah. But I want you to check on me, too, and so I showed up so you can do that. Cookie's working and Beast's busy and I just wanted to see a friend."

Not just *a* friend, but someone who knew me. Everyone at Saint was a friend and now Liz was a new friend, but this restlessness in me needed a touchpoint grounded in more than just the here and now. I needed the history of friendship, the honesty of shared service, the vulnerability of shared pain.

Stone moved away while I hugged Bear—the dog was nearly ninety pounds of black and white fluff Stone kept shampooed and brushed and pampered. He required hugging.

"Let me get us a snack and some tea."

I smiled into Bear's thick winter coat which Stone really must've just washed because it smelled fresh and clean in a way a dog almost shouldn't.

"He's such a good host, isn't he?" I asked Bear.

"Just making sure you're fed. You look skinny." His words came out in a scowly grumble as he rustled around in the kitchen, which made me ridiculous levels of happy.

I shouldn't have been so pleased by his concern, but I remembered times when he could hardly manage to eat, let alone worry about anyone else. His fussing over me was evidence of his triumph.

"I'll have you know I'm not skinny. I'm just not a giant like you and Beast. Some of us are normal human sized." At just over six feet tall, I was, by many metrics, one of the shortest male members of Saint Security. That said, Beast stood a bit over six-foot-four, and I was fairly certain Stone clocked in around six-three, so they were the big boys of the crew.

I stood and slipped down the hallway to the bathroom. After washing my hands, I returned to the living room to see Stone setting a little tray with teacups on saucers and two dessert-looking things on a plate in the middle.

"Shortbread cookies and mini lemon bundt cakes."

My mouth dropped open. I made no effort to hide the amazed and delighted grin on my face.

"This looks amazing and also I have a feeling you baked those both from scratch and I think it's finally time you tell me what's going on with the baking."

He'd started doing it a few years ago here and there, but lately he'd leaned into it. He'd showed up with a platter full of some cookie or biscotti or homemade cracker during our Monday all-hands, and it'd taken us all a while to realize *he'd* made them.

"You came here for a reason, so let's start with—"

My obnoxious and maybe slightly exaggerated groan of ecstasy when I popped the entire mini lemon cake thing into my mouth cut him off but honestly, there was no exaggeration. It was delicious. Somehow buttery and light at the same time. Soft and spongy but like, with a nice give.

I needed to watch more *British Bake Off* and remind myself of the proper terminology.

"Decent, then?" he asked, looking a little less scowly as I swallowed and took a dainty sip of tea, pinky out.

"That was incredible. Honestly. I could eat a hundred of those and still want more." I held my fingers out, dramatically circling the plate he'd filled with the sweets, and plucked up another one.

"Good to know." He pulled out a small notebook and scribbled something with a pen he'd magically produced.

I blinked. Who was this man? I mean, I knew him. I did. But this part of him felt unfamiliar.

"Yeah, I guess. So, are you thinking you'll sell baked goods? Or is it just a hobby?" I reached for one of the shortbread cookies.

He didn't answer, only watched me as I chewed. Good grief, the man knew his way around a baked good.

I may have made another mildly inappropriate sound in appreciation of his gifts and talents.

His staid face cracked the tiniest bit, a smile sneaking in at his crow's feet and the corners of his bearded face. He might try to hide it, but he liked knowing people enjoyed his goodies.

He also had no plans to chat about said goodies, and so I needed to suck it up and be honest.

"So. I did that weekend mission." He'd likely heard of it since I knew he and Cookie had hung out Saturday.

He waited, sipping his tea silently, his eyes telling me he was listening.

I wanted to squirm. I wanted to run.

Instead, I just let 'er rip.

"I was with Liz. Liz Malcom. And she's so..." I let out a pent-up breath and pulled my hat off my head, ran a hand through my hair, then settled it back down. "She's freaking great."

He set down his teacup. "Not here for long, though, is she?"

I slumped back against the couch, eyes on the ceiling. "Nope. Maybe a few months, but something tells me she might leave sooner. Seems kind of restless."

I couldn't quite pin down what I sensed in her other than discontentment. Whether it was at being here or with her job or the situation she'd vaguely mentioned had driven her to come back stateside and moonlight with Saint... all was not right in Liz Malcom's world.

I pinched the delicate curve of the teacup's handle, wondering if I did so hard enough, it'd break.

"So? Are you going to ask her out again?"

Stone knew, like most everyone at Saint now, that I'd struck out with her before. It wasn't like she'd broken my heart, but since it was the first time I'd attempted taking someone out whom I was actually interested in, it had been noteworthy.

I laughed but it sounded less joyful and more tired. "I also ran into my family in Vegas on the way home."

His brows rose. Not everyone knew about my family's messy story, but those closest to me did.

"You okay?"

My heart squeezed, aching for the pain I always used to feel just thinking about my family. I appreciated his care for me, relieved he was able to ask me that, and loving him for it.

"I am. Surprisingly. It was a crap show for sure and I hate that it happened in front of the client and Liz, but I saw G and ultimately it reminded me I don't need them to be my family. I have a new one and it's not contingent on performance or achievement or anything else. I'll never regret something that reminds me of that."

"Me neither."

Our gazes held for a moment. Did all the times we worried he'd forgotten it flash through his mind, too?

Whatever the case, eventually, I snagged another short-bread and ate it in bliss before asking him the question we both knew was coming.

"Time for some *Bake Off*?"

He nodded, flicking on the TV, and we began. I needed

the distraction from the mission, from my jumbled thoughts about Liz, and maybe a little from the wanting. I tried not to live a grabby life, reaching for more and more. I'd achieved a lot and hoped to have many years to go. I didn't want to live in a state of hands out, gasping for more, more, more. I wanted to hold and honor and cherish what I had. Contentment was what I really wanted.

Even if, sometimes, it felt like there were pieces missing.

CHAPTER NINETEEN

Elizabeth

The day with Kenny had been so emotionally challenging, I debated canceling on my dad.

Then I gave myself a pep talk and got over it.

Because I'd had a wonderful time with Kenny. I couldn't think of another time in many, many years when I'd felt so happy, comfortable, emotionally safe, and yet also excited. Like around the next corner, there might be some surprise.

The surprise, though, had been the man next to me and every gesture he made to show me around town. The quiet, gorgeous overlook of Silver Ridge had provided the most poignant moment for me, but I didn't stop feeling both delighted and dismayed by him until he dropped me off back at the apartment.

Even then, I replayed much of the day and felt the same

dissonance. He was honestly so wonderful, and yet it unset-
tled me.

I couldn't tell why, exactly, and mystery wasn't something I liked in my personal life. There was enough about
my work that naturally remained unknown. I liked order,
predictability, routine, and clarity in my day-to-day, my
personal interactions, and even in my thoughts.

Kenny Carmichael had thrown all of that to the wolves.

Mixed up in my angst about being shoved out of my job,
and all the frustration and maybe even grief, I was realizing
that there was this sense that so much else around me was
good. *Too* good.

Despite this troubling mental state, I recognized how
the choice to cancel on my dad would be hazardous to our
relationship. In the last six months, we'd had some hard
conversations. We were repairing the years of damage and
distance, most of which honestly came down to my refusal
to engage with him. I'd been gone and purposefully evasive
and distant for so long that showing up had become
unnatural.

So here I stood, stomping the snow off my boots on his
and Jane's welcome mat, bracing for impact.

The door flew open as I reached for the doorbell.

"Elizabeth, so glad you could come."

I was supposed to meet my dad around lunch. Somehow, my call to enquire if that time was okay morphed into
an invitation to dinner at his place.

Jane's warmth extended out to me via her smile, and she
stepped back, gesturing me inside. She wanted to hug me.
She was a hugger by nature. But she held herself wrapped
up tight for my benefit.

I both appreciated and loathed this. Part of me was

relieved not to feel obligated to hug anyone but Jojo, but another part wondered what might happen if I just unwound a little. If I let my mind and body be at ease instead of vigilant all the time.

You were at ease with Kenny...

Not a helpful thought, so I shoved it away.

"Thank you for inviting me. I'm glad to be here," I said, hoping she could tell I meant it, even if my voice stayed mostly even.

Maybe Kenny could teach me how to get that tail-wagging enthusiasm imbued into my voice like he always had.

And maybe we can go for a full ninety seconds without thinking about Kenny, hmm?

Once we reached the kitchen, I found my dad with an apron and mitts removing what looked to be a roast chicken from the oven. It smelled amazing and I would've done a double take if we hadn't talked about how he'd learned to cook after the divorce. My mom had always done the cooking and he'd expressed regret he hadn't helped her more.

It was small, but a helpful note. Apparently, he'd told her this, too. I knew they didn't talk often, but knowing he'd said something reparative had warmed me.

"Welcome, welcome. Everything's ready so we'll just serve from over here. Keep it casual." My dad spoke over his shoulder as he turned off a burner on the stove and Jane reached for a stack of plates and handed me one.

"Here you go, honey."

I accepted the plate, enjoying the informal nature of things. I hadn't expected something grand, but I'd wondered if we'd all be sitting in stolid silence, only occasional forks scraping on plates. This wasn't how any interaction with them had ever gone, but my mind had wrapped as much negative potential around the evening as possible and that was one scenario.

In a few minutes, I'd loaded my plate with roasted chicken, mashed potatoes, haricots verts, and a salad of field greens. Jane set a woven basket with a beautiful teal cloth in the center of the table and pulled back the edges to reveal steaming rolls.

"These are a little gift Sadie sent over. She wanted to make sure we got our bread portion for the day." She snickered.

"I think if I live here for too long, I'll end up being ninety percent bread made by Sadie." In no instance would I turn down homemade warm rolls and fresh butter. I might be a badass who would have to pass a physical fitness test upon my return to work, but I was also human.

"I love my daughter-in-law no matter what, but I can happily say I deeply love her baking skills." Jane bit into a roll and closed her eyes as she chewed.

"I'm very happy to have inherited so many wonderful step-children and grandchildren," my dad added as he bit into his own roll.

My chewing faltered for a moment. *Step-children.* I'd heard and thought the words before, but it hit me differently. Painfully even, as I was the only child without a partner. Jo and Adam weren't married yet, but it was only a matter of time. They wouldn't wait long to tie the knot.

"Do you know when you have to go back?" Jane asked, pulling me from my thoughts.

"No later than end of March." Maybe sooner.

I tried not to feel the anxious energy this thought created, but another one followed.

Maybe never.

In my dreams, maybe. But not returning and facing what'd happened wasn't an option. I didn't run from my problems, and I wouldn't have left now if my supervisor hadn't forced me into this sham of a sabbatical.

In what universe do you not run from your problems?

I huffed, not appreciating the reality check. Because in truth, I'd been running for years. I'd run from the messy family dynamic when I left for college, left the uncertainty of youth for an all-encompassing career that took over my life and made all my decisions for me. And now, I'd run away from work.

Granted, it had been a bit of a forced thing, but I needn't have come this far for my leave.

We chatted about all manner of things having to do with Jane's sons and their spouses and children, the activities coming up in town, and a signing the bookstore would host. They kept their questions about Saint Security surface level, which told me they'd learned how to navigate that with Wilder and Adam.

"You two stay and talk. I'm on clean-up crew," Jane said, collecting our dessert plates with the industrious energy I'd come to associate her with.

"I don't mind helping," I said, feeling awkward after being served so much delicious food and now not even cleaning up.

My dad's hand covered mine where it rested on the table. "It's okay. You don't have to work in exchange for food, we promise."

He winked in a way he used to do when I was a kid—it's always reassured me and made it feel like we had a joke together. Something inside and special that Jo and my mom didn't even know about.

But this also felt pointed. Like he could see how uncomfortable it made me to simply accept the meal without offering something up. There was no exchange here, and I lived my life on the premise that knowing what someone wants and figuring out how to give it to them would unlock doors for me. I'd done it for years—it's how the spy world worked—and here he was, just laying it bare.

"I know it's hard after the way you've been living, but I want you to just relax here. Just be here and take this time. I wish I'd done something similar."

The concentrated expression in his eyes made my throat tight. "What do you mean?"

He shook his head slightly, gaze wandering before it made its way back to me. "I got so wrapped up in work, I let my whole life implode. Before I knew it, I was divorced and had one daughter so distant she hardly lived at home, and another who was so tenderhearted and hurt..." His lips pursed. "I wish I'd taken a break and allowed myself to stop. To think about whether my job actually meant as much to me as I acted like it did."

"Explain." The demand slipped out between my clenched teeth, my whole body tight with recognition.

"I loved my job for a lot of years, but I also hated it at times. I think that's normal. When I look back, I don't wish I'd worked harder or more—I wish I'd worked less. I wish I'd showed up for you and Jo more, and even your mother. I don't regret our divorce so much as how we all functioned after it. And I deeply regret that it took me over sixty years to allow myself to be really, truly happy and not feel guilty about it."

My heart rate climbed, and my jaw must've been wired shut because I couldn't open my mouth to speak right now for all the money in the world. My dad seemed to sense this and exhaled softly, patting my hand again before sitting back.

"Forgive me if this is too much, my Lizzy, but I only want your happiness. And I worry deeply that you haven't been happy in a long time. I'm all too familiar with what that life looks like, and I hate the thought of you missing out on more."

I nearly choked as I coughed, my throat finally defeating the dam of emotions. "And what is more? A husband and kids? Is that what it'll take to make you believe I'm happy?"

His eyes shut and his neck bent—a defeated expression so stark it slapped at me from a foot away.

"No. No. It's not about what I believe, Elizabeth. It's about what's true for you. If you want a husband or wife or children, then have them. If it's a job change, have that. If it's staying in the same job and working your way up, do that. But please, do me the honor of believing I want the world for you, and I don't want you to feel stuck if what you're doing now won't give it to you."

I nodded, incapable of words. Some small flame of hurt and shame and hope and fear had been blown into a bonfire by this conversation and his well-meaning words. He'd touched on exactly my fears—that the pull towards Silverton and the people here, my family here, was telling me something real. It wasn't just the frustrations piled up with this mess *for now*—it was hinting that the life I'd made for myself wasn't much of one. And if that was true?

If I'd failed so spectacularly at making a meaningful life for myself, then what had even been the point of all of it? Of living away and missing out on time with Jo and even missing my parents, changed as they were?

Jane interrupted and I used the intrusion to excuse

myself with a mumbled thanks and followed an agonized, stumbling path to the car.

I want the world for you.

What did that even mean? How was that attainable? And what was next? The moon and stars?

CHAPTER TWENTY

Kenny

I wandered down the street, enjoying the way the white Christmas lights still lit all the trees in this part of town. They kept the trunks and branches wrapped with white lights until the end of ski season, likely knowing the quaint quotient for downtown increased that much more when tourists could wander in the dreamy atmosphere of our small mountain town.

I'd take it.

Most of the stores were closed save the restaurants, so the windows of Glazed and Cut and Bloom were all dark as I strolled by on the way to my car. I glanced up to see the stars twinkling brightly overhead, the day's clouds hiding somewhere else so the sky could show off.

I stopped and breathed in the chilly winter air and—

"Oh," a voice said as someone collided with my back. Their hands wrapped around my chest like they were searching for purchase, then disappeared in an instant when the person regained their footing.

"I am so sorry I—"

Liz's mouth was wide open, and she dropped her face into her hands.

Wait. *Wait.* That was not a normal response to bumping into someone, even if it was a bit of a rough one. I'd been the one to stop in the middle of the sidewalk. I hadn't heard her behind me.

I moved toward her, tugging on her arm gently once, twice. She exhaled out a gusty sigh and the light from a nearby tree caught tears glittering in her eyes.

"What's going on?"

She swiped angrily under her eyes. "I'm fine. It's just been a day."

I'd spent much of said day with her, so this didn't give me much hope she returned the feelings I'd less than eloquently hinted at to Stone, but that wasn't really the point.

"Tough family dinner?"

She wrapped her arms around herself. "It shouldn't feel like it, but yeah. It was just my dad being this emotionally intelligent, engaged father and for some reason I feel like—" Her voice wavered, and she snapped her lips closed.

I waited, knowing she needed to finish the thought. *Begging* her to finish whatever it was she was saying.

"I just feel like such a failure." She looked up at the sky, avoiding eye contact with me, or maybe simply being drawn in by its beauty like I'd been moments ago.

I wanted to make this better—to give her space to keep talking and processing, to be the person who helped her, and to maybe give her a little more of these stars. I wanted her to have whatever she needed, whatever would give her access to the person she wanted to be, not just the default version she seemed to fight against.

"Can I take you somewhere? Are you free?"

She huffed a disbelieving laugh. "Uh. Sure. If I go home, I'll just wallow."

I flashed her my most charming grin and held out an elbow. "Well, we can't have that, can we?"

The resounding silence of my house didn't bother me the way it often did when I came in after dark. Not hard to guess it had everything to do with Liz being right here with me, and yet I didn't want to acknowledge how much I liked leading her down the short entryway.

"Your house."

She had been completely silent on the drive.

"Yes." I wasn't going to be a chatterbox if she needed the mental space. "Trust me. I have a plan."

She was surveying my living room—a cozy space I enjoyed, though the house could use some work. I'd told myself I'd do it myself, but turned out, I didn't really like being a home renovator all by my lonesome. I'd contracted Warrick Saint to work with me on it and come spring, we'd be tearing up the kitchen.

"It's dated, but it's mine. More than I ever had before," I admitted quietly.

Her gaze found mine. "That's amazing. It's really nice."

It was. There were wood floors, and the bathrooms were actually not terrible. It was a three bedroom, so I had plenty of space. The cabinets were worn and there was wallpaper in a few places. The carpet in the living room was also out of style, but it was mine. A home I'd paid cash for and then nearly puked after I signed at closing.

I'd saved every possible penny during my time in service, and I'd been paid well thanks to being in the EMU relative to others of my same rank in the military. I'd lived modestly, in a small apartment that had never impressed a single person, but it'd let me save some of my housing allowance every month, too, once I was far along enough in my career to live outside the barracks.

This house was mine and there'd been points in my life when the idea of owning my own home had seemed about as far-fetched as being king of America.

I cleared my throat, a little emotional over the place and what it meant. "Yeah, thanks. Anyway, I just need a minute to collect supplies."

She raised a brow.

"Trust me, Malcom. I got you."

She continued to wander around slowly, taking in the handful of photos I had up, the cookbooks I kept around, and the other stuff she could see while I gathered things, tossed them in a basket, and pulled open the sliding glass door leading to the backyard.

After flipping on the lights back there, I stepped out. "Come on. I promise I'll make sure you don't freeze."

Temps had dropped but we'd be fine. I pulled off the cover I used for the little patio set I had out here and gestured to it. "Have a seat and grab one of those blankets from the basket."

In another minute, I had the firepit snapping and crackling with orange flames dancing in front of us. I broke out the SMORES ingredients and held out a metal skewer to her.

"Wanna toast a marshmallow?"

Her lips pinched just a little, but then her pleased smile spread them wide. My heart flipped, so I redirected my attention to the bag of marshmallows and threaded one on the stick while she did the same.

We sat in silence, slowly roasting each side of the sticky-sweet goodness until mine caught on fire and I squawked. She instantly cracked up and victory flooded my veins despite the singed treat. Was there anything better than helping someone feel better when they'd been brought low?

"I have graham crackers, Hershey's bars, and for your consideration, a cookies and cream chocolate bar." I produced the plate with the items and flashed my brows.

"Cookies and cream, huh?"

"I actually discovered these courtesy of Bruce's sister, Kiley. She made a s'mores bar last summer and had these and they changed my s'mores future." I said this in the most affected, dramatic way possible.

"I'm so happy for you," she said, meeting my sense of drama head on, then sliding her marshmallow between two graham crackers and a very plain, very not cookies and cream chocolate bar.

"I see you're taking my advice."

She took an endearingly large bite of her creation and chewed it, eyes shutting for a moment before she swallowed and smiled. "Don't mess with perfection."

Oh, dear, I liked that. I liked the little attitude popping up and the discovery that this woman genuinely liked s'mores. I mean, they were good, but this was really just something to do to give us the excuse to sit outside and look at the stars and have a fire so we didn't freeze.

"Fair enough," I said, eyes snagging on the chocolate still on her bottom lip.

Blame the cold or the feelings seeping through my resolution to stay friendly or the fact she had the most gorgeous lips... whatever the cause, I lost all hesitation and reached up and swiped my thumb across her lip, then licked the chocolate from the pad of my finger.

Her mouth dropped open and her eyes followed my movements, narrowing on my mouth when I licked away the chocolate that had just been on her lip.

The moment stretched between us, a galaxy of stars above us and the fire crackling, bathing us in heat, and my heart galloped. *Kiss her. Kiss her.*

If I did, it'd change everything. And even though she was giving me those eyes, looking at my lips like she wanted them on hers, it could ruin everything. Not just our working relationship, but her whole time here. Maybe she wouldn't be able to have that rest and peace she so clearly needed if she felt like I was here drooling after her, waiting to kiss her.

The breeze shifted and along with it, the smoke, which broke the tension and confirmed it was best to leave it be between us.

No matter what I wanted, this was for the best.

CHAPTER TWENTY-ONE

Elizabeth

It wasn't until after we'd sat there and took in the mountains and stars with only the sounds of the fire and night to accompany us that we actually talked.

He'd joked around and I'd laughed because he was silly and funny enough, I'd wanted to. Despite being rather different people, we had a lot in common in terms of simple things, like how we liked to relax and the things that brought us rest. But nothing real came up until we were back in his car, shivering against the cold on the way back into town.

"You said you feel like a failure," he said, apropos of nothing that'd happened in the last hour or so.

"Uh, yeah."

My cheeks burned, and I was grateful he couldn't see it. Why had I said that aloud? It wasn't like I particularly wanted my failures celebrated and when I had them, I certainly didn't shout it to the rooftops.

"I don't mean to bring it up if you don't want to talk about it, but I feel like I need to say something. And please believe me, this is not trying to make you feel better if what you need is to feel bad. I've fallen into that trap where I spin things so hard I can't see straight, and it doesn't help in the end."

I swallowed hard, hearing the veracity in his voice and wishing I could touch him—steady him and make him know I believed him.

"Okay," I finally said once I realized he wouldn't continue until I made it clear I was ready.

He pulled into a spot right in front of my building's door, put the vehicle in park, and turned to me.

"I need you to know that even though I don't know what happened to get you here, you are not a failure. Even if you had *a* failure, *you* are not a failure. You are not what you do, Liz, and I know that's hard to hear and even harder to believe. But you are..." His gaze shifted toward the windshield, out toward the mountains, like he could see for a hundred miles while he searched for the right words. "You're an impressive woman and you're showing up for your family now. The past does matter, but it's not the only thing. What you do *does* matter, but it's not the only thing either."

My pulse fluttered in my neck and at my temple and I felt so overcome by this kind, genuine person who seemed to know just how to cut right through the fog and say something meaningful and a little painful, but important, too.

I so rarely acted on impulse, but my gut carried me in the moment, and I did follow it. I reached for his face, his skin warm in my chilly hands, and I pulled him into me as I surged forward, pressing my lips to his.

At first touch, my heart lit on fire, but after a second, horror struck.

He wasn't kissing me back.

He wasn't pushing me away, sure, but he still seemed stunned. His hands were tucked close to his body, not urging me toward him. His lips were frozen, not coaxing mine open.

He didn't want me, or this, and I'd quite possibly just ruined *everything*. Maybe the surreal feeling of my time here had fried my brain and I couldn't read signals or navigate any interaction in a healthy way.

I pulled back with a gasp and instantly reached for the door.

"Liz!"

He scrambled out of the car after me, but I was already at the building's door. I couldn't face him and see the apology or pity on his face—not right now. Not after he'd said all those things, *done* so many kindnesses for me, and I'd just folded myself into an origami heart and shoved it into his hands.

Without turning toward him when he said my name again, I spoke as I opened the door. "No. No. Sorry. I'm so sorry. I shouldn't have done that, and we will never speak of it again. Thank you for the s'mores. Good night."

I slipped in and he didn't follow me—I knew he wouldn't.

After locking my apartment door once I got upstairs, I threw my purse to the counter and stumbled forward, dove face-first into the couch, and screamed.

CHAPTER TWENTY-TWO

Kenny

I stood there for a stupidly long time.

Had Elizabeth Malcom, the first woman who'd elicited something in me in a decade plus and who I'd wanted for years, just kissed me?

Astoundingly, yes.

And had I just... sat there?

Like an idiot?

Like a complete and utter fool who had never been kissed instead of a man who would happily devour her?

Also, heartbreakingly, yes.

I paced back and forth in front of her door, debating calling her and begging her to let me come up and at least tell her with words that her kiss wasn't misplaced.

Regret and fear flashed through me at the thought she might never do it again. She really might not. She didn't strike me as the kind of woman to do something rash in the first place, and if she did and it didn't go her way, she wasn't likely to make the same mistake again.

Had that been my one and only shot with her, and I'd just tossed a grenade on it with my hesitation and disbelief?

I groaned, scrubbing my hands over my face and pleading with the stars for an answer. I'd loved every minute of tonight—well, maybe with the exception of her hurting to start it. But I wanted to support someone like this, to distract them a little and then speak gently to them. That's what a partnership was, wasn't it?

But this wasn't a partnership. We weren't dating or together or doing anything... *Especially not if you don't kiss her back, idiot!*

And there was the very valid point that this was all temporary. She'd leave and I'd be here, so avoiding all physical contact was probably smart. It was where I'd started with this and probably where I should end with it, too.

But... I'd never wanted to follow my own advice less.

The urge to laugh hysterically or maybe cry hysterically snuck up like fingers walking up my spine, one after another, a little more pressure mounting as my mind whirled around what'd just happened and how exquisitely I'd just bungled the moment.

A tiny squeak broke through my self-loathing. I glanced around, searching for the source of the sound. Nothing obvious that I could see, so I stopped pacing and held my breath.

Meow.

My gaze darted toward a small pile of detritus near the trunk of one of the trees a few feet away. Had I actually heard something, or was my brain calling to mind all the things I wanted but couldn't have in this perfect moment?

Meow.

My pulse quickened, and I moved instantly to the pile, startled by a tiny feline face coming into view amidst the random pile of stuff.

Death by cuteness. Was that possible?

Through the handle of a plastic bag, two yellow or maybe green eyes peered back at me. It was hard to see in the darkness.

"Well, hi there, little friend," I said, bending slowly so I wouldn't frighten it. The temps were below freezing, and it had to be dangerously cold. The ears pointed out in dark triangles and the head was covered with what seemed like a dusky gray color of fur.

"Meow."

"Are you lost?" I slowly reached out a hand, not wanting it to bolt. The poor thing wriggled, but then I saw how the handle of the baggy had been looped at least twice around its little neck. "Ouch. Let me get that off there."

Slipping my glove off, I held out a finger, and the cat sniffed my skin for a minute before I inched the plastic over his head. It had definitely gotten stuck in this tangle and my heart squeezed at the thought of him being here all day twisted up like this, too tiny a voice to be heard over the normal din of business and cars and people.

In another few seconds, I got him unwrapped completely and expected him to scamper off, but he stayed put and gave another pitiful little meow.

"Not feeling too good, huh? Let me see if I can get you to a doctor."

I dialed Tristan, whose alarmed answer would've made me chuckle if I didn't have an agenda. Once I explained the situation, he gave me his vet's emergency number, and I thanked him. Normally, I would've called Beast for all things cat-dad related, but I didn't want to give him anything to worry about. Despite appearances, knowing there was a freezing little kitten out here would absolutely send the giant of a man into anxious pacing until I could confirm he was okay, so I'd try to get that part of the equation solved before I notified him.

The vet said he could meet me in a half hour and since I was likely about seven minutes from the destination, I had to get this tiny guy out of the cold.

"Okay, please don't hate me for moving you from what has become your safe place, but I don't want you to freeze and you seem like you need some help. So I'm going to pick you up, and then we're going to go get in my car. I'd really prefer it if you could not pee on me, but I won't hold it against you this time if it happens."

I scooped him up into my gloved hand and made an *ugh* sound when I saw just how tiny he was. His little head seemed to be almost as large as the rest of his body and he weighed ounces, not pounds, if I had to guess. Maybe a single pound, but not five or even three, certainly.

Tucking him close to my chest inside my jacket, I hustled to my truck and climbed in, doing my best not to jostle him. "You're the tiniest guy I've ever seen. And you feel like a small collection of chicken bones in a little half-full beanbag, but we'll get you fattened up, I hope."

It wasn't the safest thing I'd ever done, but after trying to set him down and having his spindly claws latch into not only my shirt but also my skin, I decided to keep him there with one hand and drive on over to the vet's office with the other.

Along the way, I talked to him.

"I keep thinking you're a boy, but I'm honestly not sure. I didn't get a good look and suspect you wouldn't be very happy with me if I tried right now, so we'll let the vet tell us what's what."

He didn't answer, nor did he stage a kitty revolt and climb me like a rope, so I kept going. "I'm hoping I didn't just tear you away from family, but you need some help right now, either way. We'll get the word out and see if we can find your family and if not..."

I trailed off and realized the truth of what I was about to say. "If not, you'll come home with me and I'll be your family."

Call me a loon or a fool or even a hopeless romantic— whatever applied best. I wouldn't deny any of those. And somehow, the idea that this little beast and I might be—dare I even think it?—meant to be.

It settled in my chest and nestled into my heart. I'd always suspected I'd know... and right now, I knew. This little guy and I were meant for each other.

Another tiny meow came as though in response.

"You like that idea? You and me sticking it out?" I focused on the road, resisting the urge to look away from the windshield and check on him. But soon enough, I pulled into the vet's lot right as Dr. Monroe was getting out of his car.

"Thanks for meeting me," I said, slipping out of the car and following him inside.

"Glad I was able to get here quickly. Looks like a tiny one." He flipped on the lights of the lobby, then hallway, then exam room as he went. "Hold right here for another minute if you can and let me gather a few things. If he's scared, he might try to run so I want to be ready."

"Okay," I agreed, fully acknowledging he knew far more about what to expect from this little creature than I did.

He returned with a stethoscope around his neck, a lab

coat on, a towel, and a few other items he set aside. "Normally, I'd have a tech to help if needed, but I'm going to rely on you."

His dark eyes settled on the little lump against my chest as he fitted his large hands into gloves. "Let's get this kitten onto the towel and see how it goes. If it starts to jump on us, I'm going to grab it."

Fortunately, the transition to the towel-topped table went smoothly once we got the claws hooked into the fabric of my shirt removed. I could feel the tremble in the little cat's body, but he didn't strike at us or even meow again. Dr. Monroe's hands held him gently but firmly, and I took note of where and how since I hadn't interacted with a kitten in years. Plus, I didn't think Beast's cat Bones had ever been this small.

"Congratulations, it's a boy," the doc said as he examined the cat's belly and underside.

"I was right," I said, a little impressed with myself and weirdly bursting with pride to have found this little guy and yet already dreading the possibility the congratulations didn't belong to me—that I couldn't keep him, be his cat dad. "He seemed like a boy."

Dr. Monroe glanced at me, then continued his work, speaking softly in his rich voice to the little one, telling him how his legs looked strong, and his belly was very empty. After another minute or two, he set the cat back down but kept a hand on him.

"You've got a very skinny but not unhealthy kitten on your hands. He's probably between eight and ten weeks old. If his mom's around, he may not have weaned, but it doesn't seem like he's had anyone watching out for him in a few days at least, so I'm thinking maybe he's been abandoned or lost. He's likely a fully black cat under all the muck, so you'll want to watch out for him, especially around Halloween. People take the lore seriously sometimes and it's awful." He frowned, stroking the kitten's head gently.

I shuddered. How could someone hurt a black cat, let alone any animal? "People are the worst."

Dr. Monroe chuckled. "Some can be. But you're a good man and I think you'll be a good cat dad to this fellow."

Cat dad.

Me?

I smiled down at the little black face with what I could now definitively see were light green eyes and yeah. Yep. I'd known it the second I heard the first meow, and it solidified in me now like orders for a new mission.

It clicked. I just... knew.

I could absolutely be this little one's cat dad.

CHAPTER TWENTY-THREE

Elizabeth

Living with the knowledge I'd kissed Kenny Carmichael against his wishes stung, but I'd prepared to deal with it at work today.

Being unable to get over the awkwardness sooner rather than later and potentially apologize again because Kenny didn't show up to work?

Highly unanticipated.

"Did you have a good day off?"

The man everyone lovingly referred to as Cookie asked me this casually as he perused a selection of, as it happened, beautiful-looking cookies on the table in the break room. I finished filling my mug full of mid-afternoon coffee and turned to him.

Cookie was a deeply laughable name for this man—Luc fit far better. But so far, I'd rarely heard anyone call him Luc, whereas other people consistently got called by their real name. It seemed to vary, and I hadn't been here long enough to know who preferred what.

Luc looked far more like a dark fairy prince than he did a baked good, though I could recognize not everyone's nicknames were given based on appearances.

For example, Barbie failed to catch any of Kenny's ridiculous good looks. Also, was that a L. Leroy watch? I'd had an asset obsessed with watches and he'd droned on about them. I didn't recall much other than they were a French company and most of their watches *started* around fifteen thousand euros.

Again, it wasn't as though these people were working for scraps, but that was extravagant by any measure. Maybe it'd been handed down?

Anyway...

"Uh, yes. Yeah. I—" The awkwardness of how I'd pushed myself on this man's friend struck me and if I'd been walking, I might've tripped. "Kenny showed me around a bit. Silverton is a cool little town."

This was likely the lamest way I'd ever described a place, but what else could I say? *I loved spending time with your bff and I'm falling for your town, but I also foisted myself upon a man who's been nothing but friendly and generous to me and I'm pretty sure I flushed all the good feelings between us down the toilet. Oh and, I'm gnawing my cuticles off as I wait for news from my real life and real job so I can get back to it, which makes all the rest of this irrelevant anyway.*

No. Of course not.

"It is. I like it far more than I imagined I would." Cookie smiled, his gaze softening as he finally selected an item from the tray and slipped it onto a napkin.

I wanted to ask him if he'd talked to Kenny—if he knew

why his friend hadn't shown up today. But if I did that, it would be obvious I'd been wondering, which was too much attention to draw to myself and how much I'd been thinking about Kenny, so I gave him a polite nod and headed out.

"Did you meet the kitten?"

This halted my steps, and I turned, completely perplexed. "Kitten?"

Cookie dipped his head in this subtle way he had, far more French than any other gesture I'd seen him make thus far. "Kenny found a kitten last night. He took the day off to track down the owner. Turns out it's an orphan so he's keeping it."

This hit me like a water balloon to the chest—impact and then an instant spread of water except in this case it was warmth and delight.

"I didn't realize. I'd wondered where he was today." So much for not mentioning *that* little gem.

"I'm sure he'd love a visitor if you have time after work." He held up his cookie. "Have a good afternoon."

"You, too, and thanks." Not sure what I was thanking him for, exactly. The knowledge Kenny wasn't avoiding me outright? Maybe.

Although did people really stay home from work when they got a new pet? As a non-pet-owning person, I didn't know.

I did know, however, that I'd be texting Kenny after work. There'd never been a better excuse to stop by and clear the awkwardness than to see a kitten.

So that's what I did. Although it'd come not hours later, but minutes, because I'd grown restless and since I wasn't a full-time employee, I didn't really have work to do at my desk. Bruce and Wilder had been nice enough to provide me an office, but so far, I'd done every bit of paperwork from the Jack McKean mission and we'd had no updates from them. I'd made it clear I'd be happy to assist if they needed in-person help, and I'd hoped Evie or Jack would reach out if they needed anything.

So far, nada.

Also a big fat zero news from my real job, boss, or organization as a whole, which was just super annoying. I should at least be getting updates weekly and I'd had no news. The catch-up I'd be playing for weeks after returning —whenever it happened—would be mind-numbing thanks. Fun.

And therefore, I found myself leaving work at three that afternoon, anxious to see the man I'd kissed and clear the air.

I was not, however, prepared for him to jog up to the house *behind* me as I approached his porch.

"Hey," he called out.

As though struck by lightning, I jolted and turned with a far-too-dramatic gasp.

"Hey." I blew out a breath. "Crap, that scared me."

Half his mouth quirked up into a smile and he was just... oof. He looked good.

Gray sweatpants and sneakers with a hooded sweatshirt on top, a beanie pulled low over his ears. He yanked that off as he and his long legs strode toward me, his cheeks a dark red.

"Sorry. Didn't mean to. I snuck in a jog while he was conked out. Got a little restless, so I took my chance."

Our eyes met as we passed and he set a hand on my shoulder, a gentle squeeze there that made my insides tumble around in a spin cycle before he let go and practically leapt up the stairs.

"Come on in. If he stays asleep, I'm going to run to the

shower but I'll be super quick," he said, dropping his voice to just above a whisper once inside.

Following his lead, I inched the door closed quietly. "Sounds goo—"

In the few seconds I'd painstakingly closed his front door, he'd stripped off his sweatshirt—and whatever he'd worn underneath—and was holding them at his side as though the sight of his ruddy cheeks, bare chest, dark tattoos that would never not be a little bit of a thrill, and low-riding sweatpants wouldn't summarily off me when flashed around so spontaneously.

Our gazes snagged and I could've sworn there was heat flickering in his bright eyes, but he tsked, breaking the moment.

"Sorry, I overheated. I'll just be a sec."

Clearing my throat, I mumbled, "Yep. No problem."

I did not say, "Why stop at the pants?" or "Need any help in there?" or anything else that felt like rolling off my tongue because I'd already crossed a boundary with him once.

Although honestly, he now clearly knew I was interested so why would he go parading around flashing his abs all willy nilly?

Willy nilly ab flashing was not acceptable or helpful for this little... crush I'd developed.

That was really all this was, too, and I needed to remember it.

Sure, Kenny was the nicest human being I'd met in a long time and had a way of seeing through my protective quiet and pulling out things I normally would never talk about. He was caring to those around him, gentle with people, but still so magnetically masculine in an effortless way. He was encouraging and positive, but not because he ignored hard things—because he'd learned from them. I admired him.

And yeah, he was the most physically attractive person I'd ever met, and fine, maybe he had a kind of abrupt cheeriness I normally would be repelled by. But for some reason it felt like a complementary magnet...

None of that mattered to my real life. I could admire his good looks and positive attitude and the incredible way he'd handled the challenges of his past, but it needn't turn into anything more than a basic crush. I didn't know how to handle this particularly well since I wasn't a woman who *had* crushes. *That* was why it all felt so novel, anyway.

And also nothing here felt real or normal because it wasn't my real or normal life. So... also that.

I'd convinced myself of this quite thoroughly, right up until he came down the hallway with something tucked against his chest. He stopped when he met my eyes and grinned, moving one hand to reveal a tiny pitch-black kitten snoozing away in the literal palm of his hand.

"Ms. Liz Malcom, please meet my new cat, Kit."

And there it went. Another piece of my flimsy resistance to this man evaporated into thin air, just like that.

CHAPTER TWENTY-FOUR

Kenny

So apparently, kittens were chick magnets.

Or at least, they were effective lures for Liz Malcom, who visibly melted when I revealed my kitten.

"I think I believe in love at first sight now," she said, an awestruck tone to her whispered words as she gazed at my cat.

I think I know the feeling.

Pushing the thought away, I smiled even wider than I already was. "If anything can prove it exists, it's kittens."

This kitten, who'd gotten cuter by the second, even if he had torn up my arms and chest a fair bit in the last eighteen hours.

"I want to hold him so bad, but I don't want him to wake up." Her brows were pinched, and she looked pained.

This badass international spy woman was gone for my cat, and I couldn't help but be very pleased about it. I'd also need to clarify that the kiss last night was *not* a problem, only my slow reaction to it was.

And, ideally, take a minute or two to reciprocate.

"So you found him on Silver Street?" she asked, her fingers balling into a fist like she was physically restraining herself from petting him.

"Yep. Right after we... parted ways." My gaze flicked up to hers right as she looked away. *Okay.* Not going to take that opening to talk about last night.

I ran the pad of my finger over the short fur on his forehead, and his little purr started up. A strangled sound came from Liz.

"You gonna make it?" I asked, absolutely gulping down the way she was down so bad for this little beast.

She pressed a hand over her heart. "I don't know. I'm not normally this into kittens but I honestly don't think I've ever seen anything this adorable."

I chuckled and the sound startled Kit awake. Sleepy eyes blinked open slowly until he was fully awake and gazing at Liz.

"Oh my goodness, you are the sweetest thing that has ever existed."

Her voice was soft and sweet and so unlike anything I'd heard from her, it had me grinning like a maniac.

"You are obsessed with my cat." No small amount of wonder laced my words.

She only had eyes for Kit as she inched forward and let him catch her scent before gently petting his head. "I am completely and instantly obsessed. His wish is my command."

I cackled at this, and he startled, pushing off my chest and hooking a needle-like claw right through my shirt and into the flesh underneath. At least I'd cleaned up with the world's fastest shower and put on a layer—it likely saved me a few puncture wounds.

"Ah, okay. Sorry, buddy." I bent and set him all the way down. He was spindly-looking like this—all skin, bones, and fur. The thorough wiping-down I'd given him last night had revealed his black fur, but I was eager to give him a bath. Dr. Monroe had advised I wait a few days if I could, and I saw the wisdom in that.

His little meows started up and I recognized the warning sign. "Woops, okay. Come with me." I snatched him up again and hustled down the hallway to the utility room where his litter box was located.

"Come on back if you want," I said as I sat him down in the litter. He'd gotten the hang already, but he hadn't had the run of the house just yet. The vet had advised me to start him out in one room for at least a few days so he wouldn't be overwhelmed and so he could learn the box and such. So far, that was working well. He had a good little alert system for needing a litter break.

"Is this his room?" Liz asked from the doorway, surveying the washer, dryer, utility sink, and the corner where I'd set his litter box. At the far end, I'd made him a little bed of towels and a soft blanket until I could get something more official.

"This is it until he's ready for his territory to expand. I'm happy for him to have the run of the place when he's ready, but I'm told it might be a bit too soon. He's also malnourished and was a bit dehydrated, so that's the focus for the next few days."

I glanced at her, expecting to see her smiling at the little guy as he dug out some litter, but her eyes were on me.

"You are all in on this cat dad thing."

"Is that so surprising?"

A beat of wariness pulsed in my chest. I didn't like the sensation, but I couldn't pretend moments like these didn't grate at times. It wasn't necessarily people being surprised by things I did that bothered me as much as the low-lying suspicion they fundamentally didn't understand who I was. I knew exactly where that came from—thanks, fam—and normally had a better handle on logically dismissing those kinds of things. But after a pretty restless night of sleep, it wasn't coming easily.

Liz's brow furrowed lightly as her gaze tracked the kitten. "No, actually. It's not at all."

I shrugged one shoulder, but warmth spread through my chest. We both kept our focus on the little black fur puff as he made his way out of the litter box with clumsy legs.

The genuine joy radiating from Liz was irresistible, and the way she laughed and talked so sweetly to this little wisp of an animal made me want to stay right here with her and soak it in for as long as it lasted.

So we did.

Not quite a full hour passed before the kitten did as kittens do and curled up in his mound of blankets and circled into a sleepy black cinnamon roll. I stood and reached a hand out to help her up, which she took.

The contact of her palm against mine, her small hand connected with my larger one, did stupid things to my brain. I almost pulled her into me in one fell swoop, but my mind had some lingering threads of control, so I waited until she was steady on her feet and released her.

We slipped out of the room and shut the door behind us, leaving the tiny one to sleep without being disturbed. I made my way to the kitchen, intent on washing my hands and offering her a drink and ideally asking her to stay for dinner, if I could just find the right way in.

"Thank you for letting me meet him. He's precious." She took her turn at the sink while I dried my hands on a clean towel.

"I'm glad you came," I said, my voice pitched low. Temporary or no, I wanted her here. That wasn't me, not normally, but with this woman, I couldn't seem to resist taking whatever she'd offer, even if it was to the tune of a ticking clock.

Her gaze found mine as she took the towel from me and dried her hands.

"Listen, I'm sorry about last night. I never—"

"I'm not."

She blinked, mouth opening, then closing.

"Truly, I'm not. And I don't think you should be either." I wanted this to be very, very clear for her.

She set the towel aside, moving in a way that said her mind was occupied, so her movements were distracted.

"Okay. Can I ask why? You didn't seem to—" she cleared her throat "—return the interest."

Her cheeks were pink, but her eyes locked on mine.

"That was a misunderstanding." This was the point at which talking failed but doing could triumph.

"Oh?" she asked, straightening. "Because I didn't—"

In one swift movement, I stepped into her space, cupped her face with my hands, and leaned in so I was only a few inches away. Dipping my head, I waited while the tension built, her chest rising and falling scant millimeters from grazing my body.

"Let me be clear. You surprised me last night and I froze. I'm kissing you now because I wanted to then and I want to now."

And then I closed the distance between us and took her mouth with mine.

CHAPTER TWENTY-FIVE

Elizabeth

Kenny kissed like he had been ordained to do the job. Literally, it felt like he was on a mission to claim me with his lips, and he wouldn't accept defeat.

It was... stunningly hot.

Also rather unexpected.

For all the sweetness and sunshine he displayed, the gentleness and respect and courtesy, there was something demanding and almost base in the way he drove the kiss.

And me?

I more than happily hung on for the ride, opening to him when he demanded it, tilting my head when he urged me to, hooking my arms around his neck and pressing into him as he did me.

He groaned and broke the kiss, bent down, and picked me up by the back of the legs and deposited me on his kitchen counter. As he stepped between my knees, his large hands settling at my waist, I found my voice.

"Well, that was…" I didn't know. Still hadn't regained the full powers of speech, apparently, but Kenny was already shaking his head.

"Not done yet."

His voice was gruff and so full of need, it made my stomach clench, then somersault when he dipped his head and kissed me again.

We were pressed together, every slide of his lips and tongue coaxing me from solid to liquid. The sounds he made, the way he was breathing, how his big hands splayed over my ribs, grasping but not moving up or down despite my internal pleas for it. With my thighs bracketing his narrow hips and my hands in his hair, I was utterly lost to any reason this wasn't what we should do until the end of time.

Until he pulled back, squeezing my waist again and exhaling like he was catching his breath after a run.

"So. You did want to kiss me."

His smile cracked through the serious, hooded expression like the first beams of sunrise. "Only a little."

I bit my lip, but it did nothing to hide my answering grin.

His gaze dropped to my mouth, and he swayed forward, but then he let go of me and forced his head back dramatically. "I don't think I can stand there anymore."

Knowing he was as addled as I was gave me boldness I wouldn't have imagined after what'd felt like a total failure last night. He'd done the work to reassure me and I believed him.

Because of this, I asked, "Why not?"

His gaze shot to mine, and he narrowed his eyes. "I think you know."

My eyes widened, all innocence, and I pressed. "But why not? It was just a little kiss."

Heat flared in his stunning blue irises and he stalked forward, shoving between my legs and resting his hands on the cabinet behind me, thoroughly caging me in.

Well *hello.* The tattoos had struck me as surprisingly bad boy for this sweet, sensitive man, but I was getting a hint of a new dimension. That kiss, and now this rough, barely leashed energy from him, was more than a little thrilling.

His gaze was dark and full of promise. "Yes. Just a tiny, harmless kiss."

I lifted my chin, positioning my lips a breath from his. "Completely harmless."

He shook his head slowly, brushing his mouth over mine once, twice, then pulling back.

"Stay for dinner?"

"Sure." I didn't have to think about it. There wasn't anywhere else I wanted to be. And if I hung around, maybe he'd kiss me again.

He didn't kiss me again.

Not until hours later, after we'd eaten a meal he'd cooked for us, then watched a movie in his cozy living room with a sleeping kitten snuggled on the couch between us. Not until I'd stepped outside his door, certain he was going to let me go without talking about the kiss, or what it meant, or what came next.

I was certain right up until he grabbed my hand and tugged, pulling me back toward him and sinking his hands into my hair with so much stabled hunger, I couldn't imagine how I'd not felt it coming. He kissed me so thoroughly, I saw stars when he pulled back a few minutes later and it had nothing to do with the pitch-dark sky.

"Buy you a donut tomorrow before work?" he asked, releasing my hair but pinching my chin lightly before letting me go completely.

"Sounds good," I managed, amazed I could sound at all composed after the unraveling he'd just done.

"Good. Zero-eight. See you there."

So at seven-forty-five, I left the house and two minutes later ducked into the shop to find Elise sliding a fresh batch of donuts into the display case.

"Well, hello there. Back for more donuts already?" She grinned.

"They are delicious. But actually, this was Kenny's doing. I'm meeting him here in a few minutes."

Her smile widened. "Oh. Well. Very nice." She wiggled her brows.

Discomfort hit at the knowledge that she assumed we were dating or together or at least interested in each other. But then... weren't we?

My shoulders deflated at the unavoidable reality that I didn't know. And no matter what he thought, or even what I thought, we didn't have a future.

"Hmm. That wasn't the response I anticipated." Her gaze sharpened and slid over me as though checking for something, but when I blinked it was gone. "On another note, are you coming to book club?"

"Is that Saturday? Jo mentioned it again, so I've been thinking about it."

She'd actually texted me every day and had left me a paperback copy at my apartment door a few days after I'd arrived. I had read the book eagerly since the club focused on romance reads and I'd enjoyed the genre a great deal.

"Yes. We'll have wine and appetizers and even if you haven't read, it's fun. I've missed finishing the book a few times and it's still great. The weeks I can't make it just kill me." Her smile flickered and fell.

"Do you have to miss often?" I asked, that expression too different not to ask.

She waved a hand and straightened her apron. "Nah. Occasionally, I have a meeting that pops up, but not as often lately." She grinned and her brows rose. "Your date's here."

"Oh, we're not uh... well, yeah. Thanks." And yes, I had a master's degree and had briefed senior State and Defense department staff, but my composure in the face of a handsome man meeting me for donuts was apparently nil.

Speaking of, said man looked unfazed as he wandered in and flashed me a grin that made my insides twist. And right behind him, Cookie entered the shop.

"Morning, Liz," he said, his voice still rumbly from sleep.

"Morning, Kenny. Or do I call you Barbie? I'm never really sure." I sort of wanted to push and see what he said.

"How about you call me whatever you want?"

My heart flipped, and I tried my best not to read the innuendo in his tone, but it was impossible.

"Kenny, then," I said quietly.

His smile was soft, almost secret. "Works for me."

Elise stood behind the counter and beamed at us. "Aren't you two adorable?"

We both chuckled and stepped up behind Cookie, who'd finally caught Elise's gaze.

"Morning, Luc," she said with a small smile and a flush to her cheeks.

Cookie nodded and spoke so quietly I could hardly hear him. "Glazed, please."

She blinked but nodded, punching in the order and then fluttering away to get his donuts. Kenny and I eyed each other, and I was relieved he saw it, too. There was something here and it was weird. Clearly, Elise kind of liked Cookie, enough to blush when she greeted him, but he was not himself. He was on the quiet end from what I'd seen, but not like this.

Once Cookie had paid and the *complete* silence between the two ended, Kenny moved up to order, then insisted I do the same. Minutes later, we were seated at a two-top by the front window as though Elise wanted to show us off, but instead of being self-conscious, I just listened.

He told me about the kitten this morning, told me about a dream he'd had, and right as he was saying, "We should talk about last night," both our phones buzzed.

The timing couldn't be a coincidence, so we both checked our messages to find the same thing.

There'd been an incident at Jack's and he and Evie were requesting we come to the house immediately.

CHAPTER TWENTY-SIX

Kenny

J ack looked better rested than he had when we'd seen him a few days ago, but Evie looked far worse for wear.

All thoughts of Liz, our mind-blowing kiss, the feel of her under my hands, and everything I wanted with her, plus the healthy number of "how on earth can this work between us?" questions rolling around my brain got shoved into a corner while I focused on the here and now.

"Walk us through what happened, if you don't mind. I know you've already spoken with Chief Whitaker, but it'll help us do whatever we can to make sure you're safe if you can catch us up from your perspective." I hated to make her talk about anything she didn't want to, but they'd asked us to come, even after reporting the incident to the police.

Jack sat on the couch one cushion away. He gave her space, but was close enough to support her when she needed. Again, I wondered at their dynamic. Clearly not a boyfriend or even someone interested in her, or I'd suspect he'd be hovering closer by.

I sat in a super comfy yet stylish chair perpendicular to Evie, and Liz stood somewhere over my shoulder.

"I got a call two nights ago that was just heavy breathing," Evie said, eyes downcast. "I didn't say anything because it just felt like a prank or... I don't know." She shook her head, seemingly frustrated with herself. "Then I started getting texts from a bunch of anonymous numbers saying how I'm a cheater and other lovely things."

Her hands shook as she pushed a blond lock behind her ear.

"And this morning?" Liz prompted gently.

She swallowed and finally looked up, eyes meeting Liz's. "This morning, I picked up a call and it was him." She repeated the explicit and threatening message from her fiancé, the words disgustingly cruel, graphic, and concerning.

"We notified the LAPD, as well. He doesn't appear to know *where* she is but found out her new number somehow." Jack scowled, anger pulsing off of him.

"Cookie and Beast are running through all of her accounts now to shore things up and we're told your assistant is obtaining another phone for her?" I said, trying to keep things moving toward the positive.

Jack nodded. Evie sighed and slumped back with her hands braced on her belly.

Liz moved around the couch and crouched next to her, one hand on the armrest of the couch. "We're going to make it so he has no way to find you. For now, lie low, rest, and don't let this steal your confidence in the plan."

Evie's lips pressed together and trembled, and then she

threw herself at Liz. She hugged her tight enough Liz didn't fall backwards until Evie released her suddenly.

"Thank you. I'm sorry. I'm just... I'm a wreck." Evie swiped under her eyes.

"You're not a wreck. This is incredibly stressful, and you shouldn't have to deal with it at all. We're doing everything we can." My gaze shifted to Jack's, and he clearly read between the lines. Based on the tension in his shoulders and neck, he felt the same as I did.

Evie said thank you a few more times and Liz stood when she did. "Let's see if the housekeeper has something for breakfast lined up," Liz suggested, gently setting a hand on Evie's back to guide her toward the kitchen.

I watched them go, appreciating how gentle Liz could be. She seemed like she'd be cold, even with clients, but she'd been nothing but warm and thoughtful and ready to help. She'd be great at this kind of work if she ever wanted to do more of it.

"You two involved romantically?"

Part of me hated to ask it, but we needed to know. Romantic dynamics wouldn't necessarily be a problem, but if this was someone who was eventually going to step out in public with a man more famous than most people on the planet, we needed to know that, too.

Jack stiffened. "Just because she's a beautiful woman staying with me doesn't mean we're dating." He swore, clearly tired of being asked.

I held up my hands. "I'm sorry, man. I just need to know what we're dealing with in terms of going forward. If she's about to go out to the movies with you or something and get caught by paparazzi, it's good to have that on the radar."

Jack scrubbed a hand down his face. "No. She worked for me, and we became friendly enough. My house manager started noticing bruises and she tried to ask her about it, but Evie never said anything. I acted like an ass and sort of… held up my hands like it wasn't my problem and if she wasn't going to say anything, then that was it. Then she came to the house last week and I couldn't pretend I wasn't seeing it, so I sat her down. She let me help her, and here we are."

He huffed and gritted his teeth, his jaw flexing in a way that probably made women the world over swoon if it'd been caught on camera. "What's the point of being filthy rich if I can't help someone who actually needs it?"

The tone said he was actually asking me and I sensed this went deep for him.

"You're helping. You've got security in LA, you've talked to law enforcement, and you've got us here. Between all of us, we'll figure out the best way to keep her safe until this baby arrives and we'll get her set up with a new life when the time comes."

Jack nodded, face still hard.

"Evie's eating some breakfast. I think it's time we get back to the office," Liz said, pausing a few feet from us.

"We'll circle back this afternoon with an update. You call us if anything else comes up, but expect to see us on and off, too."

The local PD would up their periodic patrols in the neighborhood even though we had no concerns this sack of excrement knew anything about this location. Jack hadn't ever stayed at this house, and though he'd visited Silverton a few times, he'd visited quite a few other small mountain towns here and, largely, hadn't stayed long enough to make it somewhere even a particularly intelligent person might look.

We said goodbye and found our way to the car, both

settling in with minds full of thoughts. Cookie and Beast would be on top of any trails they could find to help out, and I'd work on some contingency plans for local action if we needed them.

"I hate this," Liz said, her voice low.

"Me, too." I didn't know whether she meant the whole situation and the idea that a man would hurt a woman like this jerk had Evie, or the way he was harassing her, but I got it. It was different than what she did, and it all felt a little futile when Evie was technically safe, but still running scared from someone so cruel and determined to harm her, even at a distance.

We drove the ten minutes to work, compiling a list quickly. I'd run back to the house to check on Kit in a few hours, but for now—

"What the hell?"

A group of people in winter coats stood at the base of the stairs leading to Saint Security chatting with Bruce, Adam, and a thunderous-looking Stone, oddly enough.

But weirder, the group was familiar, and only because I'd just seen most of them in Vegas last weekend.

It wasn't just a random group of tourists, no.

It was my family.

My pulse jumped, body instantly on guard. They'd never been to Utah, never visited me or made so much as a text in my direction, and now they were here?

"There he is, our family's favorite soldier," my mom said, beaming at me like she really was glad to see me.

My dad and brother both made silly "heyyy!" sounds, my brother slapping my back as I approached.

"Hi," I said, the confusion and skepticism clear in my tone.

"Oh, don't pretend you're shocked to see us! You invited

us to come visit anytime!" My mom pulled me into a hug as though we did such things regularly.

My gaze found Bruce's, then Adam's, then Stone's. Each man had a different degree of concern on his face, and I instantly felt at ease.

They weren't falling for this either.

Also, did I invite them here? If I did, I'd mind-wiped it from all memory.

"I—okay. I mean, are you guys planning to ski?" Didn't seem likely since skiing was definitely a rich man's sport in the US, but maybe they were in a different place financially than they always had been. They'd been at the casino when I first saw them, after all, and that wasn't a cheap place to stay.

"Nah. Just came to see you and maybe get you to show us your favorite dinner spot. We're only in town a few days," my brother said, pasting on a charming smile that raised the hair on the back of my neck.

It wasn't particularly nefarious, but he didn't smile at me. Was this all some weird show for Bruce and the guys? For Liz, who stood with a glare I imagined she'd given more than one international bad guy she'd encountered over the years.

Maybe this was some kind of olive branch? Maybe they wanted to reestablish connection. I didn't know if I wanted that, but they were here, so what else could I do?

CHAPTER TWENTY-SEVEN

Elizabeth

I wouldn't claim to be someone who withheld judgement, though I did have a fairly even keel.

That said, I'd instantly disliked Kenny's family when we saw them in Vegas, purely based on his reaction to them. One thing in this scenario was true—Kenny must be protected at all costs.

Bruce, Adam, and Stone had clearly felt the same way. I'd never seen Bruce interact with civilians in any way other than somewhere firmly in the cordial-to-charming range, but he'd been borderline stoic with Kenny's family.

And Stone had looked like he was contemplating murder. He had such a somber face to begin with though, maybe that'd just been his thing in general? The nickname certainly fit.

Kenny's willingness to meet them for dinner after everything he'd told me made me want to scream.

And also hug him.

And if I was already hugging, I might as well kiss him, right?

I did none of those things since we were standing there with my temporary, and his actual, boss, and we'd never gotten to the point of discussing what the heck we were doing in the wake of our reality-altering kiss. Maybe that was for the best, because I didn't want to make plans right now. What I wanted was to make sure his family did nothing to harm him, and the roaring need to protect him wasn't about to go away anytime soon.

But I did make sure I got an invite to dinner, too. His family had told him to invite friends as they waved and made a big thing of seeing him later as they all piled into their car and Kenny stared after them like he'd been through a tornado.

Bruce, Adam, Stone, and I had all waited for him to react. But he just watched them drive away, turned to us, and said, "This'll be interesting," and strode into the building.

Nothing had ever been more unsettling in my life than that man having virtually no reaction to his weirdo jerk family showing up out of nowhere and wanting to take him to dinner.

"I'm coming with you," I called after him, to which he turned and gave me a small smile I chose to interpret as acceptance. Bruce, Adam, Stone, and I shared a look, and then we followed him inside.

A ball would be dropping, and I would be there to watch... or catch it if need be.

After a very slow workday in which I questioned everything from my choice to wear a suit to my choice to come to Silverton to Kenny's family's sudden and very oddly timed appearance, I trod home in the chilly winter afternoon. A quick change of clothes came first, and then I checked my personal email and caught up on texts that'd come in. I typically stored my personal phone during work hours, and the habit persisted here even though most parts of Saint Security's building allowed for phones.

I promised Jo I'd be at the book club gathering on Saturday, then grabbed a jacket and headed to Guac. I'd hardly seen Kenny the rest of the day and when I'd left around four, he'd still been working away at his computer. He'd simply nodded and said, "See you then," when I'd told him I was going home to change and relax a bit before dinner with his family.

It all had me on edge. The whole situation just seemed supremely sketchy, and I couldn't shake the feeling that his family had come here to get something from him. They'd seen him with an A-list celebrity, so maybe they wanted to meet Jack? Or get his autograph or something? Seemed like a lot of work for that, though some people were enamored with fame.

Kenny stood just outside the building, gaze pinned to his shoes. His usual bounding energy was buttoned up inside whatever shroud of thought he was stuck in.

I was instantly and illogically furious the second I read the way his shoulders bowed inward instead of spreading broad and proud, the way he hunched in on himself like he might make himself smaller.

Kenny filled up a room just by entering it because he led with hard-won joy, and right now, his family's presence here had stolen that.

"What can I do?" I said by way of greeting. *Tell me what to do to make this easier for you.*

He raised his head slowly, eyes sliding up my body and meeting mine. "Give me guac and call me pretty?"

A laugh burst out of me and my whole heart just glowed for him. "I can do that."

He fluttered his lashes and grinned, but sobered quickly. "Thanks for coming. I don't know what's going on."

I slipped my hand into his, grasping firmly to show him I was unequivocally on his team. "We'll figure it out. And if all else fails, I'll yell 'fire' and we'll run."

That gorgeous smile reemerged, and he nodded. "Deal."

He squeezed my hand, then released it and took a big breath before charging forward into the restaurant. His family was already seated at a five-person round in a far corner. At least we weren't right in the middle of the restaurant with more eyes on us. Apparently, even a Thursday night meant big business during ski season as every other table appeared to be full or sporting a little reserved sign on it.

"Glad you finally decided to show," Glen Jr. said, leaning back with an arm around the empty chair next to him, a large margarita glass two-thirds empty.

I glanced at my watch—we were approximately two minutes early.

"Come sit, Ken. And, I'm so sorry, I've forgotten your name?"

His mother phrased this like a question with a sweet

smile. I wondered whether she had actually forgotten it or if this was a way of putting me—or Kenny—in my place.

Kenny pulled out the chair next to his mother for me, then sat by his brother. Glen Jr. shot him a disgusted look I couldn't fathom. In what universe did a person sleep with their brother's fiancée and then act like their brother was the problem?

A waiter arrived instantly and took our orders since apparently Kenny's family had been here for a while based on the empty chip baskets he refilled, and the drinks they'd clearly been working on. If it were just me and him, I'd request the tableside guac and we'd gorge ourselves on that before our entrees came, but I felt a sense of urgency to eat and leave, so I just requested a side of the stuff in case Kenny's order didn't suffice for him.

The small talk starting out was nothing short of painful. Kenny asked how G was and why he hadn't come. This earned a fair amount of scorn from Glen Jr.

He started by swearing and indicating what an idiot he thought his brother was, then proceeded to say, "He has school, you genius." More expletives used in completely unoriginal ways.

I'd become inured to foul language in my line of work—in fact, I could use it in several languages and mostly chose not to. But nothing bothered me so much as uncreative uses of swearing, which in my mind only proved someone's low IQ.

"Right, of course," Kenny said, his cheeks pinking just slightly.

"So why did you all come to visit now, when he couldn't come, too?" I asked, because I wasn't going to sit here and pretend like any of this was normal, and I didn't even fully grasp how *not* normal it was.

Glen Sr., predictably, said nothing and took a sip of his beer. The food arrived before Mandee could chime in, and we all dove in like we'd been starved for weeks once each of us had our plates.

Or, Kenny and I waited until everyone else had theirs, but notably, the other Carmichaels dove in the second their plates touched the table.

It was an odd, superficial thing to notice, but I did. Their manners weren't simply poor in terms of etiquette— who really cared about that? They were poor in terms of considering other people. This was primarily astounding because Kenny was a man who was so deeply considerate of others, it made no sense.

How on earth had he come from these people?

Even as I posted the question internally, I knew the answer. He'd chosen to be different, and he'd worked hard to. Maybe some of his past had forced the change, but he'd also made the choice to be grateful instead of bitter, kind instead of angry, and empathetic instead of cold.

He was honestly a miracle.

"So, how long have you been friends with Jack McKean?" Glen Jr. asked, mouth full of his queso-covered beef taco.

Kenny didn't miss a beat. "He's an acquaintance from work." Technically, he couldn't reveal he was a client due to confidentiality, but in this case, there wasn't a ton of room for creativity.

"And your work is Saint Security, right?" his mom asked.

I narrowed my eyes, but kept my gaze on my food. As usual, the chicken chimichanga was illogically good, even in the face of this nonsense set up. I would miss this when I left.

"Yes. That's the building where you guys were talking to some of my coworkers earlier." Kenny's voice had a twinge of... something in it. Curiosity?

Even now, he was leading with being curious about why they were here and clearly pretending not to know where he worked despite having been there hours ago. If it were me, I'd be leading with flame-throwing.

"Oh, that's right, of course, silly me." Mandee giggled and set a hand on her husband's for a brief second, then removed it. "Seems like a very nice place."

"Must get paid more than you did working for the government," Glen Jr. said before shoving an entire hard-shell taco into his mouth.

His father grunted as though to second his brother's comment, and Mandee chuckled. "Well, he must. That car he's driving is certainly an upgrade from what he left town in."

The dread that'd been building weighed heavy in my stomach. I wanted to take Kenny by the hand and lead him out of here before it got any worse because I could see where this was going, but he didn't look shaken at all.

"You mean my nineteen ninety-eight Toyota Corolla I worked three years to afford? Yes, I did upgrade." He took another bite, not looking away from his mother.

Her lips spread thin. "Well, this one's nicer."

His truck was nice, but nothing flashy. It wasn't giant, and it didn't have fancy rims or leather seats. All in all, it was modest, but very nice. Nicer than the car they'd all piled into, a beaten-up Chevrolet Blazer I'd guess was made at least twenty years ago.

"You got any sense you should give back to your family a bit? Maybe pay it forward for us giving you your start in life?"

I had to hand it to him. Glen Junior was just begging to get his ass kicked, and I would proudly take that job pro bono.

When Kenny didn't respond, his father spoke for the first time.

"You've always been a poor excuse for a man. An ungrateful little—" he swore, his foul mouth pulling into a sneer. "Least you could do is deign to step down off your high horse and help your people."

And that's when I dropped my fork, tossed my napkin on the table, and stood.

CHAPTER TWENTY-EIGHT

Kenny

Everything happened in the span of a few seconds.

Liz was standing, her hand on my arm. My brother and mother also stood, and my father leaned back, arms crossed, expression full of judgment and, if I wasn't projecting, hatred.

"Why don't you sit your skinny ass back down and let's see what baby Ken has to say. I'm not even sure why you're here to begin with," Glen Jr. said, pointing a greasy finger toward Liz.

That had me rising to my feet. "Now, now. No name calling. Plus I happen to think Liz's ass is absolute perfection."

No lies, plus I wasn't about to get riled up just because he was. He'd always had a hair-trigger temper and my ability to *not* respond almost always made him worse.

So maybe I was leaning into that a bit.

"You've been living like a king and can't bring yourself to help us? We're not asking for a handout, we're just—"

"You literally just did," Liz said through gritted teeth.

"You've always been ungrateful. Leaving us behind with nothing while you ran off to do whatever you wanted. Leaving your pregnant fiancée behind like the trash you are. Abandoning the people who gave you life, who raised you..." My mom shook her head like she couldn't believe I'd betrayed them so thoroughly, eyes welling with tears.

I'd never been so deeply grateful for the therapy I'd done until this moment. Historically, this interaction would've destroyed me. I could feel my insides crumbling as it was, little pillars of confidence and hope and determination collapsing in on themselves.

But I didn't have to stand here and take this. We could just leave. I was long past trying to make them see my perspective or to respect the choices I'd made. They'd made it clear time and again they never would.

I reached for Liz's hand, and she clasped it, but when I tugged, she stood firm. When I looked at her face, she was practically breathing fire.

"I have never met a more pathetic group of people in my life," she said, her voice so low and crisp it sounded almost violent in its razor sharpness.

"How dare you, you little—"

"You don't get to speak." Her words whipped at my brother, effectively shutting him up, his eyes blowing wide in shock that she'd said anything at all, much less directed it at him.

"I don't know if you're greedy or stupid, or just rotten at your cores, but whatever the case is, you should be ashamed of yourselves. Your son is the kindest person I've ever met. He's genuine and selfless and funny and *good* in a way I suspect none of you will ever understand. He's generous and I have no doubt he might have given you some money if you really needed it. But you don't get to guilt him for leaving a family who treated him so hatefully. You don't get to try to make him feel bad for joining the military and serving his country. And you will not shame him for making a life here and working at a job he loves that also happens to earn a decent wage."

Those parts of me crumbling were suddenly knitting back together, and she wasn't done.

"Kenny is the best man I know, and you should be absolutely devastated you don't know him—you don't get him in your life, and you don't deserve to. I can't speak for what he does or doesn't want to give you, but I can promise you that as long as I'm around, you won't get another chance to speak to him until you get a grip and start respecting him."

She began walking then, but stopped short, raising her chin in Glen Jr's face despite him having six or more inches on her.

"And you? You're a pathetic excuse of a human being and your desperate attempts to make your brother feel small or like less than you should eat at you. You're a faithless, dishonorable jerk and the only thing you deserve is pity."

I said nothing, following her lead as she navigated through tables, most of whom had somehow missed the dressing down she'd just given my family thanks to our out of the way table location.

My heart, though? My heart was exploding.

All I could think with every step was... her words. *Her words*.

She'd defended me. Not just defended me, but lauded me to people who didn't deserve a second of her attention.

She'd said more in those fleeting seconds than I'd heard her say at any other time and it had been all about me. For me.

As I tightened my grip on her hand, emotion built in me. Sadness and disbelief were there, the inevitable byproducts of having my family be cruel and also ask for money after not speaking for so many years, but also something far more powerful.

Adoration. Admiration. Something bordering dangerously on love. It was too soon for that, but what else was I supposed to feel?

She was fierce and commanding and furious in the most beautiful way. Did it make me a monster that I felt like she'd set me on fire as she'd shredded my family?

Maybe it did. Maybe I was as bad as they were, wanting something from her and only being satisfied when she gave it. But it didn't feel like that as we crossed the street, as she unlocked the door to her building, as we took the stairs leading to her apartment.

It felt like she'd done something for me I never would've asked her to do. It felt like she'd stood by me when she could've just walked out like I'd planned. She'd refused to leave without attempting to make the people hurting me see how wrong they were.

And by the time we got inside her place, I'd lost the reins on my self-control and had to show her somehow. I paced into her living room as she shut the door, then turned back toward her, all my energy driving me into her space.

"I hope you can forgive me for—"

I took her face in my hands and drew her into me, claiming her mouth like she'd just claimed me in front of an entire restaurant.

Our mouths crashed together, the intensity and adrenaline colliding in this crush of our bodies. She instantly responded, arms wrapping around my shoulders even as we stumbled back against the door.

We separated before impact, and I was certain I'd never been so gratified as I was right now, seeing her eyes just as hungry and wild as mine must've been.

"You're incredible," I said into her hair, pressing a kiss to her temple, then her cheek, then her jaw. I found the soft place in front of her ear, then just below it. Running my nose along the smooth skin of her neck, I inhaled the soft scent of her, wanting to drown myself in her warmth and nearness.

"You are, too. I hate that they can't see that," she said, her voice hitching when I nipped at the skin sloping from her neck to her shoulder.

I wanted to devour this woman—to give her so much pleasure she couldn't see straight. I wanted to hear my name on her lips and give her the heart she absolutely held in her hands.

I found those lips again, tasting her and getting lost in the press of my body against hers, the door an immovable boundary to the outside world and everything in it. We were lost in this kiss, in this otherworldly sensation, in this loss of all bearings...

Until she urged me back and held my head in her hands, nails scraping against my scalp as our eyes met and she jerked away.

My heart tripped.

Desire hung in her dark gaze, yes, but something else. Something that had me sliding my hands away from her body and pressing them into the door, resting my head against the wood and exhaling, willing a return of self-control.

Fear. Not pity as I might've dreaded, but fear hung in

her expression, in those blown pupils, and I'd never imagined seeing it there.

She was afraid. Of... me?

"I'm sorry," I said, finally shoving back and stepping away so she could breathe.

Had I hurt her? Had my... had I been too aggressive?

"Why would you be sorry?" she said, still breathless from our kisses.

I searched for words as my insides felt like they were shriveling up. "I—that was too much. I'm sorry. You just did this nice thing for me, and I shouldn't have taken that as... anything but you just being a good friend."

Her laugh made me turn back to her. Her head rested against the door, but her eyes were on me. No more fear there, but I'd seen it. I couldn't unsee it, or could I? My stupid stomach dropped, and my idiot heart kicked because she was so damn gorgeous, all flushed and disheveled. It was all I could do not to rush right over there and kiss her again.

"I wasn't being a good friend, Kenny." She pressed a palm to her forehead, almost like she was testing for fever. "I was saying something true that those people should know."

Those people.

It stung, but only because she was right not to call them my family. I'd found a new family in the military, and here in Silverton, and that was part of the years-long work I'd done to stand tall in the face of the people I'd come from.

At some point, I'd have to face them again. They wouldn't just leave, especially if they thought they could get something from me.

But she'd stood up for me when I would've walked away, and now I'd let myself get wrapped up in the moment and taken things way too far.

"I'm sorry, Liz."

"Stop apologizing. You have nothing to be sorry about," she said, eyes searching mine. We stayed like that, connected through our gazes but standing what felt like miles apart. "But for now, maybe we should take a breath."

She swallowed and crossed her arms, effectively creating a barrier to herself.

I couldn't even tell what I felt, but I knew I'd respect her need for space. "Of course. Thank you again and I'll see you tomorrow, yeah?"

With her nod, I left, wondering what that edge of fear in her eyes had been, wondering if she'd forgive me for being so pushy, and wondering how long it'd take me to get past all this.

CHAPTER TWENTY-NINE

Elizabeth

Kenny got pulled into a long-term planning meeting I didn't attend since I didn't plan to be in Silverton long.

Wasn't that just a handy little reminder?

I might not know exactly when I'd return to my regularly scheduled programming, nor did I especially want to focus on it right now, but I wouldn't be here *long term*.

Plus, I needed a little distance from last night. The kiss, first, and my visceral reaction to it, which had scared me because I didn't *feel* things this strongly. My tossing and turning had done nothing to quell the rioting thoughts that'd only intensified when Kenny left.

My heart ached at the memory.

His family had been so awful to him, I'd had no choice to but rage at them. I'd run the scenario through a dozen times in my head overnight and every version had me railing at them. I couldn't regret it.

Nor did I regret the way Kenny had looked at me—like I was some kind of avenging angel on his behalf. It'd felt a little like that.

And then in my apartment... he was so intense and determined to kiss me into oblivion, and I'd been a thousand percent on board until one thought had brought all the passion and enthusiasm to a screeching halt.

What if he was only kissing me because of what I'd done? What if this was more than he'd normally want from me, but he was so caught up in the moment and the emotions his family stirred up, he was lost to the reality of our situation?

And maybe a tiny whisper of a worry that those kisses would consume me and singe every part of my being and leave nothing but ashes in their wake. A pile of ashes couldn't do anything. It couldn't run, leave, go. Could it even stay?

We hadn't discussed things after our kiss two days ago, so I didn't actually know where we stood, or if there was even a way to figure that out.

What future could we possibly have?

And why the heck was I even worrying about the future?

Because your heart is wrapped around this guy and wants desperately to keep him.

I ignored the deeply unhinged voice in my mind and pushed out of the Saint building and into the cold air. I needed actual space and if it weren't icy today, I'd try for a hike. Instead, I headed for All Booked Up in search of the one person in this town who might offer me some comfort.

"Welcome in—oh! Hey!" Jo moved from behind the checkout counter and came at me with arms wide.

I welcomed her hug, and it lasted long enough, she had questions in her eyes when we pulled away.

"I'm always happy for a hug from you, but that one felt like you needed it. Care to share?"

I cleared my throat, emotion lodged there, likely due to the lack of sleep.

Keep telling yourself that, delulu.

"It's been a busy couple days. I don't want to go too long without seeing you while I'm here." Because soon, I'd be back across the world, back to the life I was living in a grayscale existence and remembering all the color here.

The more I admitted the difference between the way I lived in Budapest and what Jo and all the people living here had, the more I worried about this nameless restlessness building in me. The more the pinch of anxiety and anger at my job felt more like an ache encroaching on more than just a small, compartmentalized and temporary part of me.

I was losing touch there, the lack of briefings and updates sidelining me, and worse, I was dropping anchor in this place in a weird bid to have something to hold on to. Or was I? Because Kenny and I hadn't spoken again since that night. My dad wanted me to look at what I really wanted in life. And Jo... Well, Jojo just wanted me around. How did I do this when I myself didn't know where my feet were supposed to land?

She smiled and pulled me in for another hug. "In that case, I'll have another."

I took it, letting everything blip out in the warmth of her embrace.

We laughed at her cheesiness, and a customer came in with a question, so I milled around, picking up a new romance. I tended to read on my e-reader, but occasionally liked the feel of a brand new paperback in hand.

By the time the customer left and I went to check out, Jo was waiting for me at the desk.

"So you're coming on Saturday," she said, no hint of an actual question.

"I told you I would, and I've read the book. I'll be here."

She nodded once with approval. "Good."

The small hesitation after that comment made me study her. "What else were you going to say?"

"Nothing, I just—"

"Say what you want to say, Jojo. Don't censor yourself." She'd spent years not telling me everything and hiding away a part of herself. We'd worked through it, but occasionally, moments like this crept in and I could tell she was holding back.

"This is going to sound... whatever. I won't caveat it. I'll just say I want you to come to book club because I think you'll enjoy it, but I also want you to see what it's like to have friends and be in community with people. I know you haven't had much of that, and I just want to give you a taste."

Her glasses glinted, but I could see the veracity in her brown eyes, the same shade as mine and our mother's. There was hope there, and the longing she had for me to experience this.

"I promised you I'd be there, so I will be. I'm looking forward to it." And part of me was.

But part of me was bracing against what I'd find there because I knew it'd make going back to what I had before that much harder. At one time, I might've been embarrassed by her suggestion because it meant she clearly knew I didn't have that for myself, but my time here had at least softened those defenses. I couldn't pretend I had this fullness, this kaleidoscope of experience. I simply didn't. In Europe, I was a spy, period. That was a job title and a descriptor of my lifestyle in one, and it was spare. Here I was... me. Whoever that was.

But maybe, like she said, all of this would help me find it for myself. And maybe I'd like what I'd find out. I hoped.

Kenny didn't come to happy hour at Craic. I saw him in passing and he seemed okay, but not his chipper self. I thought about texting him, but shied away from it in hopes he'd be there tonight and I could pull him aside to talk. So when I realized he wasn't there, I did my best to stay present with my colleagues and said hello to Jo's friends, yet again promising them I'd see them at book club tomorrow, and then I left.

I went right to Kenny's house.

After I knocked once and there was no answer, I rang the bell. My pulse began to climb when he didn't answer immediately, even though I'd never been here without him. Maybe he was always slow to answer or maybe he was tucking Kit away so he wouldn't sneak out.

Or maybe his family had kidnapped him and was holding him for ransom, expecting Jack McKean to pay them for his release.

And maybe you've read one too many Josie Wade novels lately...

Before I resorted to calling the man—a thing I likely should've done before I showed up on his doorstep but too late now!—the door swung open and Kenny stood, bare-chested and bleary-eyed, cradling a sleeping Kit in one hand against his very flat stomach.

"Liz, wow. You look so beautiful."

He sagged against the door and the way his words were lazy and slow instantly clued me in.

"You have your own little happy hour here?" The question didn't really need asking. His red-rimmed, sleepy eyes and the borderline slurred speech painted a very clear picture.

His eyes widened and his smile grew. "Oh, woman, yes I did."

Oh, womin, yesh I dithd.

"Can I come in?" This man needed water and probably something to eat.

"Would you? I would love that. I would absolutely love to have you in my house again." He stumble-stepped back, and I entered his living room, half expecting to see it ransacked.

"What're you lookin' for?" he asked, shuffling in front of me, but clearly having noticed the way I was surveying his space for hints of what'd happened.

Not that he wasn't allowed to have a few drinks and get sloppy if he wanted, but it seemed quite out of character for the man. He didn't strike me as someone who liked to drink alone or to excess.

"Just trying to figure out if you're okay," I said honestly.

"Aw, that's so nice. You're really really really nice." He leaned on the doorframe between the living room and kitchen, his gaze hazy, and then he startled, looking down at the little black ball in his hand like he'd just realized he was holding his cat. "And oh my gosh, Kit is really really really cute. Like he's so cute and I love him so much and—" he sniffed. "I'm just so glad I get to be his cat dad."

"Okayyyy. Mind if I take him and get him settled in his bed?"

I reached for the kitten and Kenny nodded with so much enthusiasm, I hoped he didn't start a brain bleed. My fingers grazed his chest when I took the small creature, and with shockingly fast reflexes, he caught one of my wrists and guided my hand back to his tattooed skin.

"This feels good."

His blue eyes were laser-focused on mine and his taut skin was burning through my palm. The man was gorgeous at all times, but shirtless and unfiltered, he was deadly. He would also likely be horrified if he kept this up, but I didn't want to push him away and have him shut down on me.

"It does," I agreed, my thumb stroking along the side of his pec of its own volition.

No, thumb! Bad thumb.

"I would like to feel your hands everywhere. And your mouth." His lazy eyes widened. "And *crap,* I'm not too drunk to know I shouldn't say that out loud I'm so sorry." The hand pressing against mine disappeared and covered his mouth.

I stepped back, hiding a laugh and most definitely ignoring what those words had done to me. This was not *True Confessions,* and I shouldn't be turned on by the fact he'd just said that. He didn't know what he was saying and I wouldn't hold it against him.

"Let me get this guy settled. Why don't you have a seat in the kitchen?"

He nodded but didn't move the hand covering his mouth. I didn't bother hiding my chuckle then, though a needle of worry threaded into my chest. Something was off and I had a sinking sensation I knew what.

After depositing Kit in the laundry room and gently shutting the door, I returned to the kitchen to find him slumped in a seat in his breakfast nook, staring at his hand.

"Have you eaten dinner?" I asked softly, sensing his mood may have shifted.

It took him a minute, but he blinked me into focus. "Uh, I don't think so. I didn't eat lunch and then I was supposed to meet my family for dinner but then—" He scrubbed a hand down his face and his chin stayed low, practically glued to his chest. "So no, I haven't eaten since breakfast or maybe the guacamole."

The guacamole we had at dinner last night... yikes. No wonder he was ten sheets to the wind.

"Anything sound good?" I moved to the fridge and looked for something to make, then noticed a loaf of bread and quickly popped two slices into the toaster sitting nearby.

"I am not going to say you, because that would be inappropriate."

I chuckled, turning to see if he had a little mischief in his eye, but his chin still rested on his chest, and I could see the downturn of his lips and brow.

"Hey, can you look at me?"

It took him a minute, but the second I saw more of his face, my heart broke and I froze. His eyes were glassy with tears and all the sunshine in his countenance had disappeared completely.

"I gave them money." His voice was so brutally small and broken.

I dropped to my knees in front of him and took his

hands in mine. "That's great if that's what you wanted to do."

"I don't know why I feel so... so sad about this. I've read this book. I know this story and I'm not surprised by the ending, but it still makes me feel so... broken." His voice was ragged, and a tear slipped down his cheek.

"It's okay to feel whatever you feel," I said, fully recognizing these were words far easier to say than to adopt and believe for myself.

"I know. I just hate crying. I mean I hate crying over them. Why should they get any more of my tears? Why do I still care?" He swiped at the moisture and rested my hands on his legs.

"Because you're not the kind of person who will stop caring about other people, even when they've mistreated you."

He sniffled. "Just makes me feel like all the work I've done to get over this is failing me, but logically and probably without a few shots of tequila on an empty stomach, I would recognize that's crap."

I smiled and one side of his mouth quirked up.

"It is crap. You're an amazing person and I'd be shocked if seeing them and having them act the way they did didn't hurt you. I probably would've worried you'd been body-snatched."

A watery laugh escaped him. "Yeah but then maybe I'd be a little more what people want. A little more of a man like they expect."

He had to mean his family, and I didn't give a damn what they wanted of him, but I couldn't sit here and listen to him demean himself, even if wallowing was perfectly acceptable for a time. I stood, then shoved his knees together and slipped over them, sitting on his lap. His brows perked up and his eyes lit with awareness.

I took his stubbly face in my hands. "You are wonderful. You are loved by so many people who appreciate and admire and love you for exactly the man you are. I would be heartbroken if you were body-snatched or, more importantly, any other version of you than this one."

He gave me a full smile. "Thank you for saying that."

I wanted to say more, but maybe now wasn't the time. I pulled him close and hugged him, doing whatever I could to push truth into him. *You are loved. You are wonderful. You are exactly who you're meant to be.*

After a minute, I released him and stepped away.

"I'm completely fine if you want to stay right there until tomorrow morning."

I chuckled and wiped at the corner of my eye. "I appreciate that, but you need something in your belly or you'll be miserable tomorrow."

The toast had popped at some point, so I slathered it with butter and slid it toward him.

"Aw, you cooked for me."

This man. He was the sweetest man alive, regardless of sobriety. I didn't anticipate seeing him like this again soon, but there was something lovely about knowing he was still himself, just even more unfiltered. He was sweet and warm and funny and flirty and loveable.

I wouldn't think about all that right now, though. I'd focus on feeding him and doing whatever I could to abate the inevitable hangover he'd have. When he felt better, it was time to have a discussion.

CHAPTER THIRTY

Kenny

Stone and Cookie arrived at eight on Saturday morning, plates of goodies plastic-wrapped for safety in hand.

"Did we have plans?" I asked, scratching at my scraggly face.

They barged in without me inviting them, but they were always welcome, so this wasn't anything particularly alarming.

"We heard you might need a pick me up," Cookie said, right as Stone rumbled, "Welfare check."

That was all it took to release the dam of memory from the night before.

My family claiming to want to take me to dinner again and clear the air, but then pushing, before we ever sat down, for money, which I had already planned to give them. Their disdain and total lack of desire to know anything about me other than a routing number.

My brilliant decision to go home and watch *You've Got Mail* and take a shot every time I heard the AOL dial up tones... woof.

My heart thudded around in my chest as the next memories came through—Liz arriving, me saying something I didn't quite remember but definitely wasn't appropriate, me crying in the kitchen and her hugging me, her feeding me, and forcing me to eat even more and drink water, and then tucking me into bed, wedging me onto my side.

Then deep in the night, a kiss to my forehead and whispered words. *You'll be okay. I promise you'll be okay. I'll see you tomorrow.*

"Yep. Elizabeth let us know you had a day yesterday," Cookie said, one brow raised.

I huffed a laugh and took a seat at the table. "Yeah, you could say that."

"That why you didn't show at Craic?" he asked.

I nodded. "I self-medicated in the dumbest way after a predictably upsetting interaction with my family and then made at least one pass at Liz before crying all over myself and letting her tuck me into bed."

Stone's eyes widened and Cookie's closed slowly.

"So yeah, just nailing it on all fronts."

"She's fine. She wouldn't have reached out to us or tucked you into bed if she was upset."

Stone's confidence would normally cheer me, but I wouldn't know until I spoke to her—saw her.

"I hope so. I feel like an ass, but at the same time..." I sighed.

"At the same time, your family is the worst and you're human. I know about families like that and I'm sorry," Cookie supplied.

His words, so full of grace for me, made my throat tight. "Yeah. That."

Also, he knew about families like mine? He'd rarely spoken about his family at all. I should've asked follow-up questions, but that might need to happen another day.

Stone unwrapped the two plates of food—one of delicious-looking omelets, and one full of what looked like homemade croissants.

"First, you eat. Then you talk. Then you check in with her."

"I don't know if I have an appetite," I said, eying the food and knowing if I could stomach it, it'd be delicious.

Stone's expression didn't change. "First, you eat."

Cookie looked out the window, but I could see the jerk's grin. I could be a bit bossy when it came to taking care of my friends, so I supposed turnabout was fair play, but it didn't mean he should get so much joy from it.

"Yessir."

"None of that garbage," Stone grumbled.

"Yes, Master Sergeant?" I asked, mouth full of one of the croissants, which were, I could now vouch, absolute perfection.

He growled.

I cackled. "Uh oh. Someone's taking on Beast's role."

Cookie snickered and grabbed a croissant, and Stone glared. "No, I'm not. But we're not in the military anymore."

I acquiesced. There had been many months where that reality, the transition from active duty to civilian, had plagued the man. It was only because I knew how far he'd come, how well he was doing that I dared joke about such things.

"Fair enough. I'm just trying to sort out my crap internally before you guys start asking questions." I chewed another bite and tried to work through the messy haze of memory, the energy slowly returning to me with each swallow.

After a full five minutes, and helping themselves to the coffee that had brewed at eight o'clock despite my never setting it last night, they jumped in.

"So start with the family."

Cookie's prompt was all I needed. These men and I had been through some of the hardest things imaginable during our time in service, and then again as we got out, and in the last few years, our bond had only solidified. They were my family now, and something about sitting here sipping coffee and eating homemade croissants with them reminded me why I didn't have to stay broken by what had happened yesterday.

"Sometimes, I wish we didn't have a morality clause," Stone said, his regret audible.

Cookie and I laughed, knowing he'd never break the handful of morality-based requirements Saint Security put in place, and yet loving him for even saying such a thing.

No, Stone could not murder my family in retribution for the pain they'd caused me. But again, I loved him for even making the joke, though I'd never actually want him to do it, and he never would.

What we'd all done in service to our country had left scars on our bodies and our souls. There was freedom in knowing we'd never do some of those things again. And pain in knowing we'd never do others.

"It's small stuff. When I think of the things we saw, this is so, so small. But damn if it doesn't crack me wide open just thinking about it." Moisture gathered in my eyes, but I breathed through it. What I wouldn't give my family? Any more of my tears.

"It is small in some ways and fundamental in others. They are the people who are supposed to love you and accept you and they have failed in this. But you know it is *their* failure, not yours. It is *their* cruelty, not your fault. It is *their* loss, not your burden."

When Cookie—Luc—felt strongest, he sometimes slipped into French, so the string of words that followed was rapid and passionate. I felt the vehemence of his words despite not knowing exactly what he'd said. He seemed to know these truths well, like he spoke from experience. Curiosity flared in me, but Stone spoke before I found the right words to ask a question.

"Family wounds are just that—they are wounds. Even when they heal over, they don't disappear. Just like anything else, they stay with us. And maybe sometimes we suffer through healing them, but it doesn't take away the memory of the pain or the healing. It doesn't make us immune from remembering the pain and being affected by it."

Stone's words were weighted with so much hard-won wisdom, I never took a single one uttered for granted.

"Thank you. Thank you both. For coming. For being the family I've chosen and who has—" I cleared my throat, the emotion building up again. "For choosing me."

Stone nodded in acknowledgment and Cookie set a hand on my shoulder and shook me lightly. "*Bien sûr, mon frère.*"

Of course, my brother. And there it was.

These two men had chosen me like I'd chosen them. And there were more members of our rag tag family.

A tiny scratching sound reached me, and I jumped to my feet. "I forgot about him."

In seconds, I ran to the door and released Kit, who

scampered down the hall and directly into the kitchen. I scooped him up before he darted away again, snuggling him to me. A flash of memory from last night hit, the moment when I'd pressed Liz's hand to my chest burning through me. *Yeah, might need to apologize for that, too.*

Stone made a mildly pained sound and Cookie let out a stream of expletives in French, his eyes wide.

"Uh, what just happened?" I asked, turning side to side, looking behind me to figure out what was going on with them.

"He's so... tiny." Stone was winded and looked like a cartoon version of himself, his eyes wide and pupils practically blown as he gazed at my kitten.

"I love you, Kenny, but *ça, c'est pourquoi*—he's the reason we came," Cookie said, reaching greedy hands for the tiny mewing cat.

I laughed, a moment of pure joy filling me as these grown ass men fell all over themselves over my mangey little cat.

"The truth comes out," I said, as though I'd found out something I didn't already know.

These two were ridiculous, but I'd keep them.

And as soon as I could, I'd thank Liz for sending them to me and helping me get grounded in so much goodness before I could sink back down into the bad feelings again.

CHAPTER THIRTY-ONE

Elizabeth

Walking in dangerous places wasn't foreign to me. I'd run enough missions in the face of actual peril, I'd become familiar with it.

And yet, this dangerous ground was completely new. The perils were coming at me from all over the place and I hardly knew what to do with myself. These weren't international terrorist organizations or threats to the US's security. They weren't spies trying to infiltrate our intelligence or a crime syndicate gaining power in foreign nations that could influence anti-US sentiment.

These threats came in the form of six women with glasses of champagne and romance novels in their hands.

"Honestly, I would seriously rethink living in a small town where there are stalkers, multiple serial killers, and then some weird doomsday cult where they want the women to literally stay barefoot and pregnant and whether part of their cult or no, is all happening within a year of my moving there." Nikki, Bruce's fiancée, looked around for backup.

"I mean, you're not wrong," Winnie agreed.

"No, you have a fair point. It would be rather concerning, especially if you knew it was all happening." Dove, a petite blonde woman I'd interacted with the least thus far, snuggled into her spot on the couch, her robin's egg blue dress fluffed out over her legs.

"Okay, but we've had multiple kidnappings here. I mean literally *two of us* have been kidnapped. By that logic, shouldn't we all be running for the hills?" Jo asked, laughing despite being one of the women who'd been kidnapped.

Catherine tilted her head from side to side like she was thinking about it.

"But that's not Silverton's fault. There were perfectly logical explanations for each of those instances," Elise said, holding her wine glass up, toasting us all before drinking deep.

"And those are..." Nikki prompted.

Elise waved a hand. "Men."

I chuckled and Dove full out snort-laughed while everyone else maintained a little more composure. Jess pressed her hands to her stomach, bracing, even though I could hardly see any belly yet.

"No, I'm serious. Literally men. Like, Bruce's sister was kidnapped by her busted-ass druggy dad. Winnie was kidnapped by, my sincerest apologies—" Elise dipped her head deferentially to Winnie, who nodded back "—her hairbrained brother's debt collectors. And Jo was kidnapped by a crazed fan, also a man. Not a uniquely Silverton problem." She threw her hands up. "This is why we choose the bear."

"As someone whose husband is named Beast, I'd like to lightly object to this line of thought."

Jess had been fairly quiet tonight, but I could tell everyone was glad to have her there. I knew her a bit better than the others since I'd worked with her team in the past when she was still with the EMU.

"Just because you didn't get kidnapped doesn't mean it's not still a pretty glaring issue. Now that I think about it, maybe it *is* a Silverton thing. I'm about to pack up and get *out*." Elise slumped back in her seat.

There was something going on there, but I didn't have enough context to know what. There were a few significant looks exchanged, but then Dove jumped in.

"Yes, but it was also men—sometimes with the help of women, of course, but sometimes not—who rescued each of them. You just have to properly vet them."

Winnie grinned.

Nikki chuckled, but blushed.

Jo smiled widely. "Well, you're not wrong there."

Catherine giggled, clearly along for the ride in the whole conversation. She'd said the least, but she seemed fully engaged still and used to watching the show.

"And how do we make sure we get a good one?" This came from Elise.

"I'd highly recommend getting a Saint Security man," Winnie said quietly.

Nikki laughed and touched glasses with Winnie, then Jo.

Jess held up her glass of iced water. "As a Saint Security woman, I endorse this message."

We all laughed then, and Dove sighed wistfully.

"Got your eye on someone there, Dove?" Jess patted her shoulder.

Her cheeks pinked prettily, but she rolled her eyes. "You know me. Ever hopeful and yet tragically doomed to a life of not only being single, but not even dating."

"I think if you wanted, you could probably crook your finger and about ten guys would come running," Jo said.

"It's true. You're adorable," Elise encouraged.

Dove groaned. "Yes, everyone's dream is to be *adorable*."

"What about you, Elizabeth?" Winnie asked, her big eyes blinking back with innocence.

Or at least, she sure *looked* innocent. But, the question felt loaded.

Jo turned slowly—and rather creepily, if we're being honest—to settle all her attention on me. "Yes. What about you, Lizzy, dearest and darlingest sister of mine." She clasped her hands under her chin.

"Okay, freaky. That's enough champagne for you," I said, genuinely chilled by her.

Everyone laughed then, and Elise said, "Seriously, Jo. That was terrifying."

"Whatever. I want to know what you did when you left Craic last night." She raised her brows in the smuggest little *so there* expression I'd seen this side of her sixteenth birthday.

Dove let out an *"Ooohhhh!"* and Jess cackled and clapped her hands together while everyone else appeared to be just as interested.

Normally, I wouldn't entertain this, but after the last few days, I needed to let it out. What had keeping every thought to myself gotten me except isolation, loneliness, and a growing sense that I'd been unnecessarily keeping myself an island next to a continent of people?

"I went to check on Kenny." My cheeks heated as almost every woman, save Jess who was leaning back and braced fairly specifically in a pose she'd mentioned helped her not feel nauseated, leaned forward with interest.

"And?" Jo prompted, Dove nodding furiously next to her.

"He had a rough day. And it's not my information to share, but..." I blew out a long breath and felt the words bubbling up despite the futility of sharing them. "I really like him and what I saw last night only made it worse."

My little sister shrieked. Like borderline glass shatteringly loudly. She shot out of her seat and jogged around the small, cozy space. Dove clapped, Elise, Catherine, Nikki, and Winnie all grinned like maniacs, and I could swear I saw Jess swipe under her eyes.

"This is stupid. I'm not crying, you're crying," she said with a watery laugh. "I love this baby but the hormones." She rolled her eyes.

"I appreciate the enthusiasm, but this means nothing. It's actually more bad news than good."

There. I'd said it out loud. Part of what I'd feared all along and what I knew to be true.

Jo stopped her jog and came to sit next to me. "How so? Kenny is a love, and I dare say he's had a hand in every one of us finding happiness in one way or another."

Nikki, Winnie, and Jess all agreed with this, while even the women who weren't paired off with a Saint man nodded.

"I have no doubt that's true. But I don't live here. I—my life is overseas."

Jo's expression changed at the edges so subtly, I wouldn't have noticed if body language and human behavior weren't part of what I used in my professional life. But the slight pull at the corners of her mouth and the shift in her gaze, the large breath she heaved, albeit silently, and the press of her hands together into a knot... these were the hints I was breaking her heart by saying the truth out loud.

"I get that. It's hard to imagine what your life is like, but I get having feelings for someone here but knowing your life is elsewhere," Winnie said.

"I guess you found a way to make it work here, though, didn't you?" It was obvious enough since she lived here and was married to Tristan, happily building a life in this town.

Everyone listened intently when Winnie responded.

"I came here with every intention of going back when it was safe for me to do so. But being here changed me—and not just Tristan. So when the time came to return, leaving was what felt wrong in my gut. I know not everyone's story will go that way, but I just want to say... I don't know, maybe it's trite, but never say never."

Parts of me longed for the ability to repeat the phrase and mean it. To embrace the idea of a total life change and take a gigantic, romantic leap into the abyss of the unknown so I could live one version of my life here.

But I'd trained myself to choose the practical, useful, obvious path. I'd lived a life forging ahead according to plan. And that was simply how it had to be.

Even if my heart of hearts, I heard it echo... *never say never*.

CHAPTER THIRTY-TWO

Kenny

The bouquet might've been on the large side, now that I held it out and literally couldn't see Liz behind it.

"They're beautiful," she said, her voice slightly muffled thanks to the huge collection of blooms.

"You're welcome. They're not nearly enough to say thank you effectively, but it's a start." This was the conclusion I'd come to while Stone and Cookie had sat on the living room floor with me and Kit and we'd played and talked for an hour before the little one fell back asleep.

I needed to apologize and thank her and then see what I needed to do to convince her to go out with me. It might not have made sense for us to pursue anything together when I'd first learned about her temporary job here, but at this point, after just a few days, it seemed insane not to be with her while I could.

Was I so hell-bent on self-preservation I couldn't take a risk with someone so completely wonderful?

Because that's what she was. She was not only beautiful and physically attractive to me in a way few women had been, but she was good. And she was grappling with what she wanted out of her life in an honorable way I admired. She was an amazing friend to me already, and she'd been so tender and supportive, I just knew this was how she treated Jo and her family, too.

How could I look myself in the eye a year from now if I didn't at least try to spend more time with her? Maybe she'd say no, that it wouldn't work for her. But what if she said yes? What if we could be good together for a little while—wasn't that better than nothing?

In the past, I might've said no. I wasn't the kind of man who wanted fast and fleeting. It'd never appealed to me after something I thought would be permanent proved to be so flimsy. I wanted forever with someone. I wanted my otter.

There was some saying about it being better to have loved and lost than not loved at all. The Kenny of the moment reckoned this and didn't want to live with eternal what ifs, even if the Kenny of years ago knew just how terrible the losing part was, and that was a version of love that seemed more than a little basic in hindsight.

And maybe I could help her, too. Maybe I could give her the gift of clarity about the way forward and encourage her to value herself and invest in herself instead of shoving all her desires down past her work obligations. If she'd give me a chance, I could be good for her.

Even for a moment, but then again, entire lives changed in a moment. So... yeah. There. We could do this.

"You don't need to thank me, Kenny. Please come in."

She took the flowers and walked inside, so I shut the door behind me and followed her in.

"I don't actually know if there's a vase in here." She gingerly set the bouquet down and started looking through cabinets.

"If not, I'll bring you one. I didn't actually think about that, sorry."

She turned toward me. "You don't get to apologize for that."

I scowled. "I'll apologize about whatever I want, thank you."

She rolled her eyes and returned to her search, finally pulling out a large pitcher that would actually work well. After adding water and sliding the arrangement out of the waxed paper sleeve, she turned to me.

"How do you feel today?"

I couldn't stop myself from reaching for her hand and pulling her to me. She came willingly, accepting my hug and returning it, resting her head on my shoulder in a way that made my heart twist.

"Good, actually, and so much of that is thanks to you." I squeezed her tight once more before letting her go somewhat regretfully.

"I will take credit for feeding and watering you so you weren't so wilted yesterday," she said, moving to the living room and taking a seat on the couch.

I took a spot on the cushion next to her, pulse skittering in my veins and I would've sworn, if I'd looked, my heart on my sleeve.

"I'm a flower?"

She smiled. "Sometimes."

I pretended to brush my hair over my shoulder. "Well, then. I must be pretty."

She chuckled. "Yes, so pretty, especially when you're slurring your words and can hardly see straight."

Wincing, I scrubbed a hand over my face. "Yeah. I was a mess. I'm sorry you had to see that."

Her hand on my leg stopped me and drew my gaze.

"I'm not. I'm glad I was there."

"Me, too. I have a few things to say, if you'll let me." *Way to make it dramatic, drama king.*

"Of course."

I swallowed, hoping I could get all of this out. "First, I'm sorry for the multiple times I crossed a line and said things about wanting you—or, just, you know, all the things." I waved a hand, obviously floundering.

She laughed softly and steadied my hands with her own. "I wasn't upset by anything. You probably said some things you wouldn't have without the tequila on board, but I never felt unsafe or like you were being sketchy. If you had been, I would've put you in an arm bar or maybe choked you out."

I barked a laugh, delighted. "Good to know. Would've been fully understandable."

She grinned.

I sighed. She was so pretty, and strong, too, and it was stupid how much I liked her. The last thirty-six hours had cemented it.

"I also wanted to say thank you for listening and for your empathy. I thought I wanted to be alone, but I'm deeply grateful you were there." My throat tightened. "Thank you for taking care of me."

Those words were simple, but wasn't that what I wanted? I'd gotten to take care of her when we had s'mores after she'd had a hard day. And she'd fully come to my rescue Friday night.

We'd been there for each other, showed up for one another... that was the whole thing, wasn't it?

She bit her soft lower lip, and I had to will myself to stay put. When she spoke, her voice held such tenderness, it caused my emotions to heighten even more.

"I'm grateful you let me. Truly."

I cleared my throat yet again, uninterested in ending up tearful again. "Thanks for sending the guys this morning, too. I'm not sure how you knew, but they were great."

"You're lucky to have such good friends. I suspect they would've been there eventually, even if I hadn't mentioned it, but I'm glad they could show up for you."

She had this soft expression that made me want to shake her—to beg her to tell me who showed up for her. Jo did, of course, and I thought maybe her dad did, too, when she let him. But everything I knew about her life in Europe said she didn't have anyone else, not really, and that maybe this was something I could offer her.

I was starting to suspect I'd give her anything she'd let me.

"How are you doing today?"

Her question pulled me into the current conversation. If I wanted to get to a discussion of *us*, I might need to finish up the focus on *me*.

"I'm good. A little sore, I guess, but I'm glad I gave them something and I hope it'll be enough to let them find some margin, or whatever it is they need right now."

For just a minute, I considered hating myself for not giving them more, or for giving them anything at all, but I didn't care about money. And why shouldn't I give them something? I didn't like the idea that I had so much and couldn't be bothered to help them. That said, I'd seen them bleed other people dry when I was growing up, had dealt with a fair amount of shame about that even then, so I recognized the wisdom in having a boundary.

I wouldn't be shocked if I heard from them again, but I'd deal with that problem if and when it arose.

"That's good. If you feel good about it, that's all that matters."

Gah, she was being so sweet and soft, and even though I liked the serious, stern parts of her, too, after last night, I couldn't keep it locked up anymore.

I grabbed her hand and threaded our fingers together, drawing her gaze to meet mine. Her dark eyes were curious, and she bit that lip again.

My heart rate ticked up, up, and after a steadying breath, I took this quiet moment to ask what I'd wanted to ask for a while now.

"What about us? Can we talk about us now?"

CHAPTER THIRTY-THREE

Elizabeth

U s? Could we talk about us?

While he held my hand and looked at me with those tender, gorgeous blue eyes, and tried to pretend he hadn't been looking at my lips for the last few minutes? On the heels of letting me see him in a truly vulnerable place, after sharing an ugly part of himself in such a beautiful, honest way?

How on earth could I say no?

"Sure. Let's talk." My stomach swooped and my pulse quickened.

The smile on his handsome face was killer as he said, "I like you, Liz."

I huffed, pressure releasing from my chest with also a hint of disbelief. I'd never met anyone like him. He was so straightforward and open despite his past.

"I like you, too."

A grin exploded on his face and his sparkly eyes and blazing smile would've knocked me over if I hadn't seen it before. His joy and happiness were a sight to behold.

"I know we're in different places—that you're only here for a time."

My heart clenched. "Yeah."

I wanted to explain myself—to make sure he knew I already felt like I could live a life here, in some other version of my story. If my entire life wasn't elsewhere, my purpose and goal, maybe...

Or maybe the urge was to explain how much I liked his life here, how wonderful it seemed, and that I didn't think less of it. I didn't think my life was better.

But he wasn't stuck there, bless him.

His thumb arced over the back of my hand. "I would like to date you."

I stared at him, waiting for more. When I didn't speak, and he didn't either, I bit my lip to hide my smile and he chuckled low, shaking his head.

"This is the part where you tell me what you want."

To eighteen-year-old me or post-grad me or even thirty-year-old me, needing someone to prompt me to tell them what I wanted would've been a laughable scenario. I'd always been certain. But right now, some unknown resistance pressed against my vocal cords, making me shy away from verbalizing just that.

"I want to date you, too, but I'm just not sure..."

"I realize it might not seem worth it for just a short time. I can promise you we'll have fun, though. I can also promise last night's drunken pity fest was a one-time deal. I wouldn't ask you to go out with me if I was planning to spiral out about my family."

Ugh, this man. He was too sweet.

"I'm not worried about that. You're allowed to be human. You may have noticed I'm not exactly a party twenty-four-seven."

He grinned. "I've noticed no such thing."

I shook my head and added an eye roll for good measure. "I just mean, I'm not sure how it'll go. I've enjoyed spending time with you, but I don't know... where it goes."

How it ends.

How I walk away from you if my heart is even a fraction more lost than it already is.

I'd dated a few times over the years, but my job had always been my priority. I'd never had to question how to move forward because my answer had always been clear.

But now?

I longed for the clarity of my youth—to channel that intrepid, confident woman who knew exactly what she wanted. I wished life was as black and white as it had been then, and that I didn't feel this glaring uncertainty. I'd never liked the idea of two roads diverging—there was always a clear path. Or there had been.

"I get that. I'm sure you do very little in life without clarity and a plan in place for how everything will go. So this would be a big ask."

My brow furrowed as I attempted to understand, but after a long few days, I needed him to spell it out. "*What* is a big ask? Dating you?"

"Yes. Dating me without perfect clarity on how it'll go. Spending time with me knowing we aren't sure how long it'll last."

And what he wasn't saying—dating and possibly getting emotionally wrapped up in someone I would say goodbye to in a matter of months.

"Correct. I don't do that." But had my insistence on knowing outcomes—or fooling myself into believing I knew the outcomes of choices—paid off?

I was currently on involuntary leave after basically being forced on an extended break due to a subordinate's mistake that I'd done everything I could to prevent, and yet I couldn't control another human being. Not completely unheard of, but the lack of faith my leadership had shown me was unusual after so many years of trust... or it certainly felt like it. I'd given the CIA and Kappa Sector the best of me these last nearly fifteen years, and what did I have to show for it?

An apartment that was hardly lived in. A family who barely knew me.

A love life bereft of anything close to love.

At some point, I'd chosen to funnel any willingness of risk into my professional life and had lost the ability to chance anything personally. Maybe I'd never had that ability in the first place—perhaps watching my parents' relationship dissolve during the key years of my adolescence could be partially to blame.

But I didn't want to blame anything. I didn't want to rehash my choices. It was time to look forward. I had no idea what that meant for me when I got to the other side of this time in Utah or how I'd continue life in Europe now that I'd let so many doubts creep in.

I couldn't see exactly how this would go, but I knew in my gut I didn't want to stop spending time with Kenny. I wanted as much time as I could get. This wouldn't last, but when I went back to those realities in my life, when I returned to the existence I'd built, I'd have the memory of this time with him.

I was a spy—we didn't get to love and have families and

Happily-Ever-Afters. But a moment, a slice of this, I could carve out and hold close to my chest for the rest of my time. And I'd take it. Before, I lived with nothing, and now, I wouldn't need to, because I'd have something. Something of this wonderful man, of my time here in this alternate universe my life could've been in some other dimension.

"I don't know what to expect, but I do want this. To spend time with you while I'm here."

I had to caveat it that way aloud for myself. I didn't dream of forever with people I dated, but something about Kenny had me needing to brace against that level of risk, at least. I had to remind myself there would be an ending, and even if it was a few weeks away, it would come.

He seemed happy with this news, based on the beaming smile he cast my way.

"That's good news," he said, raising our joined hands and pressing a kiss into the back of mine.

Our gazes tangled and my stomach did that swooping thing again, a rollercoaster I only seemed to be riding around him.

"Any chance you're up for watching a movie or something? No pressure at all, but I don't want to waste the chance to hang out, if you're free."

I looked around like there might be a clue or some task I was ignoring that would keep me from enjoying him. I'd spent so long with work hounding me, keeping me on a schedule and focusing my energy and mind, and now I didn't have it. My work with Saint was casual at best, undemanding and kind of fun, all things considered, and it didn't creep into my days when I wasn't there.

So I could relax and spend time with this man who, for whatever reason, wanted to spend time with me.

"I'm free," I said, relishing the warm grin spreading across his face.

He glanced at his watch. "How about we order some food and watch a movie? I'm getting hungry, but I don't want to go out, if that's okay."

Bless the man. I'd been *out* a lot lately, and I just wanted a little while snuggled up in this little apartment, especially if it meant being with him.

"That is perfect." And so was the afternoon, especially once he reassured me Kit would be okay with him gone for so long.

We sat on the couch eating takeout from Diner and watching romcoms. Witnessing Kenny's true love of *Pretty Woman* was probably the most entertaining thing I'd ever experienced, and once that was done, I couldn't imagine ending the day. We took a stroll around the little downtown to stretch our legs and give his energy an outlet, while he regaled me with stories about every business and person we encountered.

"This is Quinn Darling-Grenier's music store. She's insanely talented and also puts up with Julian, so she's a hero," he said as we wandered past Pluck and he waved at a young woman standing behind the counter, who beamed and waved enthusiastically back.

This happened at every store—a little anecdote about the person, always complimentary, and then usually someone inside the business, if it was open, cheerily greeting Kenny if they saw him. It'd been the same the last time we'd been in town together, but I still marveled at it.

"You are just Mr. Popular. I'm amazed." I slumped into the couch, grateful to be out of the cold air and back inside.

"Nah. It's not popularity." He shucked his coat and

hung it on a hook inside the doorway, then slipped off his boots, and finally came to sit next to me.

He'd found his spot notably closer than the last time we were here, and I didn't mind at all. We hadn't kissed again, hadn't touched other than accidental grazes of knees or the occasional pat on a leg or arm. It'd all been rather friendly and not at all charged like so many of our other physical interactions had been.

Not that I was upset by this. He liked me. He'd said as much. I might not have been a dating savant, but I didn't suffer from low self-esteem either. If Kenny was choosing to be here, then he wanted to be here.

"How is it not?" I wondered.

"I make an effort. If I see someone I don't know, especially outside of the prime tourist season, I introduce myself. I join community boards and volunteer for stuff when I can. I eat locally and spend my money in these shops. It's something I always wanted, but never realized it until I moved here and had it."

The soft smile on his face sent an odd burst of longing through me. "What is it?"

"It's a community, and inside of that, a sense of belonging. That didn't come because I waited for it to be extended to me, though I do think Silverton is pretty good about welcoming people. It's because I went out and built it—at Saint, in town, even in the surrounding areas. I claimed this place as my own like I claimed Saint as my family, and in turn, it claimed me back."

My chest burned as though he'd written the words on my heart—like he'd seen a desire I hadn't known was there and had casually spoken it out loud.

Belonging. Community. Family.

Home.

All things I'd thought I'd given up on having for myself outside of work, that maybe I thought no one had, and more than just Kenny possessed here.

Maybe it wasn't impossible.

But could I have it? That was the question.

CHAPTER THIRTY-FOUR

Kenny

A few days later, I joined Jess and Beast at their house for breakfast before work. Beast grumbled as he moved around in the kitchen, and Jess gave me a look.

"Is he somehow even more irritable than usual right now?" I asked, marveling at the sounds coming from just a few feet away.

Jess winced. "I had a bad night, and he tends to be pretty grumpy when that happens. Something about worrying I'm wearing myself too thin, which is impossible, since all I do is sit around and try not to heave up my guts."

Beast froze and turned slowly—terrifyingly, frankly. If I didn't know the man, I'd be worried he'd been possessed or something.

"You are not sitting around. You've been working." His dark eyes widened and his nostrils flared.

My mouth dropped open. "Uh oh. Someone's been sneaking in work? How dare you, Pop?"

She rolled her eyes and huffed, but a smile hid in her expression. "I dare because I am so. Bored. And I miss my job. I miss the office and being surrounded by all of you goons."

I laughed, loving her orneriness. "You two are just twin beams of sunshine, aren't you?"

Beast stomped over to the small table where we sat and slid a plate gently onto the placemat in front of Jess, then practically dumped one in front of me.

"Thank you, kind sir." I inspected the omelet and toast in front of me. "This looks really good. Where's my boy Bones? I need to pay him homage." I hadn't seen the giant, lovely beasty cat yet and part of me wanted to see if he could tell I was now a cat dad.

"Don't want your Kit confused and smelling another cat on you this early, so he's napping in the bedroom," Beast said in a low tone.

Huh. Hadn't even considered it, but I didn't want my boy to get anxious over Bones's existence.

A sharp movement from Jess's direction pulled my attention, and I looked up to see her gaze directed away from her plate, neck craning.

"Uh..." I said inanely.

Beast's large hand slipped into hers. "What do you need?"

"Just a sec," she said, her voice strained. She drew in a breath slowly.

His shoulders slumped. "Believe it or not, this is an improvement."

"I'm sorry. I should've had something sooner, but I

wanted to wait since Kenny was coming." Her voice was a little watery.

My heart clutched. "Don't apologize. I'm so happy to be here, even if you hurl your guts up."

She laughed and reached for the toast on her plate, taking a bite as she pushed out of her seat. She set a hand on Beast's shoulder. "I'm just going to take a breath outside. I'll be fine."

Her gaze cut to his and there was so much warmth and love and warning in there, I almost wanted to cry. These two were absolutely meant for each other, and I loved to see it.

The merciless ache in my chest was because of that, wasn't it? Not for any other reason.

"She's so stubborn," Jude grumbled, but then his face softened and he added, "I love her so much."

I propped my elbow on the table and my chin in my hand. "You guys are adorable."

"We are."

His easy acceptance of that was one of my favorite things about them. He'd gotten better at expressing emotions other than anger or broodiness, but the way he almost giddily enjoyed their love and closeness now was just shy of miraculous. Maybe it was actually a miracle, in truth.

The drag of my own longing faded in the face of the bliss radiating from him, even if some of it came in the form of worry. It wasn't even a full minute before Jess returned, though. She sat and then took a big bite of the omelet.

"That was fast," Beast said, a half-smile on his somber face, which might as well have been a Cheshire grin.

"I told you, I'm getting better. It's in direct proportion to the desire to work, too." She took another bite, then beamed over at Beast who was now looking so lovesick and gone for her, I had to look away. If I didn't already know she was pregnant—and she certainly didn't look it yet—I'd know by just this expression.

"So you think you'll be back soon?" I asked, shifting uncomfortably and wondering why. Why wouldn't I want my dear friend to feel better and come back to work?

After a sip of water, Jess said, "Not just yet. But don't worry. Elizabeth isn't getting kicked to the curb just because I start showing up again." She waggled her brows.

Heat hit my cheeks instantly. "Right. Of course not."

The ensuing silence forced me to look up and when I did, they were both studying me with matching expectant looks on their faces.

"You guys are already too freakishly in sync. Haven't you only been married for like a day?"

Jess laughed. "Bit more than a day now."

She leaned over and kissed Beast's bearded cheek.

He leaned into the touch, but didn't look away from me. Instead, he pinned me with his intense eyes and waited another beat before saying, "Come on. Tell us what's going on."

How did I explain this? What did I even want to say? I was a verbal processor, so the fact that I hadn't laid it all out for them already was different for me. But so was everything with Liz—from the way I reacted to her, the way I wanted her so intensely and also wanted to just be near her. The way I'd decided I'd take what she could offer and not expect more despite that going against my very nature...

"I like her a lot. She's basically everything I like and then some."

"What do you like?" Jess asked, prodding a bit.

A smile came before I even spoke. "She's honestly a little grumpy, but she has this soft heart. She cares deeply about the people around her and she's very purposeful, which I admire. She's funny and hot as hell and... well, I could go on, but the point is I like her and we're hanging out a lot."

Beast's eyes narrowed. "But?"

I chuckled softly, fiddling with my fork and feeling weirdly shy. "But she's leaving."

I nudged the perfectly made omelet around on my plate, then raised a brow at him. "Go ahead."

He crossed his arms. "Don't want you to get hurt."

I nodded. His protective instincts extended far beyond Jess.

"Can we acknowledge that we don't know how this ends, though? I mean, let's say you keep dating. Maybe you even do long-distance? I know it's not ideal, maybe not what you pictured, but I hate the thought of you liking someone this much, which is the first I can think of, and not even giving it a shot." Jess tugged on one of Beast's biceps and guided his hand to link fingers with hers and rest on the table.

Good grief, they were adorable.

"That's where I landed. It's definitely out of my comfort zone, but it honestly feels like..." I exhaled, nerves swooping around my belly as I thought of Liz and how inevitable she seemed. "It feels like I don't have a choice but to try."

No doubt thinking of this situation that way was foolish. The confusion and unsteady way I was navigating everything meant I'd been slow to let anything happen between us, despite spending as much time as she'd give me together.

But I didn't want to think about that anymore, especially not when heaviness draped over my chest when I did.

So I took up my fork again and pointed at them before jabbing a piece of my meal. "Now, tell me, how's the beasty baby growing and when am I throwing you the baby shower?"

CHAPTER THIRTY-FIVE

Kenny

In the last two weeks, Kit had grown and now had the run of the house. I'd spent as much time as possible with him, and with Liz, since we'd agreed to spend time together.

And right now, looking at her from across the room was torture.

Well, okay, no. I had a friend or two who had actually been tortured, so I didn't like using that word, but crap if it didn't feel like I was crawling out of my skin to get closer to her.

Ironic since we'd spent inordinate amounts of time *close* these last two weeks, and yet I hadn't taken any real shots with her. I'd failed completely to make a move, and I had a blaring green light.

Like, honestly. Who stays stopped at a stop line when the light is green?

This guy, apparently!

We'd sat on her couch and watched movies. We'd sat on mine. Playing with Kit had entertained us for hours. We'd eaten like ten meals together, just the two of us and a handful of others with various combinations of friends. I'd snuck us up the gondola to the top of Silver Ridge peak thanks to my ski lift friend Jiff, and we'd been to see a depressing Oscar-contender movie at the theater which we both lightly pretended to appreciate until we both realized we hated it, then gleefully returned to my place to binge half of *Ted Lasso* season one in an effort to apologize to ourselves.

We'd also checked in with Jack and Evie often, who were both doing well. The baby was reportedly growing well and healthy, and I could admit, I couldn't wait to meet her little one. Not that I expected to hold it or anything, but it made me even more excited for Beast and Jess.

And maybe a touch wistful.

Liz and I had been all over town, my quest to show her Silverton and how delightful it could be continuing in earnest amidst our... whatever this was. Because as much as some of it felt like a date, it also very much didn't.

We'd gone sledding with friends. We'd gone on a jog together. We'd done so. Many. Things.

Except kiss.

Or any other fun activities that might accompany kissing.

And I couldn't tell if it was me holding back or her or both of us or some messy mix of miscommunication brought on by *not* communicating about such things. Whatever the case, it was getting old, and I was struggling to keep my hands to myself and yet also succeeding maybe a little too well.

"Any questions about the assignments in the next few

weeks? Hijack's joining us soon, Cookie's out, and we have our VIP in place for another little bit." Bruce checked his notepad, then looked up in search of anyone who needed his attention.

Thankfully, no one did. We'd been here for a quick twenty-minute debrief on a situation that'd come up overseas, though fortunately the Washingtons had it handled, as usual. Then we'd reviewed the next few weeks' schedule due to a change up with a few personnel, and then... well, honestly, I'd spaced out because Liz had worn her hair in a long braid today instead of her usual bun at the back of her head and I couldn't think of anything I wanted more than to just... mess it up.

Well, mess it up with my hands while I kissed her into oblivion, preferably naked. With her gorgeous hair cascading around us, I'd slide my tongue down her—

"Barbie? You raised your hand?"

My head snapped to Bruce and found his eyes on me, brows raised.

What? What?! My hand was not raised. No raised hands. No hand-raising. "Wh-at? No. I'm good. I'm all good."

He winked. "Good. Have a great week, everyone."

Cookie's breathy chuckle confirmed my suspicion. Bruce had totally caught me staring at Liz and had called me out in front of everyone. *Super.*

Hopefully, she hadn't noticed my eyes had been on her. Also here's hoping she didn't realize what I was thinking about because that would be so deeply less than ideal.

"You going to make it? Need a minute before you stand up?" Cookie asked between laughs.

I sent him a glare but couldn't hold it, so I shoved his

chair away. "Shut it. I'm just fine." But also, was it *that* obvious I'd been mooning over Liz?

I grabbed my coffee mug and notepad, refusing to look at her again despite the gut-deep desire to. A hand on my shoulder halted my progress right as everyone else slipped out of the room.

"Gotta cool it with that, Barbie." Bruce squeezed, then released me.

Wilder, Bruce, and Adam all stood side by side when I turned back into the conference room.

"Sorry. I know. I'm genuinely sorry." And now, a little embarrassed, despite rarely feeling embarrassment.

"Might need to tell her that. Can't imagine she didn't notice you."

Wilder's unamused expression made me shrivel up a little. He was Liz's stepbrother, after all, and he wasn't the type of man to let the *step* deter him from exercising his protective instincts.

"You gotta get a grip, man," Adam said, disappointment ringing so loudly in his tone, I felt the need to take a seat at the sound of it.

"We would love to keep her on as long as she's here. I can't imagine that'll happen if she's feeling harassed," Bruce said, his tone chiding.

My cheeks heated as mortification set in. "I didn't mean to make her uncomfortable, I—"

My words halted as Bruce's face cracked in a smile.

Pretty sure my heart stopped beating altogether when Wilder's did, too, albeit a much smaller one.

Adam's chuckle solidified the realization, and I finally sucked in a breath.

"Wait. This is a joke?" I asked, the truth dawning.

Bruce laughed. "Sorry, Barb. We had to. You were just

so transfixed. But I'm fairly certain she didn't notice, or if she did, she was very subtle about it. She's not used to our way of doing things so she had more to pay attention to."

I shoved at Adam's shoulder, and he looped his arm around my neck.

"No, no, no, none of that. You were obvious as all get out, but you got lucky. This is a legitimate heads up." He released me.

Breathing came more easily now, but my heart rate was still thrumming in the wake of the genuine dismay I'd felt. "Lesson learned. I'm pretty hard to embarrass but the thought that I'd made her feel bad..." I shook my head.

"Our boy's got a real crush," Bruce said, sounding like a proud papa.

I groaned and covered my face. "Please can we not?"

Adam shook me by the shoulders, and as much as I was annoyed and my face was likely bright red, I loved it. Because none of this was mean-spirited or to shame me. They were messing with me, yes, but also giving me a little nudge that I had work to do, and also cheering me on.

"Just lock it up at work, okay?" Bruce suggested as he and Wilder walked out right as Cookie sauntered back in.

"Got him good, sounds like," he said, grinning his pretty boy smile.

"Oh, great, you were in on it?" I asked, knowing instantly he had been.

"I figured they were going to say something when you didn't follow me out, so I hung by the door."

Adam laughed softly again, then crossed his arms and widened his stance like he was settling in. "I know you said you're hanging out and my sources tell me you've been seen coming and going from her place almost daily. You good?"

A sigh escaped. "Yeah, Doc. I am."

"Taking care of yourself?"

Knowing Adam, this likely meant a few things—everything from my head and heart to my actual body. He didn't need all the details, but I could freely say, "Yes. We're taking it so slow we're hardly moving."

In some ways, it felt like we'd taken a giant step back from where we'd been before having the conversation where we agreed to hang out and be together.

Hence the daydreaming...

"Good. Then I'm glad for you." His brow furrowed. "Just go easy. You have a lot of love to give, and I hate to see you try with someone who won't take it."

I huffed a laugh like he'd made a joke, even though I felt it in my chest. "Noted."

Adam left and Cookie and I moved, too, wandering toward the break room with empty coffee mugs in hand.

"So you seem good, but also kind of... *à côté de la plaque.*" He didn't know.

Welcome to the club.

Every minute with Liz was one I wouldn't trade, one I couldn't get back, and one I tried desperately not to spend thinking about how much longer I did or didn't have with her.

"I like her. Little too much, probably, considering." I raised a shoulder. "But you know me. I can't just... not." I'd accepted, to some degree anyway, that despite being someone who wanted longevity and a future with someone, I couldn't pass up a chance to have this time with Liz, even if I knew for a fact there was no future with her.

He nodded. "I do. And of course you can't. It's one thing we all love about you."

He filled his mug, then held up the carafe, and I slid mine over so he could fill it, too.

"And if it all goes down the drain, I'll be here. And I'm certain Dorian will make you as many croissants as you can eat." He raised a brow as though to ask whether that would be enough.

"Hey, sorry to interrupt."

My pulse spiked. *Liz.*

"What? No. No interruption. Hey. You. How are—"

"What is it?" Cookie said, ending my weird spiral of verbal vomit.

Her eyes were troubled and her posture on edge. If I hadn't been so far down the rabbit trail of talking about my squishy feelings for her, I would've seen it instantly.

"It's Evie."

That was all she needed to say.

CHAPTER THIRTY-SIX

Elizabeth

The panic I felt channeled straight from Jack's mouth into my brain.

"I can't find her. I don't know what happened," he said, voice and hands shaky. "The police know but they can't do much."

Silverton's sheriff department was eminently capable and well-staffed for such a small town, but when a woman was missing for an hour, there wasn't a lot they could do. Hence the reason he'd called Saint.

"She went to her doctor's appointment, and then was supposed to come right back here. But it's been an hour and I can't get ahold of her, her phone isn't tracking, and the driver I hired said he didn't see her." His jaw ticked and he leaned his elbows on his knees. "If anything happens to her, I'll never forgive myself. I've already failed her once and I can't stand the thought of it happening again."

"We're not there yet, man. We'll find her. We're going to fan out in town, the police are on the lookout, and odds are, this is all a misunderstanding," Kenny said, patting his back for reassurance.

"And if not?" Jack asked, the stress radiating off him. "How do I ever look myself in the eye again? How do I stand to know I could've helped her sooner? That she deserved a life free from pain and fear and if I'd just gotten my head out of my own—"

"Hey, pump the brakes. One thing we don't do is what-if until we have to. Sometimes, we have to get creative to figure out the answers, but we will figure it out. We will find her." Kenny's voice had taken on a soothing but firm quality.

Damn, he was good. There was something so completely appealing about a man who could keep his head in a stressful situation, and a person like Kenny, with all his boundless energy and joy, didn't necessarily strike me as someone who would be like this. Bruce? Wilder? Tristan? All yes. Even Cookie had a more calming energy.

But right now, Kenny was exactly who Jack needed him to be. That just made me all the more determined to be who Evie needed *me* to be.

"I'm going. I'll be back." I caught Kenny's blue eyes and we had the same thought there—*hopefully with Evie in tow.*

Kenny would stay with Jack, so Cookie and I were on the way back to town.

"What do you think?" I asked, knowing all the Saint personnel had more experience with missing people than I did. My work in Kappa Sector rarely had anything to do with missing women, abusive exes, or even hostage rescue. If the CIA had someone go missing, they were either gone, or we called in the EMU to get them back.

"I have a feeling this is a misunderstanding. Other than the phone call, there've been no indications the ex is even looking for her, let alone knows where she is. She's been cooped up in the house with Jack, who is lovely, but not her family or even her lover, and she's about to have a baby and be essentially stuck at home even more. So I suspect she's spreading her wings."

He seemed confident and it made sense. "You're certain they aren't lovers."

"Certain."

"How?"

He laughed. "They have no chemistry. No hint of heat between them. You and I have more sexual tension than she and Jack do—and you and I have exactly none."

I chuckled. "Fair. They do have a much more familial vibe. I was anticipating that they were fighting feelings, or maybe he was, but hiding them in order to keep from crossing any lines, but no... there's been no hints."

"Indeed. Now, you and Barbie..."

My stomach flipped. What could I say to that? He hadn't even said anything specific, yet it felt like a weighty insinuation. *What about me and Barbie!!? Tell me, oh wise Frenchman.*

Instead, I rather demurely said, "Mmm?"

"When the two of you are in the room, we can all feel it."

I pulled into a parking spot at the Saint building and would've liked to sit with the sentence, mine it for all possible meanings, and then ask him another question, but we both sprang out of the vehicle, a healthy sense of urgency spurring us on and keeping me focused.

"I would like to ask follow-up questions, but for now..."

"*Bien sûr.* Whenever you like. I have something to say

on the subject at some point." He stopped at the curb, waiting for a car to pass.

Curiosity roared through me. What could he want to say? Would he warn me away? *What do you mean, Cookie?!*

"I'll be ready when you are," I said instead, jogging across the street. We split then, him taking Main and me Silver. We'd then shift to Elk and extend farther. Doc and Eddie were looking near the hospital.

This experience of going store to store was far different and far less fun than it had been with Kenny. Shop owners somehow recognized me more than once and when I got to Elise's, she was so happy to see me, I felt bad.

It was the strangest response, but I genuinely felt guilty when I left. She was so warm and welcoming, understanding of my questions as I asked basic things about whether she'd seen Evie. And it made me realize she was a friend. I hadn't allowed for that to be true in my mind, but every time I saw her, she was genuinely warm and accepting. She'd been the same at the book club.

It was a distraction and not a thought I should be kept warm by as I moved through the other businesses on Silver Street, and yet I couldn't escape it. Jo's friends had become my friends. Yes, they were new, and they didn't know me all that well, but that was partly due to my choices. I hadn't engaged with them beyond the book club and seeing them on Fridays at Craic. I'd made no effort to spend time with anyone other than Jo individually.

Strangest of all thoughts—I wanted to.

I'd led such an insular life and the farther from it I got, the more confused I felt by my own behavior. Why had I isolated myself so much? Why had I felt satisfied with a watered-down version of friendship, family, and love?

The longer I stayed here, the more I suspected it'd felt

easier to let work be my whole world. Every week, I'd pop up for a phone call with Jo and catch a gulp of connection, but otherwise, I'd allowed myself to believe my work *was* community. And maybe if I worked somewhere like Saint, it would've been. But my job was naturally isolating. I reported to someone and had people who reported to me, but often, I was alone, out in the world or more likely, behind a computer. For a long time, the difference I made doing the job had felt like more than enough to satisfy me. It'd been thrilling and compelling and yes, fulfilling. But as time wore on, what had felt full looked closer to... not so full.

Now that I'd seen what these things could look like by observing Jo, my dad, and even Kenny's way of living, I knew going back to what I'd always done wouldn't be easy. I'd anticipated that it would be like a switch I could turn on and off and back again. Now, the mechanism looked a bit off. Would it even work? I didn't really want to worry about it.

I couldn't take all of the wonderful things with me, but maybe I could bring some of it along—the friendships, at least, and maybe the determination to find more for myself when I got back to the routine.

Those thoughts, instead of inspiring hope, settled in my belly like lead.

Mentally pushing away from that thread, I focused on the job. Store after store, no luck, and by the time I'd circled the block and returned to the bookstore, I got a text from Cookie indicating he had a quick lead.

Jo was inside, so I entered, having spoken to one of the employees when I first walked by.

"Hey! What are you doing out and about?" she asked, wrapping her arms around me.

I hugged her back, absorbing all her sweetness and strength before explaining. "I'm actually working. I'm looking for a woman who's missing. She's petite, light blond hair, very pregnant."

"Oh, she's here. She's in the reading room," Jo said, waving me back toward the room where we'd met for book club.

I rushed there, rather unsubtly bursting into the small, cozy space. "Evie," I practically barked, so relieved to see her unharmed I didn't manage to gentle my tone.

Her gaze snapped up and she smiled. "Hey. What are you doing here?"

"I'm looking for you. Jack's been worried and he thought—well, we've found you now. Hold on." I texted Cookie, then dialed Kenny. "Hey, I found her. We'll be back soon."

I sat in the chair perpendicular to where she sat with legs extended on the loveseat nearest the fire. She had a pillow tucked behind her back and an iced water and a mug of tea next to her, along with a paper bag featuring a Rise and Shine logo on it.

"I'm sorry. I didn't mean to scare anyone, least of all Jack." Her face took on an agonized expression, and she reached for her tea, cupping the mug close to her chest. "I went to the appointment and everything's fine. It's such a gorgeous day and the ice has melted so there wasn't as much risk of falling, and I feel great today, so I just wanted to walk."

The way her brows pinched and her lips turned down, I could tell she wasn't okay.

"You needed a little air, sounds like."

She nodded. "I'll never be able to thank Jack enough for everything he's done, but I feel like I've put my life on pause. And that's not his fault. I need to stay here to make sure I'm close to the hospital when I have the baby, but I'm ready to get settled." She set her tea down again.

"Where will you go?" I asked, unaware there was already a plan in place for what happened after the baby came.

"My cousin lives in a town not far from here. We haven't seen each other in years, but we've kept up online. I've decided I'll go there and start over. Reinvent myself and navigate the single mom life in a small town where everyone knows me. That way, if something happens with Dillon, I won't be alone."

Her gaze searched mine like she was looking for approval. I wasn't well-versed in this kind of thing—I wasn't sure what it was like to choose a path so distinctly when everything was against you. But I could tell she felt good about this plan, and that had to count for something, especially when she hadn't gotten to choose much about what she'd gone through in the last while.

"I think if the town is anything like Silverton, that's a great idea."

She laughed softly. "It's significantly smaller than Silverton from what I've read, but I agree. And that's part of it—I wanted to go into Rise and Shine and get a croissant instead of having one of Jack's assistants bring it to me. I wanted to browse this adorable book shop and then sit down and sip tea and read. I just..." She sighed heavily.

"You needed a break. And I'm glad you took one." I meant it.

"But?"

"But it's time to get back. And if you want to get out again, please just call me and I'll be your own personal but very silent and unintrusive bodyguard. As long as we haven't had issues with the press or your ex, I don't think that's unreasonable." I hoped Kenny and Cookie would agree, but I suspected they would.

"Thank you," she said, letting her legs slide off the couch and tucking her book into the bag Jo must've slipped it into when Evie paid.

Part of keeping clients safe was their compliance. I didn't have to be particularly experienced in personal security to know that—I'd seen it with assets I'd developed over the years. I could only do so much for them if they were insistent on going places and doing things that put them in danger.

If Evie needed to be getting out of Jack's mansion every few days, especially before her life changed even more substantially with her baby's arrival, I understood. She hadn't asked for any of this and she wasn't trying to be stubborn or demanding, but she had a right to live her life.

"I'll talk to the team. We'll figure out a way to get you some space."

"Thank you. I mean it. I'm not sure you'll understand how much this means to me, but it does. So, thank you."

I brushed off her thanks, but as we met up with Cookie and drove her back to Jack's, her words stuck in my ears. Her thanks was so heart-felt, so sincere, and it made me wonder if I'd ever been thanked for doing my job before.

Had I ever felt so appreciated? And did it make sense that this simple offering I'd made to Evie should garner more thanks than a decade and a half of service and true sacrifice for my country?

More and more, I had to admit, it did not.

CHAPTER THIRTY-SEVEN

Kenny

By Friday evening, I'd lost my cool.

Not that, if we're being honest, I ever had much to begin with, especially not with Liz. But at this point, I was a goner for her and every second we spent together made it worse.

Or better, depending on your perspective.

We hadn't even gotten much time together, and I was basically living for the interactions with her. It was bad and I knew it, but I couldn't seem to rein it in.

"She said she's coming, man. Give it a rest."

Cookie's hand clamped down on my shoulder and shook me, jarring my vision from where I'd pinned my gaze on the entrance to Craic.

"I know. I'm just..." In too deep?

"Obsessed with a woman you're barely dating?" he asked, and Doc, Bruce, and Beast all snickered.

I glared at them. Hard.

But also, they weren't wrong. I'd dived full into enjoying this while it lasted, and I didn't want to be away from her. If we only had a limited amount of time left, I wanted as much of it with her as I could get.

"Oh, watch out. Barbie's got his mean face on," Beast grumbled.

"Why are you even here? Shouldn't you be at home with your woman?" I snapped.

He glowered. "She made me come."

I instantly laughed at this, as did everyone else at the table.

"Not funny," he growled.

"It's actually amazing. I bet you're driving her insane," I said, beaming at my friend. His super badass wife hadn't wanted to be doted on and wanted him to have some social interaction outside of work and home—for that, I'd always love Jess. She was trying to take care of him just like he was her.

"Maybe," he admitted.

I moved to him and gave him a big old hug. Odds were fifty-fifty he'd shove me away, but something drove me to it. When his giant paws wrapped around me and squeezed just briefly, something in me settled.

He'd needed it, but I had, too.

"You okay?" he asked quietly, the rest of the table talking about something else.

"Yeah, I'm—"

Liz stepped inside the pub and my heart leapt. She wore jeans, boots, and a waist-length puffy jacket. She pulled off a knit cap and a chilly breeze rustled the long, loose strands of hair around her face as someone came in behind her.

"Noted."

Beast's tone held something—amusement, based on the soft crinkles at his eyes. Apparently, trailing off mid-sentence when you see the girl you like is a bit of a hint.

"Yeah," I said, knowing he'd get it. Confirming his observations, admitting my own feelings... really however he wanted to take it, he was likely right.

"I think we need a nickname for you," Cookie suggested as Liz walked up to the table.

"Do they give nicknames where you are?" Doc asked.

She shrugged. "If I told you, I'd have to—"

"Kill you." Everyone echoed, then laughed.

While all of us had served in the EMU, Eddie and Liz served in an agency within the CIA. Where the missions we'd done were top secret and compartmentalized, often covert, much of what she did didn't exist, nor did her unit. People had heard of the EMU. They knew we paired with the Tier 1 SEAL teams, and we were black ops. Her organization wasn't like that, entirely clandestine.

So we all appreciated the joke, even though we all understood exactly where she came from. I wondered if that made being here in the civilian world easier. She didn't have to pretend she worked for State in diplomacy or that she was an analyst for something. She could show up here and we knew she had skills.

So many skills...

"Well, do you want a nickname?" Bruce asked, more than willing to bestow one on her if she so desired, no doubt.

"I'm fine with going by name for now. Maybe something'll come up that will inspire a good one." She smiled, and then her eyes hooked into mine.

My stomach fell down a flight of stairs.

She wasn't a smiley person. She didn't toss out grins like currency like, well, me. These weren't the keys to her interactions with people like they were mine, and yet when she did it, or maybe because she more rarely did it, she was devastating.

"Hey, so... you good to go?" I asked, not trying to pull every person at the table's attention, but successfully doing just that.

Her brows lifted just a touch, but she responded right away. "Let me go say hi to the girls and then yes, sure." She slipped past us and moved to the table where Jo, Dove, Catherine, Nikki, and Winnie stood.

"Very subtle, man," Cookie said, snickering.

"You better hope she doesn't mind you announcing that to everyone," Doc said.

Of course he'd be more paranoid I'd done something wrong—he was perpetually trying to make sure he stayed on her good side.

But after getting to know her, I knew there was no bad side. She might seem severe and intense but underneath it she was just... lovely. Beautiful and funny and smart and sincere.

"I guess Elise couldn't make it?" I asked, hoping to move on from commentary about my very unsmooth announcement.

Cookie's gaze dropped to his beer as though any of us didn't know he was absolutely tuned in to what the woman was or wasn't doing.

"Haven't seen her. Nik said she had to cancel a lunch earlier this week, too," Bruce said, sending a wink in the direction of the table, no doubt toward his fiancée.

"Huh," I said, as though I cared. I mean, I liked Elise

and all, but I wasn't tracking her attendance at the weekly happy hour.

Our beloved Jean-Luc Doux, however?

Mais oui, he absolutely was.

"Anybody seen Stone this week?" Doc asked.

"I stopped by Wednesday, but he's been checking on Kit for me during the day," I said, resisting the pull to look for Liz. She would come back to the table when she was done saying hi to the girls. It was also a great thing for her to have friends here.

If there was any hope she'd come back, the more people here she liked, the better. The more at home, the better. So this was all good.

I'd been having more of these kinds of thoughts lately. More hopes she might return to Silverton for another extended leave, or perhaps suddenly retire from the CIA, even though I was fairly sure agents couldn't access full retirement benefits until a full five years after military personnel usually could at twenty.

Whatever the case, I was slipping into delusions and we hadn't even gone on a real date.

"Ready?"

I turned, instantly settling my hand against the curve of her lower back and beginning to move. "Have a good night, guys," I said to whoever was still at the table because I didn't care about any of them but Liz.

Obviously, I did care about them in a global sense, but in this moment? When I was about to have her to myself for the first time in days?

Yeah, no.

"Hungry?" she asked, a smile in her tone as I held the door for her to exit Craic.

She glanced over her shoulder as I followed her out and caught her dark gaze. "Starved."

For her. And yes, sure, I had eaten an early lunch and was quite ready to eat dinner, but I'd passed the point of being subtle. If we only had a few weeks left, I didn't want to spend them at separate ends of the couch and I'd resolved to confirm she felt the same and then... sit next to her.

Wow, real hero shit there, man.

"Where are we going?" she asked, accepting the hand I held out and weaving our fingers together.

I must've been hungrier than I realized because I couldn't think of the name of the restaurant. I couldn't think of anything other than how much I wanted to ask her that very question.

Where *were* we going? Where could we possibly go?

Thankfully, logic hadn't abandoned me entirely, so I told her the name and promised myself to enjoy the moment, the evening, the time with her, and not worry so much about those questions.

And whatever voice would normally shout at me to stop this because it simply couldn't last? That voice had been choked out by whatever dream we'd walked into together and until it ended, I'd have to embrace it.

CHAPTER THIRTY-EIGHT

Elizabeth

Silver Ridge Brewery's pub was charming and rustic but also somehow modern, and it landed on my ever-growing list of reasons to love Silverton.

My eyes fluttered closed as I savored the bite of locally sourced cheesecake with chocolate chip cookie crumbles and chocolate espresso drizzle. This was by far the most decadent thing I'd eaten in a long time and not even something I'd typically eat. But Kenny had ordered it, taken one bite, and had been silent ever since I'd taken my first taste.

I groaned, swallowing the creamy, salty-sweet morsel. It was honestly the perfect texture, flavor profile, and something I would never encounter in Europe.

"This is so good. I'm not even a dessert person normally, but I feel like I could eat this every day forever." I opened my eyes to find his gaze fixed squarely on my mouth.

I bit my lip.

"I would happily watch you eat it every day forever." His gaze flicked up to mine, then held.

We'd talked non-stop as we ate—first appetizers, then dinner, and now this glorious cheesecake. There'd been the usual pull between us, but something about Kenny had an edge tonight. I couldn't place it, but he felt more intense in a way that made me ignite and smoke curl in my belly.

"Do you want any more?" I asked, my voice a touch breathless.

He shook his head once, eyes not leaving mine. "All yours."

The pleasure I'd taken from dessert seemed fleeting compared to the simple act of meeting his gaze and the heat rippling between us. Since our talk in which I'd assumed we'd agreed to date, we'd hardly touched. Small moments of contact, maybe occasionally holding hands and pecks or kisses on the cheek, but nothing more. Part of that was because we were often with other people since Kenny had overtly stated his mission to help me feel at home and invested in Silverton.

But even the nights when we watched movies together, we sat apart and stayed there. I'd run around and around in my head about it—should I make a move?

Kenny was so straightforward with everything thus far, so the physical dry spell seemed purposeful. I couldn't guess what the purpose was, exactly, but I'd resisted pushing him, especially after all the upheaval with his family.

I was nothing like his ex, but he'd been hurt by a romantic relationship in the past and seeing his family very well may have thrown all of that in his face again. He'd seemed to be doing well in that regard, not mentioning it, no more drunken nights. But who was to say he would tell me if he were struggling with it?

He cleared his throat when I took my next bite, gaze skipping to the large brick oven that provided a centerpiece to the kitchen just visible around the corner from our table.

"Did I tell you my nephew texted me? Never even realized he has my number, but he popped up a few days ago, saying thanks for the money."

Kenny's comment felt both completely out of nowhere and also somehow exactly on time since I'd been thinking about the interaction with his family.

"That's good, I guess? What did you think?" If it was a regular point of contact, then hopefully it was good, but I worried it was a matter of time until they had the child requesting more money now that they knew Kenny was doing so well.

He shrugged one shoulder. "I don't mind having it acknowledged, but I have a feeling it won't be the last time I hear about it."

And what he wasn't saying—it wouldn't be the last time they'd ask for his help.

"I'm sorry, if that's what happens." I hated thinking of him hurt again. If I had his brother's number, I'd call him up and give him another piece of my mind.

His lips quirked. "I'm not. I'll handle it. Plus, every time I think of them, I then think of your heroic speech in my defense, and I'm happy again."

His smile was shameless, just like his words, and I couldn't hold back my own smile. "I'd do it again, you know. They needed to hear it, even if it didn't get through their thick skulls enough to stop short of what they did."

My teeth ground together at the thought, but when his right hand reached for mine across the table, his touch instantly soothed some of the irritation.

"Enough of them. Do you want to take the rest to go?" He eyed the remaining half of the cheesecake slice.

"Yes, please."

In a matter of minutes, he'd paid, received the boxed dessert, and we were walking home. I loved that in Silverton I didn't have to drive everywhere. It was something I'd worried about having to give up if I moved back stateside because even in DC, I'd ended up driving regularly. I'd avoided it in most of my European postings, and now I was realizing I could potentially avoid it, at least to some degree here.

In the dream scenario where I spend more time here, I corrected. And that was exactly the issue—I'd been having more dream scenarios and it simply wasn't realistic. Talk about setting yourself up for heartache.

The walk from Silver Ridge Brewery's pub was a chilly five minutes, but soon, we arrived at my building's door. I fumbled with the keys, my fingers raw. I should've worn gloves, but I'd wanted to hold his hand and feel his skin against mine.

A girl had to get her thrills someplace, right?

"Invite me in," he said, his low voice gruff and demanding.

Twist my arm. I'd planned to anyway, though I hadn't even thought I needed to. I figured our destination was my couch to watch a movie. We often went to his place so we could play with the cat, but tonight, we were right here.

"Want to come—"

"Yes."

I grinned, but looked away so he couldn't see it. His certainty did things to me.

After unlocking the door, we ascended quickly, then

entered the small apartment and I slid the deadbolt in place once we were both inside.

I dropped my keys and purse on the counter and turned to see him tossing his jacket over the back of a barstool and turning to me.

Something about his attention felt oddly predatory. My pulse skittered in my veins, and I exhaled slowly in an attempt to calm myself.

He took a step toward me, hands at his side. "We've been moving very, very slowly."

I nodded as I stepped back. "We have."

He advanced again. "I would like a little more."

I took another step back, right in line with his movements. "Just a little?"

His next step put him in my space, his body only inches from mine. I backed up until my shoulder blades hit the panel of the door and his hands grasped my waist.

"At least a little. Maybe more. But not until you tell me you want that, too." He leaned down, our lips millimeters apart now.

"I do."

"You do what?"

His tone was silk over gravel, somehow smooth and rough at the same time. No longer was this Cheery Army Barbie. This was a man whose entire being spelled out his desire and there had never been anything on the planet more attractive to me.

Not simply that he was taking charge and guiding us toward what he wanted—what we *both* wanted—but that this was the same man who had a heart so big it held dozens of people, the same man who'd rescued a little black kitten and who wasn't afraid to support the people he loved ferociously.

The same man who'd been determined to show me how full life could be, who cared for me in small ways and with kindnesses he didn't even realize were special. And the same man who refused to be felled by those who mistreated him or by setbacks he couldn't control.

All of that wrapped into the person in front of me, whose hands were inching up my sides in a firm grip, his nose gliding along the line of my jaw, and waiting for my response.

It was lethal.

And I had no choice but to answer him truthfully, dream or no.

"I want more with you."

CHAPTER THIRTY-NINE

Elizabeth

When Kenny's lips touched mine, I didn't hold back. And hallelujah, neither did he.

He teased with soft, short presses and I responded in kind. When he coaxed my mouth open, I willingly complied. His hands burned a path long my ribs, then skipped to angle my head so he could take the kiss even deeper.

My hands were on him, too, snaking under the layer of his button-down and then the soft cotton undershirt beneath it to press my freezing hands into the warm, taut flesh of his abs. He gasped and broke our kiss, a laugh ringing out between us before he bent and hauled me over his shoulder.

"Hey!" I shout-laughed as he jogged into the living room, and I marveled at both how easily he moved with an entire human over his shoulder, and his joyous cackle.

He might've been intense and extremely sexy while doing so, but he was still *him*.

I loved it.

I love—Nope. Not going there.

He flopped me over his shoulder and onto the couch, then instantly kneeled on either side of my body, hands resting on either side of my head.

The mirth had been replaced by heat, and the combination of the two was undeniably compelling. I tugged at the bottom of his shirt, and he leaned up, wrenching both shirts over his head in a move I wouldn't have thought possible with a button-down, and dropped back to all fours.

"Better?" he asked, that silky-sensual voice back.

I reached up to trace a tattoo that snaked along his collarbones and nodded. "Yes."

His gorgeous blue eyes bore into mine as he pulled one of my hands away from his body, then pressed a slow, deliberate kiss to my palm.

"Better warm you up," he said.

"Guess you better," I said, only half solid as the rest of me had liquified.

A dark, low laugh rumbled out of him as he nipped at the heel of my hand before returning it to rest against his chest.

His gaze caught on our hands, the three fingers of his left hand pressing over mine and a flash of something crossed his face, interrupting the steady stream of confidence and desire.

"What?" I asked in a whisper.

"Does this bother you?" He furrowed his brow when he held up the hand that'd endured such trauma.

I instantly moved to take it in both of mine and pressed it to my chest, just over my heart. "No. Sometimes, it breaks my heart a little to think of what it must've been like to heal from this, body and mind, but to me, this is proof of life. Proof you survived something and chose to keep going. I honestly don't think of it at all, other than that it's you."

He nodded. "It was a bomb disarming gone wrong, for the record. That was an awful day, and it hurt a lot of people I love, so I like to make it something lighter."

I brought his hand down and kissed the side of it. "Shark attacks are hilarious."

He laughed, eyes twinkling.

I sobered. "Thank you for telling me. And please believe that it doesn't bother me. I'm sorry for what you lost, but I am so grateful the rest of you is here." Heat flushed as I raised his hand and pressed a kiss to his palm. "I think of how I want both of your hands on me all the time."

His throat bobbed, and I thought I might combust before he moved, but then bless him, he did.

His lips found mine and he kissed me with dizzying focus. My hands on his skin—now pressed back against his chest, then his shoulders—warmed, while his fingers explored with feather-light pressure along my collarbone. I urged him closer until he settled into the slim space next to me, our bodies flush with heat far beyond the room's warmth.

Every part of me he touched burst to life, blood humming and nerve endings firing. His hands roamed, as did mine, and I wondered if I'd ever get tired of his taste, his warm, clean scent, his touch.

We kissed for what felt like hours and I couldn't recall the last time I'd simply kissed someone like this until my mind was fuzzy and all I wanted was to get closer. But where I would've moved ahead, he pulled back, and where I pressed for a little more, he held us steady, not depriving but not driving beyond a certain pace.

At one point, with my hands in his hair and his lips against my neck, I made a sound of both pleasure and frustration. It was one second, maybe two, and then he sat up and pressed his hands to his head, exhaling slowly with his elbows on his knees like he might be sick.

Concern filled me and I sat up, too, setting a hand on his arm to urge him in my direction, but he kept his head in his hands and his gaze cast down.

"I'm sorry, Liz, but I can't keep going. I want to, but I just..."

When his eyes met mine, my heart clutched.

I wasn't someone who pretended I could read everything about someone by looking in their eyes, but Kenny might as well have spelled the words out with marker across his cheeks. He was in agony, but not simply because he was holding himself back physically.

He was in love.

With me.

I knew it as surely as I had ever known anything in my whole life—maybe more. The surety I'd had when I decided to go to Georgetown. The clarity I'd felt when I signed my employment documentation with the CIA. The confidence I'd embraced when I accepted the job in Kappa Sector.

And now, this.

This sweet, sexy, wonderful man was in love with me. And for reasons I didn't totally understand, but knew on a gut-level, it was tearing him apart.

"I'm sorry," I whispered, wanting to both draw closer to him, urge him to be with me right now, and also to run away. That was my thing, wasn't it? So how could I stay when I *would* leave him?

His jaw flexed. "Nothing to apologize for. Nothing at all. It's me. I'm not... casual. And I don't... I don't think I'd survive it."

If we slept together and then I left.

A bitter laugh slipped out, but I wasn't upset with him. It was this situation, or maybe with me. With the reality that I would go back to work and leave him here, even when it was breaking my heart, too.

Because I would go back. That life was the only one I knew. This here, it had been an interlude. I had built my entire existence elsewhere.

"I get it. I really do." It was all I could offer him. I squeezed his arm, fleetingly admiring the smooth curve of his bicep and the swirls of ink covering the upper side and onto his shoulder.

He was so beautiful, every part of him.

"I should probably go. But I..."

His jaw flexed again and then he reached for me, drawing my face to his with a warm palm at my cheek, claiming my mouth in a kiss that seared into my mind and my body, and didn't stop until I felt so thoroughly undone, I had no words left.

He stood and pulled on his undershirt, making quick work of unbuttoning the shirt and slipping his arms into it, then his jacket. I stayed put, watching his movements, hoping I didn't look too pathetic as he left, heart aching even though I understood. He was right.

I finally summoned the wherewithal to stand and walk him to the door. He leaned in and pressed a kiss to my cheek, my temple, and then ducked for one more at my lips. He tucked the hair that'd become wild behind one ear and gently touched his forehead to mine before pulling the door open.

"Call me tomorrow, if you're free." And then he left.

And for the first time in as long as I could remember, I returned to the couch and cried myself to sleep.

CHAPTER FORTY

Kenny

Kit knew something was off the minute I got home last night. He curled up next to me in the bed, and though I'd tossed and turned, he hadn't left.

Now he was curled into a ball on the floor near my clothes from last night and some sick part of me wondered if he'd done so because those clothes smelled a little like Liz. And she generally smelled great, so why wouldn't he? Plus he seemed about as obsessed as I was whenever she came over.

"I know. I knowwww. I might've completely shot myself in the foot, which would be really annoying to then have another limb difference." I thought of her assurance last night, how clear and direct it had been, how reassured I'd felt about something I hadn't even realized I was worried about.

The little beast didn't so much as raise his head and I

smashed a pillow over my face and let out a groan. Flashes of memory assaulted me—the taste of her, her body next to mine, the places I'd touched her and she me. Good grief, it was far less than a teenage make out and yet it'd been some of the hottest moments of my life to date and had left me desperately wanting more.

And yet knowing with utter and crushing certainty that if I took what I wanted—and that she wanted to give—I would be crushed myself. Being with her like that on top of all these feelings... I was a fairly simple man and that would gut me.

Was it cowardly? Maybe. I could admit it. I was increasingly terrified of what it'd be like when she left despite how much I wanted everything with her while she was here. I'd been on this path, barreling toward this end with absolute certainty, and I'd somehow managed to accept it. I'd allowed myself to live in a dream and deny the loud voice saying this wouldn't work. And now, surprise surprise, here I was, facing down heartbreak because sure enough, the temporary thing was in fact temporary.

"Listen, I don't blame you for your silent judgement, but I could really use some loves," I said, waiting for the sounds of him moving. He tended to be pretty responsive to my voice, but the fact he hadn't rejoined me on the bed yet had me continue talking.

"I promise I'll talk to Luc and Stone. I swear. And I mean, hopefully I'll see her today, even though I feel like an idiot and a jerk and a total..." I didn't know. Would she hate me? She had seemed to understand without me saying the words, but in the light of day, would she get it?

And would she want to spend time with me if sex was off the table? Thus far, it hadn't been an issue, but I could now recognize the reason I hadn't made a move. Some part of me had known this was how I'd feel and I hadn't wanted to confront it and risk ruining the time we had left.

"Dude, I need some kitty loves." I scratched my fingers on the duvet cover, hoping to lure him in, and propped up my pillows higher to glare down at him.

And then he trotted into the room and launched up onto the bed and I may or may not have let out a screech.

"Where the crap did you just come from?" I glanced down at the little black spot I'd been talking to and had fully believed was my cat, then at the actual cat, who took a swat at my feet as they moved under the covers.

I jumped out of bed and went to investigate, then cracked up. At first, it was a small chuckle, but then, when I picked up the black boxer briefs I'd left discarded with my jeans last night when I'd changed before bed, I laughed so hard it freaked out the actual cat on my bed and he bolted back out of the room.

"Guess that's part of the charm of a black cat," I said, wiping at my eyes and glad for the laughter. I'd felt so heavy and restless all night. I'd hardly slept and all I wanted was to hear from Liz, but all I worried about was the very real possibility I wouldn't.

I went about making some breakfast and getting coffee. It'd been a while since I'd sat out on the back deck and took in the space so I bundled up and slipped out onto the porch, shrugging off the memories of the night I'd brought Liz here for s'mores.

We had a surprising number of memories for the not quite two months she'd been here. Granted, I'd been a persistent little pest in her life, but she'd been willing to have me there, hadn't she?

My phone buzzed and I grabbed it, answering before I

fully registered it was an unknown number with a Nevada area code.

"Hey, Kenneth. How are you?"

My mom's voice startled me, and dread held me in place in my chair.

"Mom." No point in pretending I was glad to hear from her.

"Well, how are you, son? You still hanging around with that celebrity, Jack something? He still in town?"

My hackles rose instantly. Did she think I was an idiot? I knew she wasn't, despite how she'd played it over the years. She knew how to shape people, how to manipulate them, and it'd taken me years to see it.

"Why are you really calling?" I braced, waiting for her to say.

"Can't a mother call her son?"

"Not when she hasn't done so in more than six years. Don't you think it's a little odd, this call coming after so long?"

"We've just reconnected. I thought we could do it different this time," she said, enough pleading in her voice to make me second-guess myself.

"I don't know if that's possible," I said, not all that interested in trying, but enough of an optimist I couldn't simply hang up on her.

"You've gotten used to spending your time with people you think are better than us, is that it? All your fancy Army friends and all those celebrities and such? Never knew I raised such an ungrateful boy."

Ah. There it was.

The irony here, aside from the fact that several of my "fancy Army friends" had grown up poorer than me, was in how I'd never been all that interested in material wealth.

From the youngest age, I'd wanted security and I'd wanted love. When I thought I'd found it with Shay, I'd clung to it. And when I lost it? I had no reason to stay connected to her or my family, who'd tossed me out like they had not only no love lost for me, but no use for me.

The truth was that she'd called to get something from me and now she'd heard I wasn't going to offer up another check or anything else she could use, she had no use for me.

Sounds about right.

"I think we're done here, Mom. Have a nice life." I hung up and leaned back against the Adirondack chair, my gaze rising to the towering mountains, and reveled in the feeling of being dwarfed by them.

Right now, my family, Liz's imminent leaving... they felt like monstrous problems to face. But sitting here in the shadow of these peaks that'd been here for centuries, it reminded me my problems weren't so huge. They weren't lasting. They wouldn't outlast me just like I wouldn't outlast these mountains.

And that gave me hope.

I headed back inside and knew what I needed to do. No more moping around alone, no more wishing I could change my past, my family, or what felt like my inevitable future heartbreak. No more *thinking* about the problems.

I needed my friends, a few romcoms, and maybe some high-quality home-baked goods.

CHAPTER FORTY-ONE

Elizabeth

I felt like sludge climbing out of bed Saturday.

I'd eventually left the couch, regretfully moving from the space we'd spent so much time enjoying each other —whether last night or even over the last few weeks when we'd simply been watching movies and chatting—and huddled into the temporary sanctuary that was my bed.

Then I had continued to cry until my throat was hoarse and my eyes were swollen enough I'd remembered to take my contacts out before I finally passed out.

When I woke, I wasn't ready to see Kenny. I was raw, and both deeply honored and soundly rejected in a confusing way, so I poured myself, as I always did, into work.

Tragically, there was only one email from work and it did nothing to distract me from the disaster with Kenny. Instead, it sent me into a new round of tears, which I hadn't thought possible after crying a Danube's worth of tears last night. It pointed out just how inevitable our end was, and now it would come far sooner than I'd hoped for.

Good news for my job. I'd been exonerated from any blame and the junior agent was found fully at fault. It would still be there, in my file, but I could return to work. I could get back to the life I'd built. This should've made me feel better, shouldn't it? They'd gone through the process and they'd seen me for the reliable, trustworthy agent I was. They knew me.

That was what I'd wanted, and what I'd come here *needing* them to do. But now...

I couldn't help but think the good news for my job was bad news for my *life*, but how did that make sense?

The knock on my door sent me leaping from the table where I'd sat with my laptop and racing to unlock it. I could practically feel the excitement and relief until I yanked open the panel to find my sister smiling back at me and Elise and Dove beaming next to her.

Well, she was smiling right up until she took me in and then her eyes grew wide and she rushed at me, the other women close on her heels.

"What happened? Are you sick?"

She reached up to feel my forehead, and I swatted her hand away.

"Maybe she has a winter cold?" Elise asked.

"What are your symptoms?" Dove asked, reaching for my wrist to check my pulse, but I pulled away.

"No. I—" My throat instantly tightened, and I cleared it, then bit down on the sob threatening to climb its way out of my throat. "I just got this email from work. It's—I'll be going back sooner than I thought."

Dove and Elise were quiet, but Jo's disappointment came instantly.

"Oh, no. I was hoping it'd get extended. I don't want you to be in worse trouble, but it's been so good having you here." Tears welled in her big brown eyes and she hugged me to her.

"I wasn't in trouble," I clarified. Well, she didn't know the full of it, but I'd never hinted at trouble to her, just a sabbatical.

I cradled the back of her head, hating that anything I was doing was making her sad.

Jo held me by the shoulders and demanded I look at her.

"You don't have to go back. You know that, right? I mean, I know this is your career, but it doesn't have to be for twenty or thirty or whatever years. It can just be... what it has been. And you can do whatever you want."

I was already shaking my head. "It's not an option."

She didn't understand. She'd never had just one thing she wanted. She'd stumbled into her dream career and I couldn't have been happier for her, but she didn't get what it was like to have given so much to something and then consider walking away. I'd worked for too long to just give it all up, even after seeing the holes in the fabric I'd woven.

Hadn't I?

And I was making a difference. On the big scale. On the macro level. I was making the world a safer place for people, for women in general. Women like my sister and her friends —I'd helped dismantle a network of human trafficking in Europe. Tell me that didn't count! In the worst moments, I reminded myself that eventually, those outcomes did show out. And now... I was clinging to them with claws out.

"But it could be. You could make it an option. And you could—"

"Jojo, please."

She must've heard the devastation in my tone, because she stopped instantly. "I'm sorry. I just hate the idea of you being this miserable going back."

I shook my head, knowing if I even hinted at Kenny, I'd start bawling again. And he was so much of it, but not all of it. It was her, and my dad, and even Jane, who was so lovely. It was being even farther away from my mom, whose Pacific time zone made me a full nine hours from her. It was these mountains feeling more and more like something I could call home and this town charming my face off.

And none of it was enough to stop me from myself. From this stubborn path I'd set out on years ago and felt nothing short of trapped by now. I was making a difference, and that's what mattered ultimately. I got to do it this way, and unfortunately, not in any other form. So be it, because it counted for something.

"Alright then, that's it." Elise snapped into action, digging around in my kitchen until she found a trash can and plucking it up. "We're leaving this lovely little den of sadness and we're going to give you a good day."

She held the trash can up and slid the pile of tissues I'd accumulated into it, then grabbed the empty glasses I'd left there and bustled back into the kitchen, placing dirty things in the dishwasher.

"Great idea," Dove agreed, clapping her hands. "Let's get you into some clothes and maybe a quick face wash, and we'll get it organized."

Jo urged me along into the bedroom and promised me it'd be okay. I let myself function on autopilot, pulling on clothes, washing my face and brushing teeth, a soothing numbness descending now that I wasn't having to fill my whole day. A few minutes later, I was out on the street, then piling into Jo's car, headed toward distraction.

Forty minutes later, they'd kept up a steady stream of chatter about topics my mind wouldn't fully latch onto—some mention of Elise's ex-boyfriend, Dove's grandmother moving into an elder care facility in town, and Jo's latest update on her and Adam.

They were kind enough not to pressure me to say anything, though I couldn't have even if they'd insisted. Static like an old TV fuzzed my thoughts enough, I had a reprieve. But the lack of clarity made me restless, too.

When we pulled onto the Escape Spa property, I wished I could beam myself back into town. I didn't want to lie on a table with some stranger's hands running over me.

The only hands I wanted touching me were Kenny's. My heart clutched at the thought, but I breathed through it as we exited the car.

Even at this time of year, when most plants had died, the property was gorgeous. It looked like an inn, but I'd seen a few outbuildings as we'd turned up the long drive.

"I know you're thinking I'm crazy, but please trust me," Jo said, her hand hugging me to her and releasing all in a flash.

"Okay," I said, no pith or pushback left.

A strikingly pretty woman welcomed us from behind a long reception desk when we entered the cozy lobby. A fire roared in the fireplace and a wall of what I guessed were live plants grew at the far end of the space.

"Welcome. I've got everything set up, so go on back and they'll get you ready." The woman smiled at each of us.

"Thanks, Gen. Really appreciate it," Jo said, tapping the countertop as we walked by.

Jo's life here was so full. She had a network of friends,

small business owner colleagues, and of course, Adam. Then there was the Saint family, whom she'd gained by our dad marrying Jane Saint.

I should've been happy with these truths, and some other time I would be, but right now all I felt was jealousy and longing and a pathetic self-pity that asked, "Why can she have that and I can't?"

Big picture difference, Liz. Macro level. International bad guys.

Sometimes I wanted to slap myself in the face for those internal chants, but right now, I also needed them.

In the changing room, we were each given a stack of clothes. The material felt odd for a robe...

"Please leave everything on and place the suit over your clothing. Please change into the boots before you exit. We'll have your protective eyewear just across the way." The pretty blonde who'd materialized out of nowhere smiled brightly, then handed each of the other women neat bundles of clothes, though not all our instructions were the same.

I tried to catch Jo's eye, but she was listening intently to her own instructions. Place the suit *over* my clothing? What kind of massage or mud mask was this?

A few minutes later, Elise and Dove emerged in plush robes and Jo and I stepped out in coveralls.

"Do I get to know what we're doing?" I asked my sister, who looked as utterly ridiculous in the full-body bright white outfit.

She grinned. "Why you certainly do. Follow me." She wiggled her brows, and Dove and Elise told us good luck.

Good luck?

Jo followed a hallway to what felt like a back door, then we crossed an outdoor space on smooth paver stones set into the earth, and she knocked on the door of one of the buildings I'd seen when we drove up.

"Welcome. Please leave these on while you're in the house. Whenever you're done, we'll be here to assist your exit. Volume adjusts by the remote on the left."

Jo thanked her, and I accepted the plastic eye protection glasses, then stepped inside after Jo.

She shut the door, and I looked around. It appeared to be a normal kitchen, though smaller than what you might find in an average single family home, and there were rooms branching through two different doorways.

"This is a smash house. I know you've got a lot going on in that head and lying on a table for a massage would probably have driven you crazy, so we're going to dance and smash stuff, and then if you want, we can go relax, or we can just call it. Whatever you need."

I blinked at her. "Smash house?"

Her mouth slid into a wide grin and she reached for a plate sitting on top of a pile I hadn't noticed, then slammed it down on the linoleum floor. I jolted when the dish shattered, the small bits of ceramic sliding across the floor and bouncing off her steel-toed boot.

"Yes, Lizzy. Smash house." She handed me a stack of plates.

I took them, a sense of excitement and another little wisp of heartbreak mingling, before I threw the first plate at the wall.

CHAPTER FORTY-TWO

Kenny

On the table in front of me sat plates with a decimated pile of croissants, profiteroles, cookies, miniature quiches, and a little tea pot we'd mostly drained of a nice black tea.

My friends each sat with their attention on the TV and Kit was curled up on my lap. Stone had brought Bear, who lay prone next to him, one paw on the man's socked foot.

"I love this part," I said, allowing the emotion to rush in.

Yes, I'd cried today. But not much.

No, I didn't regret it.

I'd seen these men, especially Stone, but Cookie once or twice, too, at their lowest. I wouldn't say this was a low, but I was struggling, and I couldn't have been more grateful not to have to do it alone.

The fact that my support team came equipped with an actual gourmet tea party didn't hurt.

"I feel weird that you're tearing up and they've just accidentally collided while naked," Luc said, giving me an expert side eye.

My eyes burned. "It's fine. I'm fine. It's fiiiiiine."

He chuckled, and Stone's lips pulled up into an almost-smile.

"It's just the lack of sleep. And also the beautiful inevitability that Sandy B will absolutely fall for Ryan Reynolds, as we all do. She just doesn't know it yet."

Luc let out what I liked to think of as his adoring groan and Stone reached for a croissant.

"Are you going to talk to us about it? Or are we going to pretend to watch *The Proposal* all morning?" Luc asked.

I gasped, hand to my heart. "How dare you."

He rolled his eyes. "I know you love it, but it's not my favorite and you'll just have to accept that about me."

"I don't like how she tries to feed Kevin to the eagle," Stone grumped.

Bear's head popped up, and he eyed Stone, then dropped back down, almost as if to say, "I'd like to see an eagle eat me." He weighed northwards of eighty pounds and could rest his paws on Stone's shoulders if he stood on his hind legs, so good luck to the apex predator.

All their griping had me smiling, which I had to appreciate. There had been enough times in my life when I could hardly summon a flash of teeth, let alone a genuine smile. These men were with me whether I was sunny Barbie or broody or tearful Kenny, or anything in between.

"We can talk about it." I paused the movie because I wasn't about to talk over it. "I just don't know that there's much to say."

"Try," Stone demanded in that low, quiet voice of his. It was not unlike Beast's approach, although there wouldn't have been much gentleness in Beast's order, or at least not until recently.

I inhaled, wondering where to begin. I should update them on my mom's call and all of that nonsense, but what I really wanted to talk about was Liz.

"So I'm in love with her." I swallowed, relief and a little flame of terror at saying it aloud burning bright in my chest.

Both men nodded like they knew this already.

Um, okay. "Was it that obvious?"

"Yes." They spoke in unison, an event I would've appreciated a great deal more if it had been almost any other moment.

"We went out last night. Had a great meal. Went back to her place..." My eyes fell to my hands and I swallowed hard. "Had a nice time."

"But?" Luc prompted.

"I'm not sure there's a but. That's the stupid thing. We didn't sleep together, mostly because of me. I just had this moment where that's where we were heading and I felt, like, destroyed."

When I glanced up, Stone's eyes narrowed on me, clearly waiting for more, and Luc took a drink of his tea like it was a shot.

"I want everything with her and it's already breaking me that she's leaving. And I hate that because she's still here. I knew if we went any further it would be so much harder to move forward once she goes. It makes me a coward and selfish and probably not much of a man or whatever, but I couldn't push for something I knew I'd only have for a while and then lose." I exhaled sharply, the words tumbling fast enough I wasn't breathing normally between sentences.

"What did she do?" Luc asked.

I sighed long and slow, slumping back into the couch. "She saw it all over my face. She's incredibly intelligent and of course, she saw right through me. I didn't make excuses and I didn't explain. She didn't fight me or shame me. She just let me go."

Even that had hurt in a way—both in how I would've loved for her to fight for more information or some kind of explanation, and because her very choice not to push me for my reasoning meant she understood me.

She might not love me back, but she cared for me and hadn't liked seeing me hurting. She got it in the moment, and whenever we talked, I hoped she'd still understand.

"First, this has nothing to do with manhood. Not rushing into sex is wise and any person's prerogative, and I'm going to give you a pass on that statement earlier because you've just had all your feelings dredged up with your family's visit." Luc's face was stern and almost unlike himself, but one thing he wouldn't tolerate was his friends in pain of their own making.

"You're right. I don't believe it was 'beta' or whatever. It's just who I am, and I'm not ashamed of that. I like myself most of the time, and I think she does, too. It's just one more little thing contributing to the mess in my head."

Both men nodded, understanding my point.

"You need to talk to her," Stone said.

I scrubbed a hand over my face. "I know. But I don't really want to tell her I love her. I don't want to complicate things any more. And I'm afraid it's just going to spill out the second I look her in the eye. Plus, she *is* leaving, and I don't want to ruin the time we might have with those feelings clouding everything, which is also assuming she'll even be willing to spend time with me after this."

Stone's glare was pointed and Luc huffed.

"Your feelings are not a problem."

My lips pressed together.

"It's okay to feel however you feel. If she's no longer interested in spending time with you—"

"It's her loss." We all said it together like we'd choreographed it in an official support group.

I chuckled even though my throat burned with emotion. "I know. It's just not that simple. She's not going to be mean or dismissive. But she might say it's better for both of us, and she might be right."

They waited, quiet, letting this truth settle in the space around us. Kit's ears perked up and he stood, then bolted from the couch and down the hallway.

"That's what she's gonna do, if she's smart," I said, smiling after the weirdo little beast. He was more of the gangly teen instead of a tiny kitten these days, and he'd gotten both more snuggly and more edgy.

"No, she's not. If she doesn't want to date you, that's okay. You'll handle it. But assuming she's going to say something without asking her isn't respecting her or even yourself." Luc gave me a good ol' fashioned stare down for a minute before he stood and held his arms wide.

I rose and accepted his offering, hugging him tightly before he released me and shoved me toward the couch.

With a chuckle, I pulled the blanket over me and grabbed the remote. "Any more pieces of wisdom, or can we get back to this cinematic jewel?"

We watched the movie and, I tried to soak in the antics of the cast and the delight of Ryan Reynolds finally calling Sandra Bullock's character on her crap and insisting she marry him so he could date her. But after a while, I sent Liz a text, knowing I needed to see her before we went back to work on Monday or I'd be a wreck and not get anything done.

She responded instantly, saying she was glad to hear from me and she'd love to get together. She had plans with her family tomorrow, which genuinely made me happy even if it sent a sliver of dread through me that I'd have another whole day before I got to see her again and could feel out how she was feeling. We agreed to meet at Diner before work on Monday morning, and I promised myself I'd be ready.

Whatever that meant.

CHAPTER FORTY-THREE

Elizabeth

The pandemonium that had been Sunday family dinner at Jane and Darcy Saint's house—yes, my father had taken his wife's name in an amazing and rather significant gesture—was finally dying down.

I'd met Jane's children and their partners and kids before, but seeing them all together again, especially after the email I'd gotten indicating my time here was truly coming to a close sooner than I anticipated, was truly bittersweet.

"Great to see you guys again," I said, hugging Calla, then her husband Wyatt, who was Jane's oldest son.

"It was great to have you with us," Sadie said, right as her giant husband, Warrick, Jane's youngest, engulfed me in a hug. He was a tactile person and a giant teddy bear. I kind of loved that he was my stepbrother now.

"Malcom," Wilder said, the only one I knew in a professional capacity since he'd been in the EMU and was now technically my temporary boss at Saint Security.

"Saint," I said, using both his last name and nickname.

"It's been so good to see you. Let's get lunch sometime and I'll leave James with his daddy," Sarah, Wilder's wife, said.

"I'd like that."

"I want to come, too!" Jo said, slinging an arm around my shoulders.

Sarah laughed. "Of course you're coming."

She and Wilder followed the others out. I was peopled out in the best way and ready to get back to my little apartment.

Actually, what I really wanted was to get back to Kenny, but there wouldn't be any of that... at least not like before.

"You okay?" Jo asked, after we'd said goodbye to Jane and our dad and walked to the car. She'd insisted on driving me up here to get extra time together, and likely because Adam wouldn't be here. He'd been on a weekend assignment, which was well-timed since she was all the more available to keep me company.

"I am. I'm just..."

What word could describe what I was? Exhausted, but not physically. I was pleasantly worn out after taking a run with Jo this morning, and weirdly sore in unexpected places after spending a half hour throwing plates at the spa yesterday. Or maybe the soreness came from the deep tissue and stress relief massage I'd had after.

I'd been supported and loved by my sister, my new friends, and today, my family. It should've made me feel better and on one level, it did.

On the other, it made me feel like my heart was collapsing in on itself. Every wonderful interaction and

supportive thought someone shared became one more privilege I'd be leaving behind when I went back to my old
life.

I'd be getting another update tonight on timing for my
official return—the office admin would book my tickets and
then the final date would be set. I promised myself not to
open my work email before breakfast with Kenny, though. I
didn't want to have that looming deadline in my mind while
I was with him.

Jo had loaded in, but my dad called to me from the
porch. "Lizzy. Have a minute?"

Warmth suffused my chest at his use of the nickname.
He hadn't called me that in years, and now this was twice in
a matter of days. Only Jo had kept up using it and it'd
always felt like an emblem of the distance between us.

I jogged back toward him and mounted the stairs.
"What's up?

He smiled softly, his gray beard far less pepper than salt
these days.

"I just wanted to tell you how wonderful it's been to
have you here. I'm not sure when you go back, and I'd like to
be kept in the loop there, if you're willing, but just wanted
to make sure you knew."

I studied him, wondering if he knew my days were
numbered. I should've had close to a month left based on
the original dates I'd given him, but this comment felt too
pointed. Jo knew I was leaving sooner rather than later, but
I was sure she hadn't said a word to him, nor had I.

"Thanks. It has been for me, too. I'll be sure to let you
know."

"Good. Night, Lizzy."

"Night," I said, giving him a quick hug before hustling
down the steps.

"Don't be afraid to change if it doesn't work for you," he hollered after me, halting my progress before I got to the car.

I slowed, then turned to look at him, but he just waved and stepped inside. He meant the timing of when I went back, of course. He knew it'd shifted and he was encouraging me to stick to my plan if I needed to stay longer.

But as we made our way from their house back downtown under the light of a nearly-full moon, I wondered if maybe it wasn't that simple.

Maybe it wasn't just the travel he wanted me to be brave about. Maybe he meant... all of it.

Miraculously, I'd slept a few hours last night and was now ready for work. I hadn't checked my email, so I didn't have a specific drop-dead date for my return, and I'd managed not to sweat through my clothes while I paced my tiny apartment and tried to imagine what Kenny might say.

Before I landed on anything specific, my alarm trilled, and I held back from bolting out the door.

I didn't run or even jog. Nope! I stayed calm and walked with measured steps toward Diner, ready for some coffee and maybe some eggs, and maybe to mention to Kenny Carmichael that I was a little bit in love with him.

But also *not* mention that because who did such a thing when they were about to leave? Who?

Movement out the corner of my eye pulled my attention, and I turned to see a small crowd of people with big cameras sporting lenses of various sizes all hustling down the street away from me.

"That's bad news," Kenny said from next to me.

I jolted a bit, completely oblivious to his arrival until he'd spoken. "Seems like it."

"I have this awful feeling that my family tipped off the press Jack's here. I really hope I'm wrong, but if they could sell that information, I wouldn't be surprised. My mom seemed like she was fishing for information about him every time we talked."

His jaw ticked as his gaze followed the small group running away, hopefully to head out of town.

"I hope it wasn't them, too. But there's nothing you can do about it if they did, and that's part of why they have security and part of Evie staying put. You didn't tell them anything they could use, so you can't take that on."

I reached for him, wanting to set a hand on his arm or grab his hand, but I veered away at the last minute and started walking next to him. *Awkward*, but touching him after not seeing him in what felt like weeks but had been mere days seemed like it might've been crossing a line.

He tapped his phone and held it up, quickly relaying what we'd seen to Cookie, who would report into Jack's team and anyone else at Saint who needed to know. By the time we sat down at Diner, he'd finished his call.

Catherine wasn't here, but the other waitress took our orders right away, then delivered steaming mugs of coffee and a little pitcher of cream and left us to ourselves.

"So... how are you?" His eyes searched my face like he might find clues there.

Would he see the dark circles under my eyes born from tears first, then lack of sleep? I'd covered them up a bit, but I wasn't a miracle worker.

"Alright. How are you?"

He huffed a little. "I'm sorry for Friday. I—"

"I don't want you to apologize for doing what you needed to do, okay?" I reached out and took his hand in mine. Steam from my coffee mug curled between us and I pushed further. "What we're doing—what we've done—isn't easy. I'm so grateful for the time we've spent together, and I'll never forget it."

His throat bobbed and he reached for his water glass, drinking down several gulps before he spoke again. "I appreciate you understanding. And you're right, it is different. This whole set up has been. Neither one of us has been a casual dating type of person, but we've tried to treat this that way. And it hasn't worked. And I think part of that reason is—"

"I'm going back sooner than I thought."

He jerked like he'd been shot, a shockwave running through his body before he stilled. "Oh."

I didn't know what he'd been about to say, but I'd known I couldn't hear it. I simply wouldn't survive if this man gave me any more of himself and showed me what I could but couldn't have. So I'd halted all of this, every bit, with nothing more than the truth.

"Yeah. It's unexpected but I'll find out today when I fly out. They told me to expect this week."

I was a fool for not checking to see exactly when already. I'd do it as soon as I left here. As much as I'd felt like delaying, now that I was faced with the shadowy expression taking over his face, I knew I should've gotten it over with so we could both handle everything and be done with it.

He blinked, taking in my face like I was his, and licked his lips.

"This week," he said, almost in a trance, and just the sound of it crushed me.

CHAPTER FORTY-FOUR

Kenny

This week.

I'd thought I was worried about her calling everything off between us after I ran away on Friday, but this was worse. Had she initiated returning early? Was it really part of her job?

"It's ultimately a good thing. They wrapped up the inquiry of the incident early and..." Her finger traced the edge of the table before she made eye contact again. "It just means I can get back to work. Back to real life."

I nodded, swallowing down the objection rising in me like lava. "Right. Yeah. Well, congratulations on everything turning out well and... being done. I'm sure it's a relief."

The words were hollow, just like me. I felt so empty and almost cold hearing her news. I should've been a better friend, and genuine in my statement, but for now all I could offer was verbal support.

"Thanks, yeah. It's... what I was anticipating, but you never know."

"Okay, folks, breakfast is served."

The waitress set down our plates, and I wondered how quickly I could eat and leave. I didn't want to run away from Liz, but I didn't know how to stay and do this—to chat like she wasn't going to disappear from my life in a matter of days and leave me to go back to life before her.

What a stupid, stupid ending. I officially hated this story.

"This looks great," she said, smiling up at the waitress, though there was strain at her eyes and in the set of her jaw.

We ate for a minute or two, forks tinking against our plates and the quiet between us utterly gutting. As the food hit bottom and I took a minute to breathe through the bad news of her now-imminent departure, I saw a better way.

"I've been over here feeling sorry for myself, and I shouldn't be. But it's just because you're so great, and I'm going to really miss you when you're gone." I wouldn't confess everything, but I didn't need to be cold. That simply wasn't me.

But I needed to let her go without dragging her down. I wouldn't be a source of regret or hardship for her. I wouldn't stifle that part of her that needed the work and focus of her career.

"I'm going to miss you, too, Kenny. So much." Her eyes filled, but tears didn't run over right away. She pressed her lips together and her chin wobbled before one tracked down her cheek.

My hand shot out and I wiped away the tear, savoring the chance to touch her even in this small way. My gut clenched at the realization that this was amongst the last times. Even if I touched her a hundred more times, we were barreling toward the end, and I hated that.

"Please don't cry or you're gonna make me cry. You know I don't mind all that much, but if I start, I don't know how I'll stop, and then Beast'll get all pissy and Cookie will probably hug me and make it all worse."

She chuckled and sniffed, then took her napkin to dab at her eyes. "Sorry. I'm fine. And if you were just a little less wonderful, it'd be much easier to go."

If I were a little less in love with you, it'd be much easier to let you.

But I wouldn't say that.

This was a woman who knew her mind. She'd explored what small town life was like and seemed to enjoy aspects of it, but she had a mission. She had a sense of purpose I couldn't contend with, nor would I want to. I admired her drive and her need to serve in a way she was uniquely suited to.

But damn if I didn't wish there was another way forward.

"Well, what do you say we finish up here and get to work. We'll see if there's an all-hands and if not, we can go drive by Jack's and check on him and Evie, just to be sure," I proposed.

She finished chewing another bite of food, then wiped her mouth and tossed her napkin down. "Let's do it."

An hour later, we'd checked in with everyone and found out the all-hands would be a working lunch, so we opted to go visit Jack and Evie right away. They were both fine, and Jack's agent or someone had already alerted him he'd heard rumblings from press people he followed that there was a rumor Jack was moving to Silverton so they weren't shocked or even scared. Evie wasn't feeling great so we didn't stay long, and after a little admin work, I joined everyone else in the conference room just in time to see Bruce, then Wilder, then Tristan giving Liz handshakes before everyone took their seats.

She knows.

The realization hit like a fist to my solar plexus, the air vanishing from my lungs. I stumbled to my seat and tried to keep my mind on the meeting at hand. I summoned a laugh at the right time, chewed the tasteless sandwiches catered for the lunch, and ignored the pointed looks from nearly everyone at the table who could read me like a paperback.

The meeting wrapped up with one final, devastating comment from Bruce.

"A huge thanks to Elizabeth, who generously stepped in to bridge the gap for a while here. We've loved having you and whenever you're ready to retire and give up your life as a spook, we're here for you."

He smiled his pearly grin and gave Liz a nod, which she returned. Everyone clapped for her and I had the oddest urge to scream at all of them.

Her eyes met mine as she left her seat, our gazes locking like they so often did before she blinked away. Was it pain I'd seen? Anger? Weariness?

Someone's hand clapped me on my back.

"Jo's going to take it hard, too. Sorry, Barbie." Adam's consolation was genuine, and I could only imagine how Jo would feel. She's just had a glimpse of life with the sister she so dearly loved, and now it was disappearing again.

My heart ached, but I also felt embarrassed I hadn't really thought of other people losing out on time with Liz, too. Her sister, father, and all her stepsiblings and nephews and... heck, even Wilder would likely miss her in two ways, as a stepsister and as an employee.

"Guys' night on Wednesday?" Cookie asked, his demeanor subdued.

"Yeah. Sounds good," I said, clearing the gravel with a rough sound and offering him a flaccid smile.

"I'll let Stone know." With that, he left the room, and I followed him out, stopping only when Bruce's voice reached me.

"You'll be okay," he said, giving me one of those patented Bruce Camden looks that held so much weight and faith in me.

My throat had tightened again, so I cleared it. "Yeah. I guess that's the option."

His kind, familiar smile greeted me when I glanced up again.

"It is indeed. And we're all here for you, no matter what."

We went our separate ways, and I wandered back to my little office, avoiding looking into Liz's temporary one when I passed. I didn't want to see her packing up stuff. I didn't want to know if she'd already left for the day.

It was a few hours later when she knocked on my door. I stood instantly, heart hammering the second I saw her.

"Hey," I said, somehow winded just by looking at her. She wore her hair in her signature bun and had on a button-up and gray slacks. I had the inane thought that I was glad I got to see her dressed like this because it'd be easier to imagine her back at work in a few days.

"Hey. I'm heading out."

I squinted. "Good. Yeah." I rounded my desk, summoning whatever bravery I could find. "I just want to say I'm glad you came here. I'm grateful for the time we had together. And I hope you have a beautiful life."

Her lashes fluttered and she sniffed. "Thank you. But,

hey, I'll see you again, right? I don't leave until Wednesday. I've got stuff lined up with family and everything, but I'd love to see you at least one more time."

I forced a chuckle. "Of course. I'd love that. And I hope you enjoy the time with family. I'm sure Jo has something fun planned."

This was all so surface level. So mundane and it felt like such a waste.

It felt like my heart was army-crawling its way up my throat.

She smiled, too. "Yeah. I've got to eat as much Mexican food as possible in the next few days."

We talked another minute, lame small talk stuff, and then she left.

I sat back down at my desk and stared at the screen, willing myself to find something to do to channel this genuine angst trying to choke out my good sense.

What I'd said was true, though. I was grateful. Even now, the agony of this distance growing between us, both emotionally and physically, I was grateful for every second she spent with me.

Eventually, I'd sit here and not think of her standing in my doorway. At some point, I'd look up at Silver Ridge Peak and not think of the times we'd spent in my back yard by the fire with the stars overhead and the shadowy mountains setting the scene.

Someday, maybe I'd want to touch someone else, and want to be touched. I'd long for a kiss from someone who wasn't her. I'd hope for a future with someone else.

And for now, I'd let it hurt, because I knew what happened if I didn't.

CHAPTER FORTY-FIVE

Elizabeth

I'd eaten my body weight in guacamole but abstained from tequila despite the very real temptation to drown my sorrows in the drink. I didn't expect to have much of an appetite, but sitting with these women—these friends—had relaxed me enough to enjoy the company and food.

Nikki, Winnie, Catherine, Elise, Dove, and Jo had taken me to dinner, and now only four of us remained. Nikki, Winnie, and Catherine had all begged off to get home, but Elise, Dove, and Jo stayed with me, laughing over nothing and prolonging the night.

"I can't believe you're going to go back. Didn't we charm you enough to lure you here for good?" Dove asked, head resting in her palm.

"And if not us, what about Army Barbie? He's gorgeous, ridiculously sweet, and completely in love with you. What more do you want?" Elise said, though her words were a little squishy because she had indulged in a margarita or two.

Dove giggled and Jo hid her smile.

"He's wonderful. You all are. Silverton is. Being near family is," I said, making sure Jo could see I really meant it. "But this is my job. It's been my life for my entire adulthood."

"Seems to me that's the problem. Your job is your life. You have friends there? Family? A lover?"

My stomach flipped at the word *lover*. True enough, I could've had that here.

"No. I don't have any of those things, which is exactly why it's been such a treat to be here and witness my sister and dad having them, and getting a little taste for myself."

Jo gave me a look but patted the table. "I'm going to run to the bathroom and then we're all going home. We're getting a little too morose for my taste."

Once she'd slipped out of the booth, Dove and Elise leaned in. My eyes widened because this was most definitely a coordinated attack.

"You're making the wrong choice," Elise said, right as Dove piped in, "This is really a bad call."

"Going back? To my life and job, which I always planned on returning to?" No doubt the incredulity shone through every syllable.

"Yep. You're going to regret it," Elise said, looking at her nails like she didn't really care, but also needed me to know.

"You just told us seeing your family happy has been a treat. Do you really think life should be miserable? So miserable you have to 'treat yoself' to normal human relationships and interactions when you're on vacation?"

I leaned back, feeling more than a little attacked but also... well, maybe a little convicted by their words. Had I meant that? That this time had been a treat, and I was back to a diet version of life when I left?

"I don't think I've felt that way before living here. I've been happy."

Jo slid into the booth and set a hand on my arm. "Have you, though? When you visited last summer, you certainly didn't seem all that happy. Isn't that why you came here instead of traveling or even hanging out in DC?"

"I—" I tried to swallow, my mouth dry as dust, then reached for my water. No one spoke as I guzzled the liquid, my mind floating and not landing on a single word until I set down the drink. "I don't know."

Jo shook her head ever so slightly. "I think you do. And I think it scares you that you do—maybe you don't want to."

My teeth ground together. "I don't expect you all to understand. You have a wonderful little community here and an amazing group of friends, but that's not what everyone wants. That's not—" I cleared my throat, unable to force out the words I'd planned to say and instead rerouting. "That's not what everyone can have."

The life of a spy is lonely, by definition and also on purpose. We lived apart and only reconnected for bursts to recenter ourselves.

I'd done just that during my time here and now it'd come to an end. *Such is life. My life.*

A bus boy came and cleared the table. We'd paid long ago and they were ready to close up. I'd forgotten it was a Monday and even during ski season the restaurants closed by nine on weekdays.

I hugged Elise and Dove goodbye, each of them wishing me safe travels and extracting promises that I'd Zoom into their book clubs at least every other month.

Jo walked me to my door. I'd see her again at family

dinner tomorrow night, but my heart thudded in my chest like this was goodbye for us, too.

"I know I'm your little sister and I've always made very different choices than you have. I know you want to believe that your destiny or fate or path or *whatever* is to go back to your job and toil away until you retire, but I want to call bs on that." She shifted on her feet and tucked her hands close to her chest. "I want to beg you to consider that you could do something different and it might be amazing. I know it feels final and scary and just... maybe completely insane. Maybe it is. But I don't want you going back because you think it's the only option. You have choices and if you decided to, you could have a very different life."

I took her in, this woman who'd grown and changed in incalculable ways. I'd missed so much time with her, but I'd regained some, too. We'd broken through walls we'd erected over the years when I first visited Silverton last year for her book signing, and that closeness was what had prompted me to come back.

"I know it's hard for you to understand. You've chosen a career path that is so full of joy and gives you life." I squeezed her hands. "I love that for you and am so grateful you've found your way."

"But?" she said, shaking my hands where she gripped them right back.

"But I don't have anything like that. I don't have a secret passion I've been neglecting. I don't have aspirations I'm ignoring. I'm doing the job I always wanted to do." My mind jarred at the admission, the words hitting me like a metal mallet to a gong.

"Okay. That's fair. But I'd like to suggest that since you've been doing the job you've always wanted and you don't seem anything close to happy, you—"

"I am happy, Jojo, I—"

"Please, at the very least, stop lying to yourself, okay? Choose the job. Choose the life you've worked hard to establish. Absolutely. But please don't pretend you're happy and living a life you imagined for yourself at thirty-five."

Her big brown eyes were pleading and though the words were harsh, they came from the depth of her. They emerged from that big heart she'd always worn on her sleeve and that I so admired.

But if listening to her feelings had been her forte, functioning in a pragmatic reality had always been my specialty. "That's the thing, though. I've never imagined anything other than what I have."

Her brow furrowed and she shook her head like she couldn't decide what to do with me. Then she yanked on my hands and pulled me into a hug.

"I love you so much, even when you're more stubborn than a mule."

We laughed softly together as we pulled apart.

"Thank you for caring about me and wanting the very best for me. I don't deserve you," I said, tucking a strand of her long chestnut hair behind one ear like I used to do when she was little and I felt grown.

She sighed. "That right there's what I'm trying to get you to see. You do deserve me. And Dad. And Jane. The whole Saint crew and Elise and Dove and the girls. You deserve a workplace that appreciates you. And you, my dear sister, deserve to be loved by someone like Kenny Carmichael."

The frown covered the wobble of my chin, or so I hoped. She patted my cheek gently, then a touch harder just like *she* used to do, and we laughed at the callback, breaking the tension and the emotion creeping into my throat.

"Thanks for tonight," I said, meaning it with every bit of me.

"Thanks for choosing to be here, at least for a while."

We parted and I climbed the stairs to my apartment. Wednesday would be here too soon. Everything felt too soon.

But what else could I do, really? I had a commitment to fulfill, and it wasn't like abandoning my career of nearly fifteen years and moving to a small mountain town was actually an option.

Was it?

I spent an hour packing up everything I could before surrendering to tossing and turning in bed. I didn't want to think about all the people I wouldn't see. I definitely didn't want to think about all the things in Jo's life I'd miss.

And that wasn't even touching Kenny, which I stoutly did my best to ignore.

My work made a difference. It saved lives. What I did helped make the world a better place. The people at Saint did it here in Silverton, but my job had an impact on the global scale. This had to count for something... and someone had to do it. Take one for the team. That it was me... I could live with it. I had for years. Mostly.

I finally surrendered to sleep around two in the morning, but a banging on my door woke me around four. I jolted out of bed and sprinted to the door, yanking it open after seeing Kenny through the spy hole. His whole energy was wired and distressed. Maybe he hadn't slept?

"What are you—"

"Jack and Evie are gone."

CHAPTER FORTY-SIX

Kenny

Liz didn't hesitate.

She said, "Give me three minutes" and raced away, fast enough I couldn't truly appreciate the tiny sleep shorts and barely there shirt she was wearing. I shouldn't be admiring her right now anyway, or maybe not at all anymore.

My phone rang and I took the call, getting an update from Cookie on local police responses. Beast would be into the office soon and he'd help us pinpoint them if Cookie couldn't manage it before then.

They were unlikely to have their phones, but we might get lucky. We'd know in the next minute or two, and we'd also attempt to activate Jack's beacon. Since he was a VIP client, he had additional coverage with us while he was in town. Our main hope was that would lead us to his location.

Liz jogged out of her room in black pants, utility boots,

and a long sleeve T. We'd gear up at Saint, so these were a good start. We hustled out of her place, then jogged the block and a half to the Saint building, where Tristan was waiting for us with gear.

"Still working on location but we got a call from the Juniper View Sherriff saying one of his residents had made a call about something suspicious he thought we might want to know about," Tristan explained as we walked to the tactical room where Bruce and Cookie were gearing up.

"I let him know we had a situation before I went to get Liz. He's a good dude and if he's got a flag raised, we should look closer."

I'd gotten to know the Sherriff of Juniper View in the last few years as he served on a county-wide advisory board I'd joined. After that, we'd ended up playing soccer against each other in a casual adult soccer league and discovered our shared military backgrounds. He had a reputation for being wise and fair, and his popularity was likely unhurt by the fact that he was also a single dad and decent-looking. Knowing he was clued in and letting us know what's going on was incredibly good news.

A few minutes later, we'd gotten no official word. They couldn't get a signal on the beacon, but after talking to the sheriff, my gut said we needed to move.

"I know we can't roll on hunches, but this one feels big," I said, watching Beast and Cookie rolling through information at a pace I couldn't even pretend to emulate. Having two fewer fingers on my left hand was part of it, sure, but their ability to follow a thread electronically was masterful.

Bruce ended a call. "Police are out in force here and Sheriff Ryan has patrols going in Juniper View and the surrounding area. But it's time to move. Malcom?" He looked at Liz.

"Kenny's right. Worst case, we spend time driving out there and if something changes, you signal and we haul back." She glanced at me. "But you guys do this. You know what fits for a domestic or even celebrity kidnapping, so I'm following your lead."

Bruce snapped at Kenny as his phone rang again. "Go with it. Stay in touch. Take a sat phone just in case and I want reports in every twenty once you get there." He ducked his face to the phone and spoke.

We moved.

In minutes, we'd loaded up into a vehicle and were on the road. Sunrise was still a little more than two hours away, though we'd have the sky lightening up for us in an hour and a half.

"What did we miss?" Liz asked from the passenger seat. She'd brought a tablet with all the case files and information on it.

"I'm not sure we missed anything we could've caught. This is one problem of being law enforcement adjacent. We're not officials so we can only do so much—legally, there's even less we can do."

The temptation to stop problems before they started was always there. Not necessarily take someone out entirely but maybe intimidate someone—scare 'em straight, so to speak. But the moral compass of the Saint leadership, and I dared say every one of the team, was unflagging.

"Was anyone watching the ex? If the LAPD haven't found him yet, that seems like a pretty bad sign." She swiped at the screen.

"Agreed. Seems like he's here and he probably has Jack and Evie. There must be more than one person involved, though, because Jack isn't dumb and he's not a small man. He just spent time training with the SEALS and EMU prior to shooting a movie where he plays a Tier One guy, so he's even got some decent self-defense skills."

It didn't make sense, honestly, and second only to having them safe was the need to understand what'd happened.

We drove in silence for a while, me doing my best not to let my mind stray from the road ahead and her reading through the information on the case. When the sat phone rang, she answered.

"We're... ten minutes out from the edge of town," I said, estimating being able to cut some minutes this time of night when we came out of the canyon.

She relayed the information and in the corner of my eye, she perked up, energy sliding through her in a jerky movement.

"We're going. I'm ready to copy." She then tapped out coordinates, repeated them, and we ended the call.

"There's a signal coming from this location. It's five minutes out of town." She took the GPS and adjusted our destination. Seven minutes now.

Five.

Three.

We parked blocks away from a small house on the end of a street that abutted a national forest. My heart thundered in my chest, the adrenaline amping up, pouring into my bloodstream and readying my body. The years of training kicked in now, even when I only got to do this kind of mission every so often.

I took a breath and steadied my pulse, my heart rate, my breath, my mind.

"Ready?" she asked, appearing so damn calm I would've thought she was asking me to take a leisurely stroll.

So attractive. Completely *not* the time for the thought, but it settled into my silly little brain anyway.

"Go."

I moved, she followed. Though she was immensely capable, I had more experience. If we'd brought personnel, we'd have a breaching group to do this job with a bit more heft, but that was the challenge of spreading out to follow a hunch. Fortunately, this one appeared to be right.

Every bit of me hoped it was. I wanted to open that front door and see Evie and Jack sitting uninjured on a couch and have all this mess be done with.

Light shone from a window at the back of the house and we moved, sliding along the west-facing side of the house toward it. I peeked in and didn't see anyone, but the window was high and there very well could be someone right there. We crept closer, grateful this part of the yard wasn't snow-covered or we'd be announcing our arrival by crunching along in the snow.

There was a storm door and a back door which was cracked slightly—an easy way in. But also, likely the way our bad guy got inside. Liz's instincts were good—she grabbed the metal handle of the storm door, ready to swing it open. It looked rusted, and I didn't have what I'd need to stop the squeaking, so we were about to announce our arrival. I held up a hand as we made eye contact, then dropped it. She yanked the door open and I slipped in as she did, kicking the main door and scoping for threats.

The only person in the room was Jack, who lay on the ground, bound and apparently unconscious. I swore under my breath but after checking his pulse and feeling it was strong, we kept moving to clear the house.

In minutes, we'd moved through the entire two-bedroom home and found no evidence of anyone else, let alone Evie.

Liz called in to Bruce and the command post while I cut through the duct tape at Jack's hands, feet, and gently removed it from his lips. The movement roused him slightly and he blinked, instantly reaching for his shoulder. Might be dislocated based on the way he was moving.

"You're alright, Jack. We're still looking for Evie. Paramedics are on their way."

His speech was slurred but he nodded, and after another minute, he could speak and passed some tests that told me he was groggy from being drugged, not recovering post-stroke. My pulse slowed as he told me who the president was, what month it was, and so on.

Tristan came on the line then. "We got a call from Sheriff Ryan a few minutes ago. He was in pursuit of someone speeding who ran a red light. They ended up abandoning the car and running into the woods. He stopped to check on Evie who'd been abandoned in the car, and she was in distress, so he stayed with her. We need you guys to get to him and offer support until medical can get there."

"She's hurt?" Liz asked, her jaw hardening as she likely imagined all the ways she'd make Evie's ex pay.

"Not sure. The main issue is, she's having the baby now."

CHAPTER FORTY-SEVEN

Elizabeth

Two ambulances had been dispatched but in a town this small, it would take a minute.

Kenny had explained they didn't usually have anyone on duty, just on call. We were racing toward the location on foot once Cookie mapped it and found we'd be best off that way. We'd have backup from Saint coming in the next fifteen minutes, and we'd left Jack once we could see the sirens of another local deputy approaching and Jack assured us he wanted us to go.

"She'll be fine. She's gonna be fine," Kenny said, almost chanting it like he could will it into happening.

I wasn't about to stop him. I needed Evie to be okay. We'd seen Jack, and he was going to need a little therapy maybe, and something for the shoulder at least, but he'd be okay. Next up, Evie.

And then, catching the idiot who thought he could get away with this in the first place.

We froze when we heard a rustle in the trees and a loud thump, then cursing. Another voice rang out.

"Pipe down!"

Aside from the fact the person had whisper-yelled the words, they were being fairly quiet. Not by any trained standard, but for a bunch of criminals in the woods, sure.

The moonlight gave us enough light we could see each other, but it was the modified night vision we both wore now that allowed us to move. I was grateful I'd spent some time under NODs despite not typically using many of my tactical skills.

Kenny directed me with hand and arm signals. We moved forward, fanning out slightly, and he got the drop on one of the men while I took down the other. I held out my leg and shoved him forward, guiding his shoulder down, wrenched one arm, then the other, behind him. I quickly zip-tied his hands, then rolled him over to make sure none of the ground cover was causing him breathing difficulties.

"Good?" Kenny asked from where he shoved the second guy over on his back. He must've done something very similar to what I had. He walked over. "Let me stick with them and you push ahead."

Get to Evie, he meant.

A small hit of relief spread through me. I'd been worried about catching these geniuses, but the fact they were on foot and this forest was about to be swarming with local PD and Saint Security staff meant I wasn't worried they would be found.

I was extremely concerned for Evie.

She wasn't a friend, exactly, but I cared about her. I wanted her to have a shot at a life that made her happy. She and her baby deserved to be safe and cared for. I touched his arm, squeezed, and ran.

I worked on pulling off my equipment and letting my eyes adjust as I ran—not an easy feat, but as I approached the road, I could see police lights flashing and we'd heard the ambulance arrive right as we'd taken down the two perps.

Even knowing she and the sheriff had reinforcements, I pushed as much as I could until I reached the road, rounding the car and nearly choking when I glanced at the ambulance and saw Evie sitting on a stretcher cradling a tiny baby.

I couldn't even see the baby's head, but she was gazing down at the little person in her arms with such love that had to be it. Someone was checking her blood pressure and someone else was moving her into the vehicle.

"Evie!" I yelled, running toward her.

A large—and I do mean actually rather gigantic—man stepped in my path. "Ma'am, I'm going to have to ask—"

"It's okay. She's with the security team. Please, Grant. Let her through."

The large man nodded and stepped aside, and I rushed to her, shoving my weapon into its holster and securing it before I made it to her side.

"You had your baby," I said, announcing the most obvious thing of all time.

She giggled, then tears pricked her eyes. "I did. In a car. It's a boy."

I laughed. "Oh my gosh, congratulations, but are you okay?"

"We're taking her to Silverton Hospital to get her and baby checked out. In fact, ma'am, I'm going to need you to step back so we can get the baby secured and get her taken care of."

Evie squeezed my hand. "Thank you for coming for me. Is Jack okay?"

"He's conscious. He'll be okay."

She nodded, lips pressing together.

"I'll come visit when I can."

"Okay." She smiled, and it cut right to my heart. This woman was brave as hell and had just done something incredible in the worst circumstances.

One door swung closed, but before the other one shut entirely, Evie yelled, "Thank you, Sheriff. I'll never forget this."

For his part, the large man tipped his hat—an actual sheriff's hat—and cleared his throat.

"I guess you're Sherriff Ryan. I'm Elizabeth Malcom. I've been working with Kenny Carmichael."

His face split into a small but very handsome smile. "Ah, Kenny. I assume he's around here somewhere?"

"He's got the perps. I'm assuming the rest of the crew will be marching them right here to you any minute." I craned my neck to see into the woods, but it was too bright out here to see much into that darkness.

"Appreciate the help," he said, his face serious again.

"Seems like you handled things as well as you could. Did she... I mean, I guess everything went okay?" I asked, not sure what he could tell me. It was amazing the paramedics were here to help.

"First time I've delivered a baby roadside, but she was amazing, and the baby seemed as healthy as could be despite the odds." His brow dropped low, his face severe. "He's got a good one in Evie, that's for sure."

"He does. And... thank you for helping her."

"It's my job." Garbled voices came through on his radio and he dipped his head and mumbled something into the mic on his shoulder, then looked at me. "Want a ride to the other site? Your team's there now."

He shuttled me around the forest to the neighborhood where we'd found Jack and met up with the rest of the Saint team, several members of the Silverton Sheriff's department, and Kenny. Silverton had already read the two kidnappers their rights, and they were being loaded into a vehicle.

I reported on Evie, and Kenny and I agreed we wanted to check on Jack and Evie as soon as we could. Since we weren't the police, though, we wouldn't have access to them right away while they were getting attended to, so once back in Silverton, we went our separate ways to get cleaned up.

In the ensuing hours, the police discovered Evie's ex had learned she was in Utah after paparazzi photos of Jack appeared online. While his assumption that she and Jack were lovers and he'd taken her to be his wife and live here with him had been wrong, he'd been unnervingly successful at gaining access to Jack's home after just a few days of planning. The Saint staff were already working to address the issues they could, as the house hadn't been under their contract thus far.

When Beast had learned it'd been a Mandee Carmichael who'd tipped off the paparazzi about Jack McKean's whereabouts, my heart sank. But Kenny nodded, like he'd known. I wondered if he had, or had simply gotten to a place where he refused to be surprised by his family's betrayal. I hated it for him, but thankfully, the overall outcome was a good one.

We visited Jack first, whose driver arrived to take him home after he'd had his shoulder examined. A dislocation and inflammation already, but he'd likely be fine with lots of care.

We also saw Evie, who let us each hold the baby. I hadn't been prepared for that, or how tiny he was, but the moment Kenny cradled the swaddled shape into his arms and spoke in a whisper, a part of me came alive.

I couldn't verbalize why the sight of this man whispering tender words to a baby who wasn't his made me want to weep, but it certainly did.

We left not long after, afraid to stay too long, but not before Evie held my hand and pinned me with her wonderfully peaceful eyes.

"I know this is all in a day's work for you, but I have to say thank you again. I'm so grateful for your help, your protection, and the way you believed me and wanted to help and protect me from the minute we met, even from someone like Jack if he'd turned out to be a jerk."

We laughed, both fairly aware Jack wasn't at all a jerk.

"I'm so grateful to have met you, Evie. I hope you have an amazing life full of all the things you've ever wanted." And I meant that down to my toes.

"I hope the same for you, Elizabeth."

I thanked her and walked out, joining Kenny in the hallway and slowly moving toward the hospital exit, my heart fairly burning from the events of the night, Evie's thoughtful words ringing in my head, and what had to come next.

It was noon by the time we stepped out into the cool early March air, and I'd promised Jo I'd be at my dad's house by three. I needed to finish packing and return the apartment keys.

And worst of all, I needed to say goodbye to the man I was completely in love with.

CHAPTER FORTY-EIGHT

Kenny

What an incredible night.

Call me old-fashioned, but nothing made me love a girl like seeing her take down bad guys and successfully execute a hostage rescue.

But really, working with her only cemented one more thing in the arsenal of skill, beauty, and kindness she possessed, and it threatened to undo me.

Especially now that this really was goodbye.

"Thanks for letting me tag along," she said, toeing a rock near her shoe.

"My pleasure, really. We make a good team." She had to see that, didn't she?

"We do." Her eyes bored into mine, seeing past the smile I only barely felt straight into the heart of me.

It was on the tip of my tongue to ask her to stay. Maybe

she could be happy working here. Maybe she could be happy with me.

But if I asked her to walk away, what kind of man was I? What kind of person asks someone he loves to leave what she loved? To sacrifice what she wanted most for him?

Not me. I couldn't do it—wouldn't.

Elizabeth had a successful career that was far from over and she could stay and let the years roll on, continuing to make a difference on a potentially global scale.

I knew the pain of having that purpose torn from you, and even if I wanted her desperately, I wouldn't foist that on her. I couldn't.

"Thank you for all the time you gave me," I said, my voice rough from the long night and yeah, maybe a little emotion, too.

Her hand rose to press against my stubbled cheek. "Thank you for giving me this glimpse."

A hundred things raced into my head to say—an argument to make her stay, a joke to lighten the moment, a declaration of the truth—that I loved her so completely I didn't know how I would function once she really left. That I would give her not a glimpse, but a lifetime, if she'd just let me.

But before I could land on anything, she pulled me in for a hot, fierce kiss, then turned and left.

I watched her go until she turned the corner to the parking garage. I debated running after her and stealing another kiss, or maybe dropping to my knees to beg her to give me another moment with her. But I'd determined to let her go so she could leave without guilt.

Resolved not to have a breakdown at work, I decided to have lunch at home before returning. I'd let myself take a minute and feel my feelings like a healthy human being, eat the leftover soup from dinner last night, and get back to the office to start fresh. I didn't need to work a long day since we'd started early, but the thought of staying here didn't fit.

I got home and stumbled to the couch. Kit sniffed along my arm, then jumped and settled his little bum right against my forehead where it rested on the couch.

"Thank you so much," I said, voice ragged with tears.

His soft meow trilled, and he readjusted, curling his little face toward me and licking my cheek. Gross, considering he bathed himself with that tongue, but still a sweet gesture I wouldn't ignore.

"Come here," I said, cradling him to me. I settled back, resting him on my chest, and watched as he circled, then snuggled down into me. A sliver of the agony shredding my heart eased as I watched his little body rise and fall with his breaths.

After crying, then calming, I returned to work and powered through the last few hours of the day. There was enough to do in terms of writing up a report of what had happened last night, and it was best to do it when it was fresh.

And hey, I only teared up like twelve times while writing it. Yay, me.

That night, I somehow convinced everyone—especially Cookie and Stone—that I was fine. I'd been up much of the night, and I truly just wanted to sleep. To wake up and decide to live the new day, so I did.

Only problem with that plan was knowing her flight had taken off and every minute of the day was taking her farther away. It just felt so wrong.

"Do you want to look at the assignments board with me?" Bruce asked, interrupting my dazed stare into a coffee mug.

"Sure," I said, no excitement whatsoever for the idea, but knowing I needed to get some plans on my horizon. I had to.

I followed him into his office and took a seat. Wilder was there, too.

"Hey, Saint."

"Barbie."

"Elizabeth was pretty subdued at the family dinner last night."

Pain lanced through me. "Yeah. Leaving has to be hard."

Wilder nodded. "Especially when you're leaving loved ones."

Loved ones. Why did everything he said make this hurt worse, not better? "Yeah, I bet."

"And especially since she's leaving a place I don't think she wants to leave."

My head snapped up to inspect him. "What does that mean?"

He waited like he thought it might occur to me naturally, but acquiesced and explained. "She clung to Jo and Darcy with everything she had. She was as close to distraught as I can imagine that woman being."

My heart hurt. My *soul* hurt. "I hate that."

He nodded. "Yeah. It was awful."

Bruce clapped as though we'd gotten off-track and he was redirecting, as though he was completely oblivious to the gut-wrenching conversation going on directly in front of him.

"Not sure what you're thinking for my next assignment, but—"

"Did you know there's a listing for Europe right now?" Bruce asked.

I blinked.

"Hijack's popping back for a bit and we need someone out who's flexible. But that person could, should they have a reason to stay in one place, choose to live in any city that's near a major airport."

A glimmer of light slipped into the darkness in my chest. "That's... interesting."

Wilder just stared, but Bruce nodded meaningfully. "Isn't it?"

"But I'm not sure if... um, well, if the city would want me there."

Wilder huffed softly and said, "The city wants you."

Bruce grinned. "I think the city wants you any way the city can get you. And we want you, too. So we'll work with you to make this work."

Throat tight, I swallowed hard. "What are you saying?" I couldn't afford to misunderstand this.

"They're saying you can be with her and keep your job at Saint, too." My head snapped to the doorway where Cookie leaned in. "They're also about to say that you're booked on a flight to Budapest first thing tomorrow, so you better go pack."

Everything clicked into place and I knew. They were right. I couldn't leave my family at Saint Security, but the idea of living without Liz was unbearable. I didn't know if she'd want me, but I had to try. I had to offer up this compromise that didn't take from her and allowed me to keep the things dearest to me.

I cackled and shot out of my chair.

"I'll take it."

CHAPTER FORTY-NINE

Elizabeth

Somehow, I'd survived the last forty-eight hours in one piece.

Well, all except half my heart and some pieces of my soul, which I'd left in Silverton, tucked away with the people I loved.

Returning to my drab apartment and my sterile office only drilled the choice I'd made home. Then walking into the office and getting back into the thick of things had felt... oddly thin. Because work hadn't stopped without me here. Leads had been uncovered and followed, assets had been reined in, tips had been investigated. All without me. Without a shred of input or insight from me, from my position and job.

I'd always thought I was a cog in a big mechanism, but had felt like I mattered in that context. Turned out, the mechanism hadn't even needed me, let alone missed me. Sure, my boss and colleagues seemed glad I was back, but after the weeks in Silverton, all those faces felt practically unfamiliar to me. They certainly didn't know *me*.

What did it say about my life, my purpose, my whole reason for being? Every move I made here made this ring in my head, and every step I'd taken away from Silverton and every old routine I'd run through in the last few hours pushed me toward one very clear conclusion.

I didn't want this anymore.

This life had begun as a dream for me. Truly, I'd been exhilarated by the work for a long time. The thankless long hours, the risk, the distance, the feeling of being an *other* in any given country I lived in despite speaking the language and knowing the customs after preparing for months... I'd loved it all.

Until I hadn't.

Sometime in the last few years, I'd lost that focus and sense of purpose. At some point, all of the hard things just started feeling harder, and the good things didn't balance them out.

And then I went to Silverton.

I saw the possibilities I'd never even fathomed. They weren't pictures I'd ever seen or dreamed of in my childhood. They were a version of life I couldn't have imagined and wouldn't have believed if I hadn't seen them myself.

I saw Jo so completely in love with Adam and witnessed his sacrificial, encompassing love right back. I'd seen my dad happier than he'd ever been in my memory, not only loving Jane and her family, but working in the bookshop and reinventing himself.

And I met Kenny.

Just the thought of him brought a fresh and very unwelcome round of tears to my eyes.

He'd been genuine. He'd pursued me but didn't pressure me. Kenny had shown me so much beauty—in his town, in the people there, in his cobbled together family at Saint, and in his care and love for me.

I'd known it the night he left me with apologies, and I'd known it each time we parted in the last few days. He loved me.

I'd willed him to ask me to stay. I'd almost begged him to say anything to deter me from coming back to this life, and yet he'd encouraged me. He'd been glad for me, even.

The anger I'd felt at him for that was real, but somewhere over the Atlantic, I'd realized he never would've done anything else. Kenny would never stop cheering for the people he cared about, nor would he do anything to deter them from pursuing their dreams.

Hadn't he come from a dynamic that discouraged and put down? Hadn't he faced a family who sneered at his desire for more, at his pursuit of service and anything beyond what they already had?

Of course he wouldn't sentence anyone else to those same experiences.

Plus, his past was full of betrayal from the people he should've been able to trust. He needed safety and security in a relationship. We hadn't had a relationship, exactly, but it'd felt like it. Within the little cocoon of our time together, I'd been willing to share things I'd never told anyone.

What he needed was someone to choose him overtly, repeatedly, and in an undeniable way.

I'd come back to work citing the commitment I'd made, but the truth rested in my gut, lodged there with an aching clarity. Coming back here was the safe bet, and it was running away, like I'd done so many times through my life.

Had I grown in any way? Matured? Learned anything at all these last few years, or even my thirty-five so far?

I thought I made a difference here, and I had. Maybe I was a replaceable cog, but it didn't diminish that I'd taken down bad actors, had saved many women's lives. But I'd also made a difference in Silverton. Evie was proof of it.

It wasn't the job that mattered, ultimately. *How long has it taken me to realize this?*

It was what I was doing with my life. Wherever I was, I could make a difference. It was all on me and not the job title, per se. I could choose how to spend my time and the things I'd learned, just like Jo chose to gift the world with books that brought joy and delight, and it brought her the same to do so.

I get to choose.

The moment this clicked, I knew what I had to do.

I got to work setting everything in motion—it'd be a long day, but hopefully by the end of it, all the details would be settled.

I made it back to my apartment, shot off a dinner order at my favorite delivery place, and got to work packing. When I'd called the regional chief and told him my plan, he'd been, not surprisingly, furious. When I'd talked to my deputy station chief, he'd been more than delighted because my change most likely held a promotion for him.

Was I planning to fly back across the Atlantic within twenty-four hours of arriving? Sure was. Did it feel a little wild? Sure did.

But there was a peace in my soul I hadn't experienced in... quite possibly ever.

Successful spies didn't often retire—it was those who couldn't stand the isolation, or the burnout, or the red tape that still cropped up sometimes. Occasionally, people at the top of their game did, and I'd seen the proof of that with my own eyes all along in Silverton, aka Eddie James-Williamson. She'd done it, had left a career destined to be a bright one, and was living her best life in this small town with friends, family, and the man she loved.

Somehow, this epitomized hope for me. Maybe I could, too...

Maybe I'd hit that wall, too. I couldn't say I wasn't burned out. But none of the why mattered when I knew the *who*. The *where*. And as soon as I could make it happen, the *when*.

I started a load of laundry, cleaned up a bit in the apartment, though it was fairly spotless since I'd cleaned it thoroughly before I left, knowing I wouldn't want to come back to a mess.

The bell rang and I shuffled to the door, eager for sustenance since I'd not managed to get to the grocery store. I pulled open the door, already saying what great time the person made as I swiped through my phone for the app to confirm it was my order.

But I froze when I looked up.

"Kenny?"

His shy smile nearly catapulted me directly into his arms, but I resisted, still nailed to the spot where I stood.

"Hey, Liz."

I laughed and it sounded a little crazed. "What are you doing here?"

His brow furrowed, but he pinned his gorgeous blue gaze on mine. "I'm here for you."

Well, knock me over with a small gust of air. I was pretty sure there wasn't anything more thrilling than hearing this man say that.

"You are? How? What does that mean?" My heart galloped in my chest. I couldn't believe he was actually here.

Wait, he was *here*, and still standing in the hallway of my building. "First, come inside." I stepped back out of the entrance so he could come in. He had only a backpack with him and he somehow smelled like himself—laundry detergent and mint and something else fresh, instead of airplane.

His eyes tracked over the small kitchen, living room, and the door to the bedroom. "This is... different than I imagined."

"Oh? Did you think it'd be nicer?"

He shrugged a shoulder. "I honestly don't know. I didn't actually imagine anything specific. Maybe it's just being here is the odd thing."

I swallowed convulsively, nerves shooting through me. I hadn't even felt elation or excitement yet because he was so serious and almost subdued, and I didn't know what to make of it.

"Um, so, I'm here because I took a travel position with Saint. I'm the new European post."

His eyes were glued to mine, and it took me a heartbeat to absorb his meaning. "You're moving to Europe."

"Yes. To be with you, if you'll have me."

My shattered heart knitted back together in this instant,

like he'd hit rewind and every little piece that'd cleaved from the whole had been restored.

I launched at him and he caught me, his strong arms wrapping me up and his mouth meeting mine with as much determination and relief as I felt. We shifted, and then he was sliding his hand down, urging me to jump and I did, only halting the kiss for a moment to wrap my legs around his hips before I dove back in, wanting to be closer and closer to this man I loved.

He stumbled, tripping over something, and caught himself on the wall near my bedroom.

"Sorry. I'm really not trying to destroy your place," he said between kisses.

Your place.

That phrase smacked me upside the head, and I pulled back, knowing he needed the truth more now than ever.

"I really don't want to stop you from having your way with me, but I also really need to say a few things," I said, breath heaving in the wake of his glorious kisses.

His smiling face sobered slightly, and he stole another kiss before setting me down. "Please say whatever you need to."

I took his hand and led him to the couch, where we sat side by side. I kept his warm hand clasped in mine as I spoke.

"When I left, I was genuinely hoping you'd ask me to stay."

Pain lanced across his face. "I'm so sorry. I should've. But I didn't want you to feel anything but glad to go back to the life you've built. You have an incredible career you've fought for, and I didn't want to be someone trying to take away from that in any way."

Ugh, this man. He was so deeply good and loving. "Thank you."

He huffed.

"But also, I need you to know, especially in light of what you just told me, that I've just resigned my position and am no longer living in Europe as of about twenty-four hours from now."

CHAPTER FIFTY

Kenny

This woman would likely never fail to surprise me.

I might've wished for something like this, but it did not compute.

"I'm sorry... what?" I truly didn't fully understand what she was saying.

She grinned, shifting so she straddled my waist and cupped my face. "I love you, Kenny Carmichael, and I want to be with you. I'm tired of doing this job and tired of toiling in isolation. I don't know exactly what comes next, but these last few months have given me a picture and it's so beautiful."

I could barely let her finish before surging forward and kissing her beautiful face. Good grief, had she really just said that to me? Was I hallucinating somewhere over the ocean and I'd end up arriving here to find a different version of this story?

If so, please flight attendant ma'am or sir, do not wake me.

"I love you, too. So freaking much," I said between kisses. I pulled back. "I wanted to tell you, but—"

Her index finger pressed against my lips. "I know you have things to say to me, but I'm going to talk first, okay?"

My heart flipped because I did *not* mind bossy, in charge Liz, but I also loved that she wanted to say her piece. And I wanted to hear it.

"Alright then. Please proceed." I settled my hands on her waist and promised myself I would keep them there and resist the temptation to touch her anywhere else until she was done.

She grinned, then cleared her throat and regained her composure. "I haven't been happy in a long time—probably years, if I'm honest. You showed me not only what dating someone wonderful could be like, but also what life in a community looked like. And along with wanting you, kind of desperately..."

She gripped my shirt and tugged at it.

You will not kiss her again until she's done talking. No. Don't do it. This is what you've been training for!

She grinned, no doubt seeing the heat flash in my eyes.

"I also wanted that place. Those mountains. I want to call my sister while living in the same time zone and meet her for lunch on a workday. See my dad laughing and being a freaking grandpa to his stepkids' children. I want the Silver Ridge Romance Readers official membership designation, and I want to know every store owner by name."

This woman... I broke my rules and hugged her tight, wanting to cradle her close and tuck her near me until the end of time.

Okay, well, actually I had a few other things in mind, but that was a good start.

She inched away but left her hands on my shoulders, pressed a kiss to my mouth, then leaned back.

"What I don't totally understand is what *we* do next."

I hummed. "I have some very specific ideas of what we do next."

She grinned again and I chuckled, then settled back against the couch. "I resign my job as the European post right after we go back to Silverton and tell Kit the good news."

She laughed softly. "I feel like there might be a few other people I need to talk to about this."

"Fair. But Kit will need a personal debrief."

She nodded with a fakely serious expression. "Absolutely."

There was so much hope bursting through me, I could hardly breathe through it. "Bruce already said you could have a job at Saint any time and I know that's true. I have no idea if you're interested in that line of work, but I think you'd be an incredible part of the team. No—I know it."

Her hands traced over my pecs, sending cascades of sensation down my body. I caught her wrists, fully aware my ability to concentrate on this very important conversation wouldn't survive if she kept that up.

"I do. I'll take a few weeks to make the transition and really think about it, but I loved working with you and everyone else. And even though I'm sorry they went through what they did, the Jack and Evie job was kind of amazing."

I chuckled. "I get it. Like, I never want someone to be kidnapped or in danger, but I will never get tired of being the person to help someone who really needs it."

Her gaze softened. "That is one of so many things I love about you." She leaned in for another kiss.

I accepted it happily, but a twinge of worry poked at me. "So... you're sure you want to walk away from this? I mean, hear me when I say I'm ecstatic, and I also get this is not about *me*, but I hate the thought of you making this move and regretting it."

"Thank you for being mindful of that. I'm not without some anxiousness, but I also know that coming back here was filled with dread instead of joy. I kept telling myself that wasn't part of the equation—people don't just 'follow their joy.' I mean, some people do, but I didn't. I don't. That's just not the kind of person I am."

She ran a hand through my hair, and I closed my eyes, soaking in the sensation of her nails on my scalp and the affection she was giving me so freely.

When I opened them, she spoke again.

"This change isn't just about joy for me. It's about possibility. I know what the next ten years of this job looks like because I've been living it for well over a decade. It's predictable in nature even if not location, exactly. And many people truly love it and miss it when it's gone. For me, I didn't see any other options once I got this far in, and there's this lie we tell ourselves, a kind of sunk-cost fallacy where I've spent so many years here so I can't possibly stop now when, in just ten more years, I can be done. But in ten years, I'll be forty-five. Do I want to wait that long to have a home I get to keep and a partner and to live near my family? Even if you were willing to live in Europe indefinitely, my family wouldn't be here. I've fooled myself into thinking that was okay, but it's not. And I'm not going to sacrifice those things for this job, no matter how valuable, anymore. I get to choose where I make a difference and how I live, and I know what I want now."

I loved so much about what she'd just said and there was absolutely a Kenny Carmichael doing back handsprings through an endless field at her insinuation that *I* would be her partner for years.

Yes please! Me! Me! Meeeeee!

"That makes sense," I said, attempting to maintain my composure. "I could've stayed in. Did you know that?"

Her brows rose. "After the wolves came for your fingers?"

I squeezed her waist and grinned. "Yes. After the wolves came. You don't get automatically discharged for that kind of thing. There are soldiers with more severe amputations and limb differences who choose to remain in if their rehab goes well."

"What made you leave?"

"Family. I'd planned to retire from EMU and there I was, twenty-seven and barely a decade into my service missing two fingers and dealing with the aftermath of that accident, and I heard whispers that Wilder Saint was retiring and moving to some dinky little mountain town to start a business. Rumor had it he wanted as many former EMU people as would come."

Her soft smile grew and her beauty felt like a lightning bolt to my chest. "And you ended up being one of them."

I nodded. "When I found out Bruce and Tristan were going, it was a big deal. Then when I heard Adam and Beast were, I really couldn't even pretend like I wanted to stay without them. They'd been my mentors and were funda-mental to my time there—to who I was as a man. So I sat down with Cookie and Stone, and we all agreed we'd come. Stone promised and once I had that locked in, I had no reason to stay except the service. I loved my time in the Army and especially in the EMU and there are plenty of things I miss about it, but I don't regret leaving. I don't regret making the choice to have a life I love with people I love."

She swallowed hard. "And yet, you were leaving them..."

I sighed. "For you. Yes. Because they're my family, but you... Liz, you're my whole heart. You're my future, I hope, and without you, it just wasn't going to work."

The kiss that followed was so consuming, we didn't talk anymore. We didn't talk for a long, long time after that.

CHAPTER FIFTY-ONE

Liz

I'd never imagined Jo as a screamer and I'd never thought of myself as a crier, but here we were, Jo screeching into my ear and me borderline sobbing as she squeezed me so tight and rocked me back and forth.

"This is the best day of my life. Honestly. Like, I love Adam but this is the best day. I cannot believe you're moving here. I cannot believe you aren't a badass CIA woman anymore. I can't believe you're actually admitting you're in love with Kenny!!!"

Shrill to say the least, and yet she had me laughing through the tears now.

"In some ways, me neither," I said, breathing deeply once she released me. "In other ways, this feels like an inevitability. It feels meant to be."

Saying it sent me right back to the moment Kenny had explained how he felt being here was meant to be, and I laughed, a fresh wave of tears hitting my eyes at the way this feeling, this knowledge, had come to me, too.

Jo grinned and shook her head, her eyes glittering with tears as well. "I am so happy and I know it's a huge transition, but I can see *you* are happy, too. This is going to be amazing for you."

We hugged again, and she released me fully before she stepped inside my same little apartment I'd left what felt like a lifetime ago but was in fact a matter of days. It'd been six days since I'd left Silverton. I'd planned to turn around less than forty-eight hours after arriving back in Budapest, but once Kenny got there, I slowed down my timeline. We got a hotel, moved me out as I'd planned, and then spent a few days touring the place I'd called home.

I was grateful for the opportunity to spend a little longer saying goodbye to the place where I ended my career with the CIA and Kappa. I'd expected more sadness, but what I felt, more than anything, was clarity.

Did it hurt that Kenny had been willing to give up something for me? No. In fact, it reassured me in a way I'm sure I never would've felt the lack of if he hadn't, but I was profoundly grateful he'd done it.

And as I waited for my boyfriend to come pick me up for dinner—a double date with my sister and her fiancé—I reveled in the joy and excitement I felt for the future. No dread, no sense that I could predict everything coming, and yet no fear. Was I anxious about how I'd settle in and if I was really cut out for work at Saint Security? Yes.

But was I sure that if I needed to make another change and find a totally new path for my career, I could? Absolutely yes. Because I had a support system here—family, friends, and someone who loved me in a way I could feel *and* see.

Kenny and Adam arrived and Adam hugged me, then gathered Jo to him and they moved downstairs while I grabbed my jacket. The early March air wasn't as frigid as it had been when I'd arrived in January, but much like Eastern Europe, Utah didn't plan to warm up any time soon.

"Tomorrow?" Kenny asked, his whole face lit up with expectation.

I chuckled softly and leaned up on my toes to press a kiss to his lips. "No."

He narrowed his eyes. "The next day?"

I grinned. "Nope."

His hand cupped the back of mine and he kissed me hot and hard, then released me. "Fine."

He led me down the stairs, fingers intertwined, and I had to laugh, though I tried to keep it quiet. He'd started asking me to move in with him a few hours after he'd arrived in Budapest, and I had told him I loved the idea, but I felt it was important for me to move back and adjust to life in Silverton before I also adjusted to living with him.

So far, I'd deeply regretted that choice. It felt like such a hassle to go our separate ways at the end of the day. I could only imagine how frustrating it'd be when we were leaving the same workplace.

At the same time, I saw the wisdom of my decision. I was thirty-five and knew what I wanted—him. But I was also in the midst of a huge transition, and it benefited us both to take it bit by bit. As much as he teased me about it, he made it clear he understood and respected my choice.

He also promised me he'd ask every day, and I told him he could absolutely do that, and that as many times as I said no, I didn't want him to stop asking.

So far, it'd only been a small handful of saying no, but I

had a feeling it wouldn't be too long before I simply had to say yes.

He was my future, and I knew that. A small part of me knew it the minute he showed me those mountains, and we sat quietly, and my soul took a deep breath.

I loosed a sigh and he turned, so much love in his eyes I wanted to just shout "Yes!" at him and drag him back inside.

"What's going on in that head?" He drew me closer, completely unafraid of anyone on the street who might be watching his affection for me.

"Just thinking how much I like you."

He made a pathetic face. "Just like?"

I laughed. "And love. I do love you pretty madly, too."

He dipped his head and moved so his lips were almost touching mine. "I love you, too." He gave me a lightning-fast kiss, then asked, "Now?"

I cackled. "Good try, but no."

He shrugged. "No for now, but not forever."

A stupid grin covered my face. "Not forever."

EPILOGUE

Kenny

I shook out my hands and Cookie patted my back.

"It'll be good. Promise."

His words were reassuring except I kind of hated promises like that because no one knew for sure, did they? No. They did not.

"It will be. She's all yours and you're hers. It's perfect."

Stone's faith in me and Liz was not something I would ignore, and I'd heard it before. But it didn't help the absolutely dizzying nerves sliding through me.

"Are we sure the girls are ready? Everyone's set up?" I asked, my throat dry. Why was my throat dry? I also probably had to pee because I'd been drinking so much water.

"They're ready," Doc confirmed, squinting in a way that told me he was hiding his smile.

They were all trying not to laugh at me, but I got it. I was a whole damn mess and I wouldn't pretend otherwise.

But how could I not be? I was asking Liz to marry me, and even though we'd talked about it and she'd finally answered "yes" when I'd asked her if I could ask her a few days ago, as our little game had become this last little while, so this would not be all that much of a surprise, what if... I didn't know?

What *if?*

"Nikki just confirmed they're en route and it's all good," Bruce said, tapping at his phone before slipping it into his pocket.

"And Darcy's good to go, too," Wilder added.

Okay. Okay. Really, this was it.

"Incoming in five minutes," Cookie said, his voice low.

"Scatter!" I said, my dang throat dry as a July afternoon. I shuffled toward the bench where I'd stashed water and guzzled some down, willing my breathing to slow.

I'd faced down terrorist organization and bomb disposal and friends bleeding out and kidnappers and all kinds of crap, and I'd *never* been more nervous.

Cool, cool, cool.

"You got this," Beast said, his severe face imbuing me with a bit of calm as he patted my shoulder and strode away, leaving me with the stunning view of the mountains.

Maybe this was foolish and completely off the ledge, but I hoped she'd like it.

I hope she says yes.

The next four minutes passed like a kidney stone, but eventually, I heard her coming.

"Kenny? Are you—hey, there you are." She beamed when she saw me standing in what I'd come to think of as our spot. "What is going on?"

"Whatever do you mean, dearest Liz? I always wear a

suit when we come to the bench." I reached for her hand as she made it to me.

Her face was so full of humor and happiness, my heart clutched.

"Seriously, why did it feel like every single person I know watched me walk up this trail, and why are you wearing a very nice suit and I'm standing here in... normal clothes?"

The guys should be arriving back down the other side of the trail. They'd had to loop around after she started her hike, and bless them for being willing to do so. They'd have a few minutes to change... if all went to plan.

"Sit with me," I said, guiding her around to take a seat.

Nerves twisted through me, but I launched in. "The first time we came up here, I had no idea who you were."

Her eyes were wide and her hand gripped mine firmly. "Likewise. You've surprised me in so many ways."

I huffed a laugh, praying this one would be a good one. "You're an impressive woman, whether I'm looking at your résumé, your ability to make a decision under pressure, or your glorious a—"

Her gasp was loud enough to startle me, and her hand pressed against my mouth. "You were not just about to say that."

I giggled, the nervous energy spiraling out of control. "I wasn't, actually." My beaming smile had her grinning back at me, and it hit me right in the chest.

"Falling for you was the best thing I've ever done. It was scary, and I'm so grateful we've been able to stay together. I know marriage ends up being work, but I want to do that work with you. I want to do everything with you."

"Marriage?" she asked, voice quiet.

I shifted to one knee in front of her, hands grasping hers. "I love you, Liz, and I'm in love with you. I admire you and enjoy you, and I want us to be partners for the rest of our lives. I want to spend my days and nights with you, make a family." Our five-year age gap wasn't huge, but it wasn't nothing. She'd mentioned being anxious about waiting very long, and I wanted nothing more than to marry her and knock her up, as I'd told her.

It was happening.

Right now. It's all happening right now.

Emotion caught me as our gazes held, but I pushed through. "Elizabeth Malcom, will you marry me?"

She launched into my arms and hugged me, then kissed me with a passionate, but sadly fleeting, kiss. When she pulled back, she cupped my face. "Yes. I will marry you, Kenneth Carmichael."

Relief and awe and adrenaline swept through me and I kissed her again, then grabbed the ring from my pocket. "If you want to take this back and go shopping for something else, we can. But I wanted to give you something, and I thought this suited you. But it's fine if—"

"It's beautiful, Kenny. I love it."

She gazed down at the simple solitaire. The platinum band wasn't fancy, nor was the setting, but the diamond itself was a conflict-free stone so brilliant and beautiful it was something I was deeply proud to have her wear.

"We can get you something smaller for work, if you want," I said, recognizing the stone might be a bit big for certain missions.

She let me slide the ring onto her finger, and then we hugged and kissed again. I was laughing and her eyes were shining when we parted.

"There's one other thing..." Anticipation and an instant and complete crash of *this was a terrible idea* rained down on me.

"Another surprise?" Her smile said she didn't mind.

I loved that she knew me and she wasn't scared of, or bothered by, the way I liked to spring things on her. My smile was crooked and full of nerves, but I nodded.

"Yeah, so... we've talked about how you don't care about a big wedding and I only care that my chosen family and friends are there, right?"

"Right. I've never been one to dream of a fancy ceremony. I never thought I'd get married until you."

And I would never take that for granted. But it was also why this might seem... extra.

"I'm honored I could stimulate your imagination a bit," I quipped, then pressed a kiss to her lips. "And because of all of that, and the discussion we've had, I, uh... Iplannedawed-dingforustoday."

She blinked. "What?"

I chuckled, heart hammering. "I planned a wedding? For today?"

A laugh burst out of her. "Is that a question, or... you actually did it?"

I laughed, too, because what else could I do? "Not a question. I did it. Jo helped. Well, everyone helped. Your mom is here, and—"

"My mom?" She still had this expression that told me I'd truly surprised her, maybe even shocked.

"Yep. You want her here, right? So, I mean if this is too much, we'll just call it an engagement party and we'll figure out another time, but if you like the idea..."

"I think..." She glanced out at the mountains and the

perfect summer day. "I love it. I mean, I wouldn't have planned it this way, but I think my record has shown that sometimes, the things I don't plan are the best." She wrapped her arms around my neck. "Thank you."

I grinned down at her, heart so full of love I could hardly breathe past it. "Don't thank me yet. Let's see what you think of... everything. And if we're doing this—" I glanced at my watch "—then we only have about an hour to get everything done and meet at the chapel."

She laughed, then hugged me again. "It's a good thing I love you."

I held her tight, relishing her closeness. "Oh, woman. You have no idea."

Liz

I looked at the women standing hand in hand in the small circle, each wearing a cheery, summery colored dress. They were people I'd known for just shy of a year aside from Jojo, and yet they were the sisters of my heart. I never imagined I could love people I'd known for such a short time, but Kenny had proven me wrong first, and each of them had, too.

"I'm so grateful for you all. Thank you for all the work you've done for today, and thank you for accepting me. For loving me." I choked up for what felt like the hundredth time today, but it'd really only been about an hour.

Jo, Elise, Dove, Nikki, Winnie, Catherine, Evie, and my mom all grinned, several of them wiping tears. Jane and my step sisters-in-law Calla, Sadie, and Sarah all swiped under their eyes. From her seat, Jess sniffed.

"I'm not crying for you. I'm crying because this is so beautiful, and because I am so, so pregnant."

We all laughed. and I was grateful she was able to be here, and so happy I could hardly stand it. Except I'd learned to embrace happiness and not be suspicious of it. I'd learned I could work and have a purpose, but also be joyful and fulfilled in a way I never imagined. And that was all in the last seven months since first venturing here.

"I love you so much. And I want to keep chatting and sipping champagne. But I know if we leave Barbie hanging, he'll probably pass out. He's been so anxious about this." Jo chuckled fondly.

"Poor guy." Dove laughed.

I joined them for a moment before taking a deep breath. "Okay. Let's do this."

Soon, each woman was processing with whoever was escorting her down the aisle and my dad was holding out his elbow to me.

"I'm so proud of you, Lizzy."

I scoffed. "Because I'm getting married?"

"No, stubborn child. I'm proud of you because you listened to your heart *and* your head. You didn't stay stuck. You've got so much ahead of you and I'm just glad you're letting it happen."

I beamed up at him. "Me, too, Dad."

The music from a string quartet rose, and the sun shone through the windows of the little white chapel on the Silver Ridge Resort property. I took another deep breath and looked up, finding those bright blue eyes of my fiancé waiting for me. He swiped under one eye, and I laughed, already crying as I looked at him.

Whatever came in this life, I was so unbelievably grateful I'd be facing it with him.

Thank you so much for reading Kenny and Liz's story! Don't miss Cookie's book, and keep reading for a special bonus epilogue from him!

Luc

My grandfather spoke in rapid-fire French while I gritted my teeth and kept my eyes on the bright pink glow coming from Glazed.

"What do you have to say for yourself?" he practically yelled into the phone.

"Nothing new. It's the same things I've been telling you for years." My family insisted on behaving like I'd become someone they didn't recognize, but this only served to remind me they had never known me.

A string of creative curses filtered in one ear and out the other as a figure moved around the bakery. I could only see her crossing the doorway to the kitchen every so often. She wouldn't be out to stock the trays in the glass case at the front of the shop and unlock the door for another eight minutes.

After another rush of vitriol streaming into my brain that I tried not to fully register, I sighed silently and interrupted. "Is there anything else you need, Grandfather?"

A beat of silence swelled.

"You will meet Odette de Valois, you will become engaged, and you will marry her within the year," he said, his words slipping through clenched teeth.

My pulse jumped just a touch. "I will not."

"As the only male heir to this family's dynastic wealth, you will do this."

His face would be red and his entire body wired with fury. I could just see his fists and the vein in his forehead as he said the pompous words as though anyone spoke of *dynastic wealth* in real life.

"My apologies, Grandfather, but I cannot." My mind filled in everything I could about the lie spilling out of my mouth. "I'm already with someone. I'm nearly engaged to her."

"Nonsense. Get rid of her."

I exhaled sharply away from the microphone, then braced myself to end this call. "I will not. I'm sorry." Though was I?

Maybe it was just another lie I was telling.

"Who is she? What is her name? How have you not mentioned her until now? This is convenient, isn't it?"

He was seething and the child I used to be, the one who cowered in his presence when he was like this, wavered.

But the man who'd made choice after choice to show him who I was, to separate myself from his control and the games of my family, stood taller.

She emerged from the back with a tray full of donuts glazed in that same bright pink to match the walls of her store.

And I did what'd become a little too easy over the years. I lied again.

"Her name is Elise Cordero, and I imagine next time we talk, we'll be engaged."

Oh goodness. What do we have here? A fake engagement with the sexy half Frenchman and our local donut-making mistress? Read Luc and Elise's book today.

If you haven't read Bruce/Jaws, Tristan/Oak, Adam/Doc, or Jude/Beast's stories, they're ready for you today!

Read Bruce's single guardian story in Made For You.

Read Tristan's marriage of convenience story in Safe With You.

Read Adam's secret identity story in Inspired By You.

Ready Jude's enemies to lovers story in Fighting For You.

Curious about Eddie's time in the Kappa Sector and how she ended up in Silver Ridge? Read her story in Love Undercover.

Thank you for reading Known By You! Kenny has been a little sneak. His book was actually supposed to be the fourth in this series, but Beast and Jess jumped the line and Kenny was being coy! But his book came just when it should, and I'm so happy for him to get his HEA. I hope you loved seeing him sweep Liz off her feet in his most Kenny way, and also enjoyed seeing him fall for Kit.

And hmm, what's the deal with that new guy in a new town, Sheriff Ryan? And will Jack ever get his story? And will we see how things turn out for Evie? And are we going to see cute Ethan have his day? Well my friends, I guess you'll have to stick around.

Huge thanks to my family, who were going through a deeply busy season while I was writing this book. Thanks for hanging in there while we had so much going on. We've encountered some challenges and I am delighted to see how we're facing them down together. I'll always be proud of being on our team.

Thank you to Genny Carrick for giving me the anecdote about talking to black clothing and thinking it's a black cat. Somehow I knew Kenny would have that moment. And thank you especially for your insight and suggestions for this book. Thank you to Amanda Krieger for your thoughtful beta read as well.

Thanks to B.R. Goodwin for being an incredible friend and hype person in so many ways.

Thank you to Jess Mastorakos for sticking it out and nailing this cover. It was hard won, but I love it so much. Thank you for gifting me with your time and talent, and most especially, your friendship.

Zee Monodee, thank you as always for your push to give these two more. I love where they ended up!

Huge thanks to Jamie McGillen editing, both Jamie and Mollie, for your careful proofing of this book!

As always, huge thanks to my ARC readers. Thanks especially to Carol Ann, Judith, Suzan, and the many other ARC team members. To Darla, Elise, Aubrey Ann, Rebecca, Jordan, Hannah, Abby, Riley, and so many other wonderful bookstagrammers who do so much to help share and spread the word about my books. I know there are so many amazing books vying for your attention and I never take for granted that you choose to spend a bit of your precious time with mine.

Readers, it all comes down to you. Thank you for being here. Thank you for reading this books. Thank you for every moment you spend with my characters. I am honored, and I hope you found joy and delight in these pages.

Now it's Cookie's turn...

ABOUT THE AUTHOR

Claire Cain lives to eat and drink her way around the globe with her traveling soldier and three kids, but is perhaps even happier hunkered down at home in a pair of sweatpants and slippers using any free moment she has to read and cook. Or talk—she really likes to talk. She has become an expert at packing too many dishes in too few cabinets and making houses into homes from Utah to Germany and many places in between. She's a proud Army wife and is frankly just really happy to be here.

You can also join Claire's facebook reader group for exclusive content and fun: https://www.facebook.com/groups/clairecain/

Website: http://www.clairecainwriter.com

E-mail: Claire@ClaireCainWriter.com

Newsletter sign-up for new releases, exclusives, and freebies, including a free book:

http://www.clairecainwriter.com/newsletter

amazon.com/author/clairecain

bookbub.com/authors/claire-cain

instagram.com/clairecainwriter

facebook.com/clairecainwriter

goodreads.com/clairecainwriter

pinterest.com/clairecainwriter